LOOKING FOR CHET BAKER

Also by Bill Moody

◆

SOLO HAND
DEATH OF A TENOR MAN
SOUND OF THE TRUMPET
BIRD LIVES!

LOOKING FOR CHET BAKER

AN EVAN HORNE MYSTERY

Bill Moody

Walker & Company ✺ New York

First published in the United States of America in 2002 by
Walker Publishing Company, Inc.

Published simultaneously in Canada by Fitzhenry and Whiteside,
Markham, Ontario L3R 4T8

For information about permission to reproduce selections from
this book, write to Permissions, Walker & Company, 435 Hudson
Street, New York, New York 10014

Library of Congress Cataloging-in-Publication Data

Moody, Bill, 1941–
Looking for Chet Baker : an Evan Horne mystery / Bill Moody.
p. cm.
ISBN 0-8027-3368-9 (alk. paper)
1. Horne, Evan (Fictitious character)—Fiction. 2. Amsterdam
(Netherlands)—Fiction. 3. Jazz musicians—Fiction.
4. Baker, Chet—Fiction. I. Title.

PS3563.O552 L66 2001
813'.54—dc21
2001056772

Series design by M. J. DiMassi

Printed in the United States of America

4 6 8 10 9 7 5 3

CHET BAKER

looks out from his hotel room
across the Amstel to the girl
cycling by the canal who lifts
her hand and waves and when
she smiles he is back in times
when every Hollywood producer
wanted to turn his life
into that bitter-sweet story
where he falls badly, but only
in love with Pier Angeli,
Carol Lynley, Natalie Wood;
that day he strolled into
the studio, fall of fifty-two,
and played those perfect lines
across the chords of "My Funny Valentine"
and now when he looks from his window
and her passing smile up to the blue
of a perfect sky he knows
this is one of those rare days
when he can truly fly.

—John Harvey

Foreword

Chet Baker—or Jet Faker, as I often called him—and I met in the early 1950s. The musical rapport between us was immediate. We worked, recorded, and traveled together for nearly five years. In 1953 Chet, his first wife, Charlaine, and I rented a house together in the Hollywood Hills. It was there that I wrote many of the compositions we later recorded. In addition to being arranger, composer, and pianist with the quartet, I took care of all the details when we went on the road, so I came to know Chet very well.

Chet was often thoughtless where other people were concerned, *but he could play.* He loved cars and drove too fast, *but he could play.* He was a drug abuser for forty of his fifty-eight years, but *he could play.* All that is true.

It's not true that Chet couldn't read music, although he couldn't read it well enough to do studio work. But it is true that he knew nothing about harmonic structure or chords, even simple ones. If you asked him what notes were in a certain chord, he couldn't tell you. He was, however, a truly instinctive player with an incredible ear and great lyrical sense.

If anyone has doubts about this, just listen to "Love Nest" or "Say When" from the CD *Quartet: Russ Freeman and Chet Baker*. It's unfortunate that many critics and musicians were unaware of what they were listening to. Chet Baker was unique; there will never be another like him.

Bill Moody has done an outstanding job in capturing a very difficult subject. Not only is *Looking for Chet Baker* an enjoyable read, but Bill provides a further glimpse into the jazz life and the character of one of the music's most remarkable musicians.

—Russ Freeman
Las Vegas, 2001

Acknowledgments

Thanks first and foremost to Chet Baker for the legacy of so much great music he left to the world.

I've had the privilege of working with a number of musicians who were also friends of Chet. They gave generously of their time and remembrances. The late bassist Carson Smith; saxophonist Jack Montrose; pianist Russ Freeman, saxophonist Herb Geller; bassist Bob Badgely; trumpeter Graham Bruce; trumpeter, pianist, bassist, artist Terry Henry; and vocalist Marigold Hill, who played no small role in making available undiscovered recordings of Chet, done those many years ago in the basement of her waterlogged home in Villa Grande, California. Marigold remains a good friend, and as drummer Benny Barth says, "a beautiful girl for many years."

Thanks also to Dick Conte of KCSM-FM in San Mateo, for sharing memories and interview tapes. Additional information that was extremely helpful was the film *Chet Baker: The Last Days,* produced by Dutch Television, and j. de Valk's fine biography, *Chet Baker: His Life and Music.*

To George Gibson and Michael Seidman at Walker & Company for their continued support of Evan Horne, and to Philip Spitzer for always being more than an agent.

And finally to Teresa, the best first reader any writer could have.

Intro

KNOW WHAT *I did when I heard, man? Just sat there for a
few minutes staring at the TV, knew right then I wasn't
going to work the next day. No way. Fifteen seconds on
the six o'clock news, and an old photo. American jazzman Chet
Baker died in Amsterdam yesterday under mysterious circumstances. Yeah, right. You know he was high, nodded off, fell
right out of the window of his hotel. Chet was gone.*

*"Well, right then I got out some of my best shit and I got
high. You know, sort of a tribute to Chet. Dug out all those old
sides too, man, cranked up the stereo and played 'em all. The
quartet with Gerry Mulligan, the band with Russ Freeman, the
New York sessions with Philly Joe, Johnny Griffin—even the vo-
cal shit, man, and I loved his later singing. You could tell how
much he'd been through with that voice, man, like he wasn't
going to make it through the fucking tune but somehow he always did. Tear up your heart, man. Check out what he does on
'Fair Weather,' when he made that movie with Dexter Gordon.
I'm tellin' you, man, tear up your heart. Some of that European
shit too, and there was a lot of it. In Italy with strings after he*

got out of jail. 'Course even I don't have it all, nobody does. He recorded so much they'll probably never find everything.

"Know what else I did, man? Got my trumpet out too. Dug through my closet, throwing shit everywhere looking for it, and I was so fucked up by then, but I found it. I put on 'My Funny Valentine,' and tried to play along with Chetty. No way, man, that's gone for good, could hardly get a tone out of that old horn, but I could hear it in my head. Then I just cooled out and listened to Chet sing and play and scat, just like he played.

"I just sat there holding that trumpet, crying like a baby, wishing it was me who could play like that, but of course nobody could play like Chet Baker. He was the man!"

I remember all that—Tommy Ryan, crazed wannabe trumpeter, jazz fan gone computer programmer, raving on—when was it? five years ago?—as I study a signed, poster-size photo of Chet Baker on the wall opposite me. He's looking somewhere off camera, like always, never in the lens, maybe nowhere, someplace none of us can go.

"Evan?" Colin Mansfield turns around to look over his shoulder, follow my gaze.

"Oh. Chet gave me that when he was at Ronnie Scott's, not long before he died. There's a video of that performance." He studies me for a moment. "You're not looking into that, are you? I mean, with your history and all."

I shake my head. "Nothing to look into. He fell out of a hotel window, didn't he?" It was ten, eleven years now.

"Well, there was some talk of suicide, even murder," Mansfield says. I'd once met Chet's longtime pianist, Russ Freeman, and we'd talked about it. That was after my accident, during the days when I was trying to figure out why some musicians just stop playing. Russ Freeman had been one of them. All those years with Chet and Shelly Manne, and Freeman had just up and quit playing. Lived in Las Vegas now, so I'd heard, arranging, composing.

"No way," Freeman had said. "There was nothing about Chet that would make him even think about suicide." Freeman had been adamant. Still, things happen to people.

As for murder, I'd heard those rumors too, and Chet was a junkie. Hard not to travel in bad circles, even if you're a famous jazz musician who plays beautiful music. Drug dealers don't care, not if you don't pay, and there was the beating in San Francisco that, according to the story, cost Chet all his teeth and nearly ended his career. But suicide? No.

"I don't think so," I say to Mansfield.

"Hmmm, interesting, though," Mansfield says. "One never knows. But I find it fascinating—you, I mean. A jazz musician detective. I say, would you mind? I have some questions, and I'm sure my listeners would be enthralled."

I want to say, Please don't go there. But I just shrug, maybe because I've never heard a jazz DJ use the word *enthralled*, but then this is England. "Hey, it's your show."

"We're on in five, Colin." I hear the engineer's voice in my headphones. Mansfield and I both watch him do the silent countdown with his fingers.

"Good evening. I'm Colin Mansfield, and this is *BBC 3 Jazz Scene*. Tonight my guest is American pianist Evan Horne, who begins a one-week engagement at Ronnie Scott's tomorrow night. Welcome to London, Evan. Good of you to join us."

"Thanks for having me." I watch Mansfield across the table from me, flanked by the requisite CD players and turntables. He looks nothing like my idea of a jazz DJ, but London was never my idea of a jazz town either. Everything is different here. Mansfield, in his tweed coat with leather elbow patches, looks more like an off-duty Oxford don. His voice is well-modulated Oxbridge English. He checks some notes in front of him and pushes up the headphones that keep slipping down around his forehead.

"I'd like to begin with a track from your first recording as a leader." Mansfield smiles, catches my surprised look. "Yes, bit of luck on our part to find this. We managed to get a copy of *Arrival*, and we're going to hear 'Just Friends' on *BBC 3 Jazz Scene*."

Mansfield flicks off the air microphone, but I can still hear him talk through the headphones. "Have you been to Ronnie's before?"

"Yes, once on a brief tour with Lonnie Cole." Stan Getz had been the headliner.

"You'll enjoy it, I'm sure," Mansfield says. "Pete King has carried on well since we lost Ronnie. Another real tragedy."

I remember reading about it. Heart attack or stroke, but some unusual circumstances. Mansfield nods his head to the music and holds up the album cover for me to see. I look at the photo of myself and see someone I almost don't recognize, someone much younger, more relaxed than I feel at the moment.

For the next half hour, Mansfield plays music, and I answer his questions on my influences—Bud Powell, Bill Evans, Keith Jarrett—and dodge as well as I can the ones about my away-from-the-bandstand experiences. My history, Mansfield called it. No, I didn't solve Wardell Gray's death in Las Vegas. Yes, I did confirm that a lost recording of Clifford Brown was bogus, and no, I didn't stop a serial killer in Los Angeles.

"The FBI were the real heroes," I say, giving my practiced answer.

"Still," Mansfield says, "you played a significant role, I daresay." He presses the button for another cut from my album but keeps the volume low. "We'll conclude tonight's show with what I believe is one of your favorite ballads, 'My Foolish Heart.' Chet Baker's too," Mansfield adds. I give him a look with that one.

"This is Colin Mansfield on *BBC 3 Jazz Scene*. We've been visiting with pianist Evan Horne. Stay tuned for the news at ten."

The music comes up, and Mansfield hands me the album cover. "I wonder, would you mind?"

"Sure." I sign it, thinking "My Foolish Heart" or "I Fall in Love Too Easily," either could be my theme song, and both were favorites of Chet Baker. I hand the cover back to Mansfield. "Thanks for having me."

"My pleasure. I'll be sure to pop round to Ronnie's one night and buy you a drink."

"I look forward to it." We shake hands, and I make my way out of the studio to the reception area. On the way out, a young girl at the desk with spiked red hair, black lipstick, and an angelic smile stops me.

"There was a call for you," she says in a soft, light voice. She hands me a slip of paper.

"Thanks." I glance at the name and number and crumple it up in my hand. "Can you call me a taxi, please?"

"Sure, luv." Outside, I light a cigarette and bounce the crumpled paper in my hand for a moment, almost tossing it in the gutter. I should just say I didn't get the message. But that's not my style.

"Where to, guv?" the taxi driver asks me.

"I'm not sure."

1

I PUT OFF calling Ace Buffington for a couple of days, but some, perhaps misguided, sense of obligation or loyalty finally makes me give in. We agreed to meet at a pub called the Boar's Head just off Shaftesbury Avenue, near the London theater district. It's noisy and smoky inside, loud voices, bodies shouldering up to the bar for that one last drink before curtain time, and Ace is easy to spot. He towers over everyone, waving money to get the bartender's attention.

"Wow," Ace says as I come up. "Busy here. I'll get the drinks. See if you can find a table, then we'll drink to our collaboration. Beer okay?"

"Sure." I try to catch his eye. "It's not going to happen, Ace."

He looks at me, feigns puzzlement. "What?"

"Whatever it is you're going to try and sell me." I've thought about it all afternoon, anticipating the moment, steeling myself to ward off Ace's enthusiasm, persuasiveness, and persistence. He's done it before.

"Hey, c'mon, Evan. At least hear me out." He waves again at the bartender.

"Won't make any difference, Ace. You'd be wasting your time. I'm afraid to even ask why you're in London." The spring semester isn't over yet. Ace should be at UNLV, lecturing coeds on American literature and correcting final exams, not meeting me in a London pub.

"Sabbatical," Ace says. "I was eligible and jumped at the chance, especially when this other thing came up."

I shake my head and smile in spite of myself. "I'll find a table."

I turn from the bar and spot some people getting up, putting on coats. I get there just ahead of three guys, claim the table, and wait for him to join me.

I met Ace Buffington on one of my first trips to Las Vegas when I was playing and conducting for Lonnie Cole. Ace is a big, friendly guy who is crazy about two things: jazz and tennis. A professor of English at UNLV, he also has a passion for collecting old records, and a knowledge of jazz history that reflects his love for the music and impressed me. When his wife Janey died suddenly of cancer, he threw himself into work. But even department politics, which he describes as worse and more vicious than any crime family, weren't enough to fill the lonely hours. Ace got it in his head to do an article on Las Vegas, and that's what got me into trouble the first time.

Until me, jazz musicians had simply been names he'd read about or listened to, but he wanted to get inside. Ace loves having a jazz musician friend, but sometimes he goes overboard, which is why musicians often keep people at a certain distance. Civilians, we call them. No matter how much they're into the music, there's that unmanageable, impossible-to-close gap between the bandstand and a seat at a front table.

I suppose it's true of any profession. Talking, communicating, with a colleague is different than with an outsider. There's so much that doesn't need explaining. No matter how hard someone like Ace tries—and he does try—he still can't quite understand what goes on in your mind when you're on the bandstand. How it feels, what you're thinking. Still, Ace has been a good friend. It's his overzealousness that gets me in trouble.

He decided to write an article on the Moulin Rouge, the first interracial casino in Las Vegas, and more pointedly, somehow explain the death of saxophonist Wardell Gray. He enlisted me to help with the research and talk with musicians, and since he'd got me my first gig after the accident, I felt obligated, so I agreed. What I didn't know was that I'd uncover a mess from the past, butt heads with a minor Mafia figure, and almost get myself killed.

Ace's record collecting got me into trouble too, when he hired me to authenticate some supposedly lost recordings of trumpeter Clifford Brown. That time it was a looney-tune collector, and I found out how serious those can be. I vowed then that would be the last time. But Ace finding me in London meant he was up to something again, and he was going to try and drag me into it. Not this time. I couldn't afford any more misadventures, and I still had Los Angeles on my mind, although Ace had had nothing to do with that. But what had happened in Los Angeles was part of the reason I was in London.

My chops were back, I was recording again, Natalie and I were very serious, everything was going fine—until a crazed woman, bent on getting vengeance for her brother's rejection by the jazz world, started knocking off smooth jazz artists. She left a trail of clues the FBI couldn't figure out until I was brought in to help my high school buddy Lieutenant Danny Cooper. It spiraled out of control into a psychological duel between her and me, a nightmare that has left me with a hollow feeling inside. Enough so that I want to escape for a while and decompress in Europe. Ace isn't going to get me this time, but I know he will try.

He jostles his way through the crowd and sets down two glasses of lager with a firm hand. He settles himself on one of the upholstered stools and takes a long drink.

"What other thing, Ace?" He winks at me and pauses to take a big gulp of beer.

"Ah, worth waiting for," he says. He sets the glass down and gives me his full attention.

"A bona fide book deal, a tentative contract, just one minor thing to firm it up." Ace's eyes light up with enthusiasm as he explains. I've seen this look before. "Who's the one jazz musician who has been written about more, has more recordings, and is still surrounded by a certain mystique, still being talked about today?"

I light a cigarette, relieved that English pubs are not as hard on smokers as California bars. "Miles Davis." Keep this low-key, I think, so Ace doesn't get too excited.

"Close. Right instrument, wrong guy."

I shrug. "Okay, tell me."

"C'mon, Evan." He leans closer. "There's even a whiff of a movie deal. He's been compared to James Dean. You know, tragic life, sometimes brilliant career, and . . . mysterious death." He looks disappointed when I won't play the game. He holds up his hands. "Chet Baker, of course."

"Of course. A movie deal?"

"Yeah, couple of big-time actors are vying for the rights. Over ten years since he died, and he's still being talked about."

I can see Ace is only getting warmed up. I'm beginning to feel like I'm trapped with a time-share salesman moving in for the close. "Okay, so you've gotten a tentative contract for a Chet Baker book. Congratulations, I'm happy for you." But Ace doesn't sound happy. There's something in his voice, some air of desperation about him, as if he just has to make this sale or he loses the commission.

"It's fate, Evan, fate. Turning on the radio, catching you on the show the other night. We're both in London. Did you know that Chet Baker died just a couple of hours' flight from here, in Amsterdam, and here you are in London, maybe going to Amsterdam yourself. It's meant to be." I had told him about the possibility briefly on the phone.

"The Amsterdam gig is tentative." I look at Ace steadily. "And no, Ace, it's not meant to be, not this time." His pained expression makes me pause. Ace was responsible in no small way for getting me playing again, but as far as I am concerned, the books are balanced.

Ace puts down his beer and takes a breath, as if now he's going to tell me the truth. "Okay, I won't lie to you. The book deal is tentative because I promised them you'd be coauthor." He can't meet my eyes. He takes another drink of his beer. "There, it's out."

For a moment I stare at him, speechless. "Why, Ace? You didn't even talk to me about it." I try to hold my anger in check, but it's getting difficult.

"I know, I know. It's just . . . Evan, look, I really need this. If I'm finally going to get a full professorship, I need another book. I've made some enemies, but I want to run that damn department, politics or not. With you on board, the contract is a sure thing, then . . ."

He lets me finish the thought. I don't like the implication that if I don't help him, I'm responsible for his not getting promoted. I sigh and look around the pub. It's less noisy now as it begins to empty out. People are gathering up their coats, saying good-byes. "I already told you, Ace. It's not going to happen."

"Evan, we were partners, remember? We worked well together. Look what we did with Wardell Gray. Almost solved a forty-year-old murder. And what about Clifford Brown, those lost tapes? You proved they were phony. I couldn't have done that by myself. I need you on this, Evan." His voice drops lower. "I really need this, Evan. I wouldn't ask otherwise."

"Stop it, Ace. Nobody said it was your fault, but those things got me way in over my head. Are you forgetting I almost got killed a couple of times? No, I'm through with that, especially after L.A. and Gillian Payne."

"Hey, I wasn't any part of that."

"I didn't say you were."

He looks away for a moment. "She got sentenced, you know. Life without parole." He takes a drink of his beer and looks at me, quickly realizing he should change the subject. "Have you heard from Natalie?"

Once I was out of it, I hadn't followed the case. "No, but I didn't expect to. I haven't contacted her, either."

Ace shakes his head. "Well, I'm not going to go there, either." He leans forward, revs up again. "But this is different. Chet Baker is a completely other thing."

"Really? You know that for a fact? For all we know there are people who would prefer keeping his death just the way it apparently was—an accident. And as far as anyone knows, it *was* an accident." Even in the noisy pub, I hear my voice louder than I intended. A couple at a nearby table turns to look at us. "Ace, I'm sorry, man, I really am, but I have to pass on this one. I can't do it. You're on your own."

Ace smiles weakly and shrugs, and his tone changes to quiet acceptance. "Well, hey, I had to try, didn't I? No hard feelings?"

"No," I say, but that's a mistake.

His tone changes once again. I've never seen him like this. He won't look at me. "What do I have to do, Evan? I don't think you understand. I need this to happen."

"Ace, don't do this. I know it's important, but I can't do it."

He nods silently, doesn't say anything for a couple of minutes. I don't know what more to say, but I know it isn't going to be yes.

"I really didn't think you'd go for it," he says finally. "I understand. I just got carried away. The editor seemed just on the edge." He sits up straighter, manages a show of false cheerfulness, but comes off as disingenuous. "Don't worry, I'll manage. I'll just have to do such great research they'll give me a book contract anyway. But did I mention you'd have credit? Your name would be right there on the book. I mean, I don't expect you to do this anonymously. I—"

"Ace."

He puts up his hands. "Okay, okay. I'll stop." He looks at his watch. "Hey, you better get going. Opening night, huh?

Wish I could stick around to hear you, but I've got some things to do."

A gap of uncomfortable silence descends upon us that even the pub noise can't drown out. I feel like I have to say something. "Look, there must be plenty of research material on Chet Baker. If you're going to Amsterdam, you can talk to some musicians, maybe the police—"

"I know how to do research," Ace says.

The silence falls over us again. Finally I have to break it. "Well, I should go."

"Sure," Ace says. "Well, listen, if the Amsterdam gig works out, promise me we'll get together, have a beer or something." He digs in his pocket for paper and pen. "Here," he says. "This is where I'll be staying." He writes down a name and number and hands it to me. "Let me know if you're coming."

"Sure, Ace, of course." I stuff the paper in my pocket and stand up to go. "Good luck with everything." The crowd has thinned considerably as I make my way to the door. I turn back once, toward Ace, but he's still at the table, staring into his empty glass.

Then I walk out.

Soho is back behind Shaftesbury Avenue. I wind through the noisy little crowded streets, filled with pubs, sex shops, Indian, Chinese, and Greek restaurants with lamb roasting on spits in the window, tobacconists, and the occasional fish-and-chips shop. My mind, though, is still on Ace's proposal and Gillian Payne. She had killed three people and almost killed her brother. The FBI made me her contact after she promised to stop the killing if I agreed to help her find her brother. I found him, but it cost me a lot, mainly my relationship with Natalie. What was she doing now? Ace's mention of her brought memories of our times together flooding back.

Across from Ronnie Scott's I stop and grab a coffee and a cigarette, enjoying this last moment of anonymity before I walk across the street. It feels good to see my name on the marquee of one of the oldest established jazz clubs in Europe. I feel good. I want to play, and I don't want to think about anything else but music. Not Ace, not Gillian, just music.

Inside the club, there's a fair crowd already. I walk past the bar to the back room behind the stage. The grand piano awaiting me is flanked by a bass and drum set. The seating is slightly tiered, arranged in a half circle facing the stage. Somebody points at me, and I hear a voice say, "I think that's him." Backstage, Pete King, the burley Cockney manager of the club, is talking with the bassist and drummer.

"Evan," King says. "All right then? These lads are ready to go." He jerks his thumb at Gordon and Derek, the bassist and drummer.

"Hi, Pete, hi, guys." We'd only had time for a short afternoon rehearsal. They were both good, and I knew everything would be okay if I stuck to standards, a couple of blues. Derek glances up at me from tapping his drumsticks on a rubber pad. Gordon nods and smiles.

Pete looks around. "Well, all right then, shall we?" We all file onstage and take our places as the lights come up while Pete makes the opening announcement.

"Good evening, ladies and gentlemen. It's our pleasure, and I'm sure it will be yours, to meet pianist Evan Horne. He's American, but we won't hold that against him."

Pete pauses, taps the microphone, waits for the polite chuckles that follow. I catch Gordon rolling his eyes.

"Hmm," Pete says. He glances at me and shrugs. "Ronnie always did that better. Anyway, with Evan are our own Gordon Powell and Derek Runswick."

I begin with "Alone Together," medium tempo. Gordon and Derek follow easily, and by the second chorus we hit a comfortable groove. My hand feels good and relaxed, the piano is in tune, and I realize I'm in good company. I haven't done it that much, but it can be hit-and-miss with pickup rhythm sections, nothing like your own group. They're not

Gene Sherman or Jeff Lasorda, but these two have backed plenty of American visitors and both are good players.

I play another couple of choruses, then give it to Derek for his solo. I nod at Gordon, and we play some eight-bar exchanges, then take it home. A couple of ballads, an up blues, and I end the set with "Just Friends." First tunes, first set, butterflies gone, and the three of us know each other a little now. The audience is with us, and the applause is genuine as we take a break.

"Hey, nice, guys," I say to Gordon and Derek. "Let me buy you a drink." I catch the waitress and order for the three of us.

"Two whiskeys neat also, please," a familiar voice behind me says. I turn and find Colin Mansfield and another man. "Hello, Evan," Mansfield says. "Come and join us. This is Mike Bailey with the *Daily Telegraph*."

"Hi, Colin. Didn't expect you so soon." I shake hands with Bailey. He's a short, stocky man in a rumpled suit and knit tie.

"Always like to catch an opening night," Mansfield says. "Mike would like to do a piece on you for the arts section if you have time."

"Well, sure, I guess so."

"Don't worry," Bailey says with a quick, reassuring smile. "It won't hurt much."

"We can go in the back if you want. I've got about a half hour before the next set."

"Suits me," Bailey says.

"Good, I'll get our drinks sent back," Mansfield offers. He goes off to find our waitress.

Bailey and I head for the backstage dressing room. He takes out a pad and pen from his bag, and I get a cigarette going.

"Colin has filled me in on your background. This will be short, but I'd like to try and get it in tomorrow's paper. I understand you have a new recording coming out."

"Yes, that's right. Quarter Tone Records. Small label in

Los Angeles. We recorded it just before I came over. I don't think there's a release date yet, but I haven't been in touch with them for a while."

Bailey looks up. "Hiding out in Europe?"

Something in his tone bothers me, but maybe I'm being too sensitive. I've been burned by the press before—misquotes, misinterpretation, and sometimes they just make up things. "No, just getting away from the fray for a while."

Bailey nods and scribbles on his pad. There are some more questions about music, my playing, and how I like Ronnie Scott's. Then he shifts gears. "I imagine that episode with the serial killer in Los Angeles was quite an ordeal."

I pause, wondering where this is going, but I can't seem to escape it. "Well, it wasn't fun, I guarantee you."

"No, I'm sure," Bailey says.

Colin joins us then, followed by the waitress with our drinks. "Well, cheers then," Mansfield says, raising his glass, and we all drink.

"What are your plans after Ronnie's?" Bailey asks.

"Well, they're pretty sketchy. There's a possibility of a gig in Amsterdam, then we'll just see what happens from there."

"So you might stay in Europe for a while, then?"

"Possibly. Like I say, I'll just have to see what happens. I like to play it by ear."

Mansfield and Bailey exchange glances, then Bailey continues. He glances briefly again at Mansfield, and some kind of signal passes between them.

"Wasn't Amsterdam where Chet Baker died?"

"So they tell me, but that's not why I'm going there."

"No, of course not," Mansfield says.

Bailey nods. His smile seems more like a smirk to me. He makes a few more notes, then closes his notebook. "Well, I guess I've got enough. Thanks for your time."

"No problem. Are you staying around for another set?" I ask Mansfield.

"No, I'm afraid not. I have to be up early."

"And I have a deadline," Bailey says, getting to his feet. "I enjoyed your music."

"Thanks."

I walk them out. We shake hands again, and I watch them disappear toward the front door. Derek and Gordon are leaning on the bar, drinking beers.

"Mike Bailey, wasn't it?" Derek asks.

"Yeah. You know him?"

"Fucking wanker," Powell says and downs his beer.

Derek smiles. "He thought Gordon played too loud for a singer. What did he say?"

Gordon screws up his face and spits out the words like they're something that tastes bad. "Powell's obtrusive drumming lent little to the evening's performance. What the fuck does he know? He's a critic."

Derek winks at me. "Gordon's very sensitive."

"Hey, that's a good quality in a drummer."

"See," Gordon says. "I told you."

I get a signal from Pete King then. It's time for the second set.

This one gets even better. Derek's lines are just right, and Gordon's cymbal sizzles underneath me throughout the set. My only regret is that I know that, just when we're really meshing, the gig will be over and I'll be on to someplace else.

I'm staying at a small hotel in Bloomsbury, arranged for by Pete King. The room is so small I can hardly turn around, but it's clean and comfortable and includes breakfast. Over bacon and eggs in the dining room, I leaf through the paper, looking for the arts section. Mike Bailey was a fast writer. The best thing about the piece is that there's no accompanying photo.

JAZZ PIANIST DETECTIVE FINDS
PEACE AND QUIET IN LONDON

American pianist Evan Horne opened to a respectable crowd at Ronnie Scott's last night, but most of the patrons probably weren't aware they were listening to a sometime private investigator whose last assignment was to help the FBI catch a serial killer in Los Angeles.

I hate to even read the rest of the article. Bailey has dug up all the details and implies that I might be heading to Amsterdam to investigate Chet Baker's death. He makes playing piano seem a sideline, the music secondary. I try to get angry, but I'm beginning to realize stories like this one are something I can't escape, perhaps ever. There's nothing inaccurate, it's just the slant he takes. Bailey ends on a brief, albeit positive note.

> Horne's playing was a pleasant surprise. He displayed excellent technique, despite having a near-career-ending injury several years ago, and his rendition of standards, particularly ballads, is reminiscent of a muscular Bill Evans. Horne is at Ronnie Scott's through Saturday.

I finish breakfast and go for a walk, thinking about Bailey's story and wondering how much Mansfield was in the background on it, and what Pete King will think. But, as they say, any publicity is good; if it puts more people in the seats, who's going to complain?

Ace Buffington, on the other hand, does worry me. He doesn't seem at all like his old self. That cloud of desperation around him isn't normal. I'm not surprised that he tried to enlist me once again, but I am at the pleading way he did it. I know that wasn't easy for Ace, and I feel a little guilty about refusing. There is something else going on, something he isn't telling me. I can sense it, and I don't like the feeling.

Until Colin Mansfield brought up Chet Baker—and then

Ace and Mike Bailey—I hadn't even thought about how he'd died. It was just there, somewhere in the recesses of my mind, another of those jazz legends that gets embellished in the retelling, but nothing more.

I left Los Angeles in what now seems a permanent move. I left my car and a few belongings in storage with Danny Cooper and gave notice on my Venice apartment. I simply hopped a plane to New York and points east with a vague idea of going to Europe.

But now, walking through the narrow streets of the Mayfair district of London, past Rolls Royce and Jaguar showrooms, expensive boutiques, and trendy restaurants, L.A. doesn't seem so far away after all. It's always just there, just over my shoulder, with people like Mike Bailey ready to take up the thread and question my motives for being here. There are going to be more questions to answer to bring it all back, and that's something I don't want to do, not now.

I've done that already.

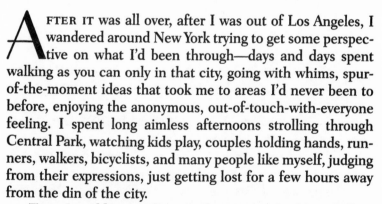

2

A FTER IT was all over, after I was out of Los Angeles, I wandered around New York trying to get some perspective on what I'd been through—days and days spent walking as you can only in that city, going with whims, spur-of-the-moment ideas that took me to areas I'd never been to before, enjoying the anonymous, out-of-touch-with-everyone feeling. I spent long aimless afternoons strolling through Central Park, watching kids play, couples holding hands, runners, walkers, bicyclists, and many people like myself, judging from their expressions, just getting lost for a few hours away from the din of the city.

True, I could rationalize, easily point to the facts. Gillian Payne was in prison, Danny Cooper had fully recovered, and Gillian's brother could now perhaps resume a fairly normal life. But there had been a price for all this. Natalie and I were probably over, and I still didn't know how I felt about that. Maybe our breakup would have happened anyway. Maybe the whole awful nightmare was only the catalyst. I hadn't called her, and she hadn't tried to contact me, so there was that to consider and add to the equation.

On the plus side, the recording had been finished and would be released soon. My hand was fine, I was playing well. It remained now for me to pick up the pieces and get on with my life. All things considered, there was every reason to believe in the future. That's how it should have been, but it wasn't working. I couldn't erase those images from my mind.

I forced myself to keep busy, looking up old friends, listening to music, even sitting in a couple of times at sessions. Cindy Fuller, my old stewardess girlfriend, had been on the flight. We'd gotten together for dinner, but Cindy had her own life now, and there was nothing to rekindle there. I'd even made a trip up to Boston to visit some of my former teachers at Berklee. I actually thought about visiting my parents, but we'd been out of touch for so long, what was the point? They had their life, and I had mine. Short, civil visits were all either of us wanted or could endure, and it had been that way for years.

It all came back to the slip of paper in my wallet, a scribbled phone number and a name, constantly dragging me back to the past like an unpaid bill.

It was part of my debriefing from the FBI, the complimentary counseling they not only offered but recommended. I could still hear Wendell Cook, the senior agent, trying to convince me, the day before I left L.A.

"Evan, at least take the number. You're going to be in New York. You've been through quite an experience. It might help to talk about it to someone who can view it objectively, and Dr. Hammond is one of the best." I dutifully took down the number, but I was convinced I'd never use it.

But after only a few aimless, unsettled days in New York, I was still unfocused, restless, disconnected from the few friends I knew there, much less the people I passed on the crowded streets.

It was worse at night. The images continued to haunt me—

Gillian Payne's twisted smile behind the glass partition in jail, the phone conversations when she taunted me, the crime scenes, her brother's look of surprise and shock as her blade caught him in the throat. I caught myself looking at the faces I passed, trying to see if they knew what I knew, if they'd seen what I'd seen. But there were no answers there.

One night I took the subway downtown. I'd planned on going to the Village Vanguard, but once there, I stood in front of the club, staring at the marquee, hearing the music filtering out to the street, wondering why I was there and no longer interested in going inside. I think it was at that moment I knew it was time to do something about it.

The next morning I gave in and dialed the number, but I hung up the first two times when somebody answered, not sure I wanted to relive the experience. Maybe I didn't want to hear some of the answers I knew were there, buried somewhere I wanted to keep them; getting them out would be a struggle, and carry consequences. Looking at them would perhaps be worse than keeping them hidden.

Realistically, I knew the whole counseling idea was no more than the FBI's way of protecting themselves from future litigation, an exercise in covering their ass. They didn't want me to turn up on a talk show a year or two or three from now, claiming I'd been coerced into cooperating with them and had suffered anguish or trauma, or whatever the label might be, from assisting them with the apprehension of a serial killer. Yet I didn't doubt Cook's claim that even seasoned agents are required to undergo counseling, particularly when they have witnessed crime scenes of what Cook called "such a violent nature."

When I called the third time and stayed on the line, they almost seemed to be expecting me. Somebody, probably Wendell Cook, had told them to be ready. I was given an appointment the next afternoon at an address on Riverside Drive.

The office was done in restful pastels, soft lighting, and I sat apprehensively in one of the two comfortable chairs, opposite the psychologist, Rosemary Hammond, a pleasant, fortyish woman in a long, flowing dress and glasses on a chain. She had me sign a document stating that I was there voluntarily, but once that formality for the FBI was covered, she assured me she was there mainly to listen objectively and possibly offer some suggestions.

"Relax, Evan. I'm not a dentist. You look like you're about to have a root canal." She smiled and leaned forward to reassure me, "I promise not to use words like 'issues,' 'relate,' or phrases like 'Feel good about yourself.' I've read your file, I know all about your background, what happened, all the players." I could see it right there on her desk, a dark green folder probably faxed from Los Angeles. "You went through quite a lot in a very short time. More than most field agents experience in their entire careers. It's understandable that you wanted to get away from where it happened. That is why you're in New York, isn't it?"

I knew how counselors worked. I'd been through a number of sessions after my accident, trying to come to terms with the idea that I might not ever play the piano again. They were earnest, their recommendations were well meaning, but to me, not much help. How could anyone understand, and why would Rosemary Hammond be any different? I was cautious at first, trying to get a read on Hammond.

"I don't know. I suppose it is, but I'm not staying here. I plan on going to Europe if I can get some work."

She didn't say, Oh, running farther away, huh? She just smiled again and said, "Tell me about it." She didn't take notes, and I saw no tape recorder. She just leaned back in her chair and focused her attention in a way that made me want to tell her everything. Maybe I could leave it all right here in her office and be on my way.

"There was Andrea Lawrence, one of your agents. That got to be more than a working relationship, or at least I felt it could have been."

"Ah, that's not in the file," Hammond said, "but it doesn't matter, this is all confidential."

"Okay, I'll get to that later."

Hammond shrugged as if to say, However you want to do it.

"I was just getting my career back together after years of physical therapy, not being able to play, when Danny Cooper called, asking for my help. Just look around the crime scene, he said, help us understand this. The killer had written "Bird Lives!" in blood on the mirror in one of the victims' dressing rooms, referring to Charlie Parker, the saxophonist. The victim was still there on the floor, blood everywhere, his horn smashed, and there was a Bird CD playing when they found him, and a white feather in the saxophone case. The police didn't know what to make of it, but I knew what it all meant immediately. The killer was sending a message. That room was filled with rage."

"And you saw all this."

"Yes. Saw it, smelled it, felt it. It made me sick. I just wanted to get out of there so I could breathe. But I felt obligated to Cooper. We're old friends, from high school, and he'd helped me in the past, so I stuck with it. When they were sure it was a serial killer, and the FBI got involved, I explained more clues for them—saved them time, so they said, and I was okay with that."

"And then what happened?" Hammond asked.

"Somebody leaked it to the press that I was involved. The story trotted out my past, my involvement with similar things. Then I got personally involved with Gillian, the killer, through phone calls, tapes, mail, even poems. She was very clever. I became the go-between. There was no way out, nothing to do but see it through to the end. To be truthful, I resented the intrusion. On my personal and professional life. I'd just signed a recording contract, work was coming in, and things with Natalie were fine. Then Lawrence—Andie, everybody called her— got involved. I had to help her create a profile of Gillian. Natalie didn't understand all the time I spent with Andie or why I was so involved in the first place, and I couldn't tell her everything."

"And did she have any cause to be worried, jealous even?"

I paused a moment before answering. "Worried? Yes, it was more dangerous than anything I'd ever done. Jealous? I don't know. Not at first, but there was chemistry between Andie and me, strong sexual tension. I admit that. I thought I was committed to Natalie, but maybe not as much as I thought. It didn't help that Andie was very attractive. She made it very clear she was available and interested."

"Did you think that was unprofessional of her?"

I shrugged. "I didn't connect it like that. I knew she was testing the waters, but under the circumstances, it was different. We were thrown together, we traveled together to San Francisco. People can't help their feelings, even if it means being unprofessional. It happens all the time, and I suppose I was flattered by the attention."

"And did you act on those feelings?"

"No, I didn't, but Natalie wasn't convinced, and that in turn made me doubt her, wonder why she couldn't trust me. I was just doing a job I didn't want to be doing. I could tell her less and less as they closed in on Gillian, but it was in part for her own protection as well. Nobody knew what Gillian was going to do. I was juggling Gillian, the FBI, Natalie, Andie Lawrence, and trying to keep my music together, all at the same time.

"In San Francisco, Andie and I were staying at the same hotel, in adjoining rooms, but something kept me from opening that door, even though I knew it wasn't locked. Natalie, of course, didn't see it that way. She suspected the worst, and nothing I could tell her would make it go away. But there was something else as well."

This was the real problem, and I'd been working up to it gradually by talking about Andie Lawrence and Natalie. Now it was time.

"What?"

"Gillian. Her phone calls. I never knew when they were coming, but she was playing with my head, seducing me in a way, mentally. I wanted . . . to know. It became an obsession to know why she was doing this, what would make anybody do what she did, and if I could stop her." I smiled at Hammond. "Makes me sound weird, huh?"

"Not at all. It was a natural feeling. You had too many opposing forces closing in on you all at once, that's all."

"I always thought music was the only thing for me, but I got caught up in those other things the same way, just on a different level. I had to know the answers once the questions were put before me. Wardell Gray's death—how did it happen? The Clifford Brown recordings—were they real or not? I wanted to know, even though I should have stopped long before I did."

"And when you found the answers, was there satisfaction?"

"Yes, there was satisfaction, even though all the questions weren't answered." I got up and walked around the office, glancing at Hammond's certificates on the wall, the art posters.

"Can I smoke?" I asked Hammond. She nodded yes. I lit up and sat down again while she poured us both some coffee. "It's hard to explain, but yes, I got satisfaction from tracking down people, finding the answers, resolving things. Sometimes maybe even as much as I get from music. And that scared me."

Hammond said, "No reason it should. You were perhaps transferring the frustration from your accident to something you had some control over. Finding those answers was up to you."

"But that doesn't explain it all, how I feel now."

"No, it doesn't. Your loyalty to Cooper and Natalie was rewarded by one, rejected by the other. Your resistance to Lawrence was not acknowledged by Natalie, at least not to your satisfaction, so your feelings for her changed."

"Yes, they did." And in that moment, I was suddenly clear about it.

Hammond paused then, considering. "When you left Los Angeles, who came to see you off? Anybody?"

It was the first time I'd thought about it. "Cooper drove me to the airport. Andie was there at the gate. I didn't see Natalie after the last time we talked, a few days before I left."

"And the case was over," Hammond said. "Lawrence had no reason to be there other than she wanted to see you."

I looked away then, replaying the airport scene in my mind, remembering Andie's words: *You know how much I'd like to get on this plane with you?* Things might have been different if I hadn't already been involved with Natalie.

Hammond looked at me then. We both knew I was avoiding what was really bothering me, however gradually I was easing into it.

"I still see Gillian, that last meeting when she was already in jail. I still see her slashing her brother's throat."

Hammond nods. "Those images are hard to erase. What you're experiencing is similar to what combat veterans go through. You know the term. Post-traumatic stress syndrome. You may never be free of those horrific images, but over time, they will fade. It was because of you that a killer was stopped. The file is very clear about that, and you should be too. If you were an agent, you'd be on mandatory leave now until we thought you were able to return to the field."

"But I'm not an agent. Am I ready to return to the field?"

"To life, you mean?" Hammond smiled then and stood up. "Perhaps that's enough for today."

"How do you know I'll come back?"

"You'll come back," Hammond said, and showed me to the door.

Dr. Hammond was right. I did go back. For three afternoons in succession. It was like I wanted to get it all out and over with as soon as possible. I drank coffee with Hammond, smoked and talked, and answered her occasional question. It seemed easy, like telling your life story to a stranger you'll never see again, not caring what they think of you. It was thinking out loud, getting nonjudgmental feedback. It felt damn good.

"What do you think draws you away from music, gets you involved with these other things?"

"It begins with doing somebody a favor, feeling obligated, helping somebody I know. With Wardell Gray and the Clifford Brown recordings, that's the way it was. But I was too good at it and dug too deep. I got more than I bargained for. Plus, as you said, I wasn't playing. It was a way to get my mind off that."

"But it's more than that, isn't it?"

I sat up straighter in the chair, as if I'd been pulled upright. "Yes, yes it is. Calvin Hughes said something similar. It's some fascination, maybe even an obsession with knowing. In all those cases, there was a point when I could have, should have, stopped. But I didn't."

"But there was a trade-off. You got satisfaction, but it cost you a lot, and perhaps made you a different person."

"Yes, it did. You're right. All those things are true. I might have been doing that the other times, but with Gillian there was no choice."

Hammond stops me for a minute and looks through my file. "Tell me about Calvin Hughes, Pappy Dean."

The question surprises me, and I take a moment to consider. "Both musicians—Pappy and I became friends. He helped me with the Wardell Gray thing. Calvin, I've known for years. He was my piano teacher at one time. We've stayed in touch over the years, remained fairly close."

"A kind of mentor?"

"Yes, I guess you could say that. Why do you ask?"

Hammond pauses, looks away for a moment. "I don't know. It's just a feeling. You haven't talked at all about your parents. Are they both still living?"

"Yes. My father and I never got along, he had no empathy for music. My mother does, but neither of them communicate much. They have their world, I have mine. I see them rarely."

Then I see where she's going. "You think Calvin and Pappy are father figure substitutes? Is that it?"

"Possibly. They're both considerably older than you are and

both musicians, so the connection is there, perhaps in a way you would have liked to have with your father."

"Aren't we getting away from the point here?"

Hammond doesn't push it. "Yes, I suppose we are." She looked at me then and smiled. I knew I'd told her more than I meant to. "I don't know if this has helped you, but my instinct tells me you're going to be okay. You acted courageously under pressure, and you were certainly an asset on this case. Your drive, determination, it's who you are, but sometimes you need to rein it in."

I knew then exactly what she meant. I leaned back, distinctly feeling a weight lifted from me. "So what do you think?" I asked Hammond, trying to keep it light. "Am I ready for the field again?"

"I think you know the answer to that better than I do," she said. She closed the file and plopped it on her desk. The sound was a satisfying one to me. "Call me anytime if you want," she said.

She was right. I did know. I'd never see things quite the same way again, but I also knew I could probably go on.

I didn't call her again, and a month later, I left for London.

April 28, 1988

Chet Baker, nodding, listens to the playback in the cavernous Hamburg studio. Only two tracks to go. His teeth are hurting, getting worse lately. He touches his jaw, feels them slip. Making it so far, though, playing good, but now he just wants to get out of there, get in the Alfa and drive as fast as he can to the gig in Paris. Just cool it for a while.

Chet's old friends Herb Geller and Walter Norris are there for the date. Herb and Walter come into the control booth to hear the playback of "Well You Needn't." Norris, the brilliant pianist, sits quietly, legs crossed. Herb, his horn hanging from around his neck, watches him, listens, checking him out. Chet, smiling at Herb now, hearing his solo. So long since L.A., from the days when he and Gerry Mulligan packed the Haig for almost a year.

"Not too bad for an old guy, huh?" Chet says.

Herb nods. "You sound great, man."

"Thanks."

"Are you okay? You need anything?"

"Just hope that guy gets back here with the teeth glue." He looks at the floor for a moment. "You know, man, if the uppers go, I can't play anymore, but I have an appointment with a dentist next week." Chet sighs, shakes his head, smiles that sad smile. "I gotta get out of here, man."

Herb nods again and smiles back. It's been over thirty years, but he knows how it is with Chet, how it's always been. "I know. Well, only a couple of more tunes left."

The engineer stops the tape as the track ends and looks at Chet. "That one is fine for you?" he asks.

Chet, glancing at Herb, catches his nod, saying, "Yes, it's fine."

As always, he hadn't played for anyone. Certainly not the record company suits who were now relaxing in chairs, in the control room, beaming at each other. They were scared earlier when he hadn't showed for the rehearsal. Chet didn't need to rehearse, but the orchestra, one of the best in Germany, did. For two days. An eighteen-piece big band and forty-three strings. Chet just played. He examined these old songs, played them, and then put them away until the next time. They would always be there, waiting for him like the women, the friends he left and eventually returned to. They were waiting too. Even if he was sometimes selfish, untrustworthy, there was something about him, that sweet nature that made people welcome him back.

The band reassembles in the studio. The audience takes their seats. Chet, aware now of the musicians sneaking glances at him, wondering, he guesses, if he's going to make it, but he's never doubted himself. He's been through too much for that now. It's just these goddamned teeth. Then a man carrying a small paper bag comes in quietly, holds it up to Chet.

"I need five minutes, okay?" Chet says to the conductor.

"Of course, Mr. Baker."

Chet goes out, taking the paper bag from the man, going to the men's room, squeezing the gel out of the tube and quickly applying it, resetting the teeth, testing, biting down while sixty-one musicians and the audience wait. After all this time the teeth still give him trouble, but there's nothing he can do about it.

He splashes water on his face, raises his head slowly, and gazes in the mirror, seeing an old man, a man older than his years, staring back at him. That face, perhaps once destined for Hollywood, is now lined, wrinkled, the cheeks sunken, the eyes sad and dark. The face of an old Indian. It's a face he knows well, but occasionally he still sees the young man in the old man's reflection. "You ain't no movie idol now, are you?" he asks the mirror.

Drying his face and hands with a paper towel, he heads back to the studio, nodding to the musicians and conductor that he's ready now. He looks for Herb Geller in the saxophone section and winks. "Okay, let's do it," he says to the conductor.

He's chosen all the tunes. They're going to call the album *My Favorite Songs*. He's comfortable with these tunes, and no matter how many times he's played them before, he finds something new, some new way to approach a phrase, hold or bend a note. He still doesn't know how he does it, but that doesn't matter. Doing it, playing, is all that matters.

The conductor raises his baton, begins a count: a lazy three-four tempo for "All Blues." Chet nods his approval, and the orchestra starts the vamp figure. He holds the horn casually as always, feels one twinge of pain when he puts the mouthpiece to his lips, but it passes quickly. He picks his spot and blows that first long tone, simple and pure, letting it settle over everyone there like satin, easy, relaxed, slipping into the tune. In that moment the missed rehearsals, the late arrival, the interruptions, are all forgotten, unimportant now. All will be forgiven when everyone hears the playback.

Chet, eyes closed, breathes life into the horn, playing, already seeing Paris in his mind.

3

I WAKE UP as the train slows and rumbles into Amsterdam's Central Station. I've dozed on and off all the way from London, glad now that I chose to go by train instead of flying. Part of it is the novelty. I can't remember the last time I was on a train. Just sitting there watching the countryside fly by has been soothing, a breather from London and hassling with the airport and the confines of a jet.

The week at Ronnie Scott's couldn't have gone better, and the Dutch promoter who'd visited the club twice confirmed the Amsterdam gig near the end of the week before he headed back to Amsterdam. I gave him Ace's hotel, and he's promised to relay the message that I am on the way. I'm not sure whether the gig is because of or in spite of Mike Bailey's story, but the end result is more work. I'm keeping the string going. It means a chance to see some of Europe, and I can have that drink with Ace, so I don't feel so guilty.

I get my bags together as the train enters the station and clanks to a halt. I follow the other passengers toward the exit, come out into a bright spring sun, and stand for a moment on the steps, taking in the bustle of people hurrying in every direction. Then my eye catches the bicycles. Hundreds of them, maybe more, most of them basic black models, many with baskets, racked, leaning against rails, chained to fences, taking up virtually every square inch of space. I've never seen so many bicycles.

"They are for the commuters."

"What?" I turn at the voice beside me and see a man in a raincoat, carrying a satchel. It's no one I recognize, just a friendly local perhaps who sounds like a tourist guide.

"People cycle to the station, leave their bicycles here, then come back and cycle home," he says. "There is little parking in Amsterdam. Bicycles are the main mode of transportation." The man nods and starts off. "Well, enjoy your stay in Amsterdam."

"Thanks," I say, wondering how he knew to speak English. "Wait, maybe you can help me." I set my bags down and consult the slip of paper with the name of the hotel the promoter has arranged for me.

"Yes?" The man comes back.

"Do you know the Prins Hendrik Hotel?"

He smiles. "Yes, you are very close." He points across the wide boulevard in front of the station. "This is called Prins Hendrikkade. The hotel is there, toward the plaza."

I look in the direction he's pointing and see the sign. "Okay, thanks. Thanks very much." I set my bags down and offer him my hand. "I'm Evan Horne."

He takes my hand and shakes it vigorously. "Edward de Hass."

"Well, thanks, Mr. de Hass. Thanks very much."

"Not at all," he says. "Enjoy Amsterdam."

I grab my bags and start walking, crossing without the lights, taking in the traffic, the people, and even more bicycles, riding in a special lane. I stop in front of the Prins Hendrik Hotel and see the irony of the promoter's choice. Next to the double glass doors is a plaque and a sculpture. The artist has captured that lined face so well.

CHET BAKER
TRUMPET PLAYER AND SINGER
DIED HERE ON MAY 13, 1988.
HE WILL LIVE ON IN HIS MUSIC
FOR ANYONE WILLING
TO LISTEN AND FEEL.
1929–1988

Next to the plaque is a list of contributors. I scan the names but see none I recognize except for a couple of record companies. It's hard to walk away, though. I look around, but people are passing by without even giving it a glance. I push through the glass doors into the hotel lobby. Inside, on one wall is a poster-size photo of Chet, taken in 1955 at the Open Door in New York City. This is the young Chet, on the rise, before his first bout with trouble, before those lines became etched in his face. All I can think is, Amsterdam is pretty cool.

At the desk, I show my passport and get checked in by a bored clerk. "You weren't here then, were you?" I ask, pointing at the photo. "When it happened, I mean."

It's obviously an old question. The clerk doesn't even look up. "No, only the owner was, and he does not come in much. Your room is C-18, and no, it is not the room Chet Baker stayed in."

"Thanks. I didn't ask if it was." I start for the elevator, then turn back. "Do you have an Ace Buffington checked in?"

"A moment, please." He taps some keys on his computer. "No, we did. Mr. Buffington checked out two days ago." The clerk looks at me and smiles. "He stayed in C-20."

"The Chet Baker room?"

"Yes."

Riding up the elevator, I think about that. Kind of puzzling, but maybe Ace already got what he wanted here, didn't get my message, was heading someplace else or even back home. The truth is, I hope he's already left Amsterdam.

I find the room small and clean but stuffy. I try to open one of the windows facing a back alley, but it's difficult. I get one of them halfway up and prop it open with this kind of stick thing attached to a chain. Below me is a cobblestone alleyway that winds back from the hotel. If I lean out, I can see one of the canals. I wonder if that's what happened to Chet Baker. Chet, high, leaning out too far, just nodding off and . . .

I put that all out of my mind then and unpack, wait for Walter Offen's call. Chet Baker, what happened to him, is for Ace to worry about, not me.

"So, you are ready to play?" Offen asks me. We're in the hotel bar. It's all old wood, carpeted, and very dark. No one is around but the bartender, and he's busy with the newspaper.

"Yes, I'm ready. Looking forward to meeting the bassist and drummer too."

Walter smiles, pushes his glasses up his nose. "Ah, you will like them, I'm sure. They are very good." He grins at me sheepishly.

"What?"

"I have one small surprise. Do you know Fletcher Paige?"

Fletcher Paige. The name comes at me from the past, the back of album covers. Great tenor player, long time with Duke Ellington or Count Basie, I think.

"Yes, I know who he is, but I haven't heard anything about him in years. I'm not even sure he's still alive. Is he?"

"Oh, yes," Walter says. "Very much so, and right here in Amsterdam. In fact, you will meet him soon. I have taken the liberty of arranging for him to play with you."

"Fletcher Paige? Really?" It's starting to come back. He went to Europe and just kind of disappeared but had a group of his own after leaving the big bands. I wonder, though, how we'll fit together style-wise. "It's okay with him?" It's an unusual arrangement, to say the least, without some prior approval. I wonder if Fletcher Paige had any say in things.

Walter is nodding his head excitedly. "Yes, yes, he knows

of your playing. This will be fantastic." He looks at his watch. "We should go, yes?"

"Fine."

"Finish your beer. I must get my car, and we will go. I am parked nearby. You wait outside, and I'll come around in front." Walter gets up, puts his coat on, still smiling, and taps me on the shoulder. "In five minutes, then."

I sit for a minute, thinking about Fletcher Paige. He was something of a legend, like Lester Young or Dexter Gordon. I knew that much at least. He'd played with everybody who was anybody, I'm sure. So he had become one of the expatriates, finding an audience in Europe and liking it, staying over here. No wonder I hadn't heard anything about him lately.

I go outside and stand, waiting for Walter, glancing again at the Chet Baker plaque. Walter arrives a few minutes later in a small car and honks. I jump in, and we're off in a squeal of tires as I get my first taste of Amsterdam driving. Walter careens around corners, over canal bridges, and through a maze of shortcuts and one-way streets, and finally skids to a stop in front of a tall gray brick building.

"I drive too fast, yes?" Walter asks.

"No, not at all," I say, finally letting go of the strap above the door. I get out and follow him inside.

The Bimhuis Club is upstairs and opens onto a long bar. To the side is a large open room with tiered, amphitheater-type seating and a fairly large stage. I stop for a moment. On the stage, a small black man in slacks and sports coat is seated on a stool, running through some changes on his tenor saxophone. Fletcher Paige.

"Come," Walter says. We go down the stairs to the stage. Paige stops playing, looks up, and smiles. He's short, slim, wears steel-rimmed glasses. His hair is salt and pepper, matched by a well-trimmed beard and mustache.

"My man Walter." He gets up and shakes hands, looking over Walter's shoulder at me trailing behind.

"So," Walter says, turning toward me. "This is Evan Horne." Paige steps up and offers me his hand.

"How you doin'? Bet you thought I was dead, huh? He did, right, Walter?"

It had crossed my mind, and Paige knows it. "Well, I . . ."

Paige laughs. "See, I told you." He points at Walter with a long slim finger, then looks back at me. "Don't worry, man, a lot of people think I'm dead. Mostly record companies." He laughs hard at his own joke.

I know we've never met, but somehow he looks familiar, as if I've just seen him recently. He catches me looking at him and smiles. "I could also double for Jimmy Heath."

As soon as he says that I see the resemblance. Jimmy Heath, the tenor-playing brother of bassist Percy with the Modern Jazz Quartet, and drummer Tootie. I nod and smile. "Okay, you got me," I say. I'd just heard Jimmy in New York before I came to Europe.

"I heard a lot of good things about you," Fletcher says. "We just have to see we gonna play together."

Walter watches this exchange and beams. He checks his watch. "Well, I must go. I will see you both tonight."

"Funny little cat, huh?" Paige says. "But he got me a lot of work over here. He's the reason I stayed in Amsterdam." He gives me a quick smile. "Well, there are a couple of other reasons, but we'll get into those later."

"How long have you been here?"

"In Amsterdam? Eighteen years. Few little side trips to Stockholm, Copenhagen, Paris, but mostly here. It's very cool for me here. Ben Webster lived here, and he *is* dead, so I figured, hey, why not?" Paige laughs again. It's infectious.

I want to know more, but we've got some music to figure out, so I save my questions for later. I look around. There's a drum kit set up and a bass lying on its side near the piano. "Where's the other guys?"

"They'll be along. I figured you and me should get acquainted first. Why don't you try the piano?"

"Okay." I sit down at the grand. It's well tuned, and the action is nice. I run through some chords, spin out a few single-note lines, aware of Fletcher Paige's eyes on me.

He nods, says, "Yeah, we gonna get along fine. We're billed as co-leaders—I hope that's cool with you. So I guess we can both pick tunes. I got some music, but for tonight, we best stick to standards, blues, shit like that. Okay with you?"

"Sure. How about 'Stella by Starlight'?" It's the first thing I think of.

"One of my favorites," Paige says.

I play a short intro, then Paige comes in with the melody. He plays with it a little, makes it almost his own composition, and makes me think I've never heard a tenor like this before. His tone is not rough and hard like Coltrane nor silky like Stan Getz, but somewhere in between. The notes flow out of his horn effortlessly, and when I veer away from the predictable changes, he goes right with me, as if we've been playing together a long time.

He drops out after a couple of choruses, and I try to play something equal to his solo. While I'm playing, he walks over, stands near the piano, then joins me for the final chorus, playing lines against my own till we meet again at the melody and go out. We both stop and look at each other.

"All right," he says, grinning, holding out his palm to me. I slap it and smile back.

Damn. Fletcher Paige.

We eat dinner at a small place around the corner from the Bimhuis, owned by a musician, so Fletcher tells me. There's no menu, just a half dozen specials printed on a blackboard. I let Fletcher do the talking and ordering. We sit by a window and watch the bicyclists pedal across the canal bridge. The food is good, and so is the carafe of red wine.

"I can see why you like Amsterdam," I say, lighting a cigarette. Fletcher joins me and blows a cloud of smoke toward the ceiling.

"Yeah, it suits me, and I don't have to put up with no shit here, if you dig what I'm saying. That's why a lot of cats stayed over here—Kenny Clarke, Don Byas, Art Farmer. Man, there's a whole history to this scene. But plenty of white ones too for a while. Phil Woods, Dave Pike—he played the Bimhuis a few times—Herb Geller, Walter Norris, Chet Baker." He pauses for a moment, thinking. "Not so many pianists, though. You might do okay here if you stay."

"It's not something I've really thought about. I just wanted to get away for a while, and these gigs made it easy."

"Yeah, it's like that at first. Phil Woods came over with three gigs and stayed five years. But then you become a local. Bread goes down, and you not in demand so much." He smiles again, kind of wistfully. "Hell, when I first got over here, it was like Lockjaw Davis used to tell me. All I had to do was tune up to get applause."

"Well, I don't have that kind of reputation to build on."

"You'd be surprised. You got your own kind of reputation, least with some folks." He stubs out his cigarette and signals the waiter for coffee. "I know all about you," he says, grinning slyly.

"How?"

"The Web, man, the Internet. My brother's a computer geek. On his last visit he got me a computer, hooked me up. Wanted a way for me to stay in touch easier. I have to admit it's cool, hear that voice say, 'You've got mail.'"

"I'm on the Internet?"

"All over, baby. Sherlock Holmes got nothin' on you. I read about Wardell Gray—I knew him slightly—those tapes of Clifford Brown you proved were bogus, and that serial killer thing in L.A. You had your hands full on that. What was she like, that Gillian character?"

I spend a lot of time putting cream and sugar in my coffee, stirring slowly. "Not something I really want to think or talk about, if you don't mind."

"That's cool, I can dig it." Fletcher watches me for a moment. "Maybe sometime, though. Might be good to talk about it."

I smile at him. "You a counselor too?"

"I'm a man of many talents," he says, grinning.

Fletcher Paige is one of those kind of people you like instantly, and I know we're going to hit it off. "So you've never been back?"

"Oh yeah, short visits, recorded a few times, but mostly I stay here. I can work all the jazz festivals, club dates, recordings, but I think about going back once in a while, when I remember Ben Webster dying here, living in a room with that woman who took care of him. Ben was lonely and depressed at the end. I don't want to end up like that, but shit . . ." He spreads his hands and shrugs. "Gotta be where the work is, man. Maybe I'll get lucky, get in a movie like Dexter Gordon and go back for the Academy Awards." He laughs out loud then.

After fifteen years in Europe, Dexter Gordon had starred in *Round Midnight* and been nominated for best actor. His career took off all over again—gigs, records, discovered by America from Europe.

"Chet Baker died here too," Fletcher says. "Course, you know that already. Walter got you in that hotel down by the station?"

"Uh-huh. Nice plaque they put up for him."

"Another one nobody is going to figure out, but it ain't no mystery. Motherfucker just nodded out, went out that window. Probably thought he could fly."

"Has anybody been around asking about that? I have a friend who was supposed to be coming here. They told me at the hotel he'd already checked out. Not like him to just disappear like that."

"Big tall professor dude? Yeah, he was around asking a lot of questions. Only saw him one time."

"Did you talk to him?"

"Little. Cat made me nervous, almost like an interrogation. Got out his tape recorder and shit."

I could imagine Ace being thrown by Fletcher, trying to be respectful but wanting to quote him accurately and thrilled to have found a genuine jazz hero.

Fletcher looks at his watch. "Come on, man, it's almost show time." He pulls some money out. "I got this one. Welcome to Amsterdam."

The Bimhuis is full when we get back. Even the bar is crowded as we push our way through to the stage. The drummer and bassist are already there, talking, laughing with friends, ready to play. Fletcher introduces us, and we talk briefly about tunes. I sit down at the piano and flex my fingers, feeling the anticipation as Walter Offen appears and makes the introductions in a flurry of Dutch. All I can make out is Fletcher's name and my own, then we're off, on a blues line of Fletcher's.

I feed him the changes for half a dozen choruses, then he bows and steps back to a round of applause while I start my exploration. Drums and bass are right with us, and during the bass solo I have to marvel at the bassist's chops. Nothing stiff about the drummer either. We do a couple of choruses of eight-bar exchanges—Fletcher and I alternating—then bring it on home. Fletcher beams at me and steps to the microphone. "How about a warm Amsterdam welcome for Evan Horne."

This part at least does feel like home. The rest of the night goes equally well. Nobody asks me about being a detective or calls me Sam Spade. Walter is pleased, and so apparently is the Bimhuis owner. We're a hit.

"You want to come by my place?" Fletcher asks as he packs up his horn. A lot of the audience is still lingering, not wanting to give it up yet.

"I don't think so tonight. I'm kind of tired, but yeah, some other time, sure."

"Cool," Fletcher says. "Hey, you play chess?"

"Not in years."

"Okay, well, we'll get you brushed up. I'm going home and read my e-mail." He laughs hard. "Wonder what Prez would have thought of e-mail. Later, man."

That would have been something. Lester Young online.

Walter drops me at the hotel. I have that wired feeling after a gig—tired but not ready for sleep. I check at the front desk for messages, but there are none. I feel a slight twinge of apprehension that there's nothing from Ace. It isn't like him at all to just take off, but maybe he finally got the message and is hot on the trail of his research. Chet Baker lived all over Europe, so Ace could be anywhere. Or maybe Ace didn't like it that I'd turned him down, and now he is going to show me he can do it on his own. More power to him. Trying to put it out of my mind, I decide to go for a walk.

I leave the hotel and head around the corner, through a maze of cobblestone alleyways that lead into the Old Quarter—bars, restaurants, sex shops, snack bars with food smells wafting into the street, and lots of people, even at this hour. Turning one corner, I come across a short street of the red-light district.

It's impossible not to look at the girls on display in the windows. That's the only way to describe them. Clad mostly in bras and panties, they smile and beckon from their perches on high stools. Some of them are quite beautiful. I pass a number of coffeehouses, which I know are venues for marijuana smoking, complete with menus, so I'd heard—but not tonight. I head back and come out behind the hotel. I look up toward my room, count over a couple of windows to the room where Chet Baker fell from, the same room Ace stayed in.

There's a drainpipe running up the side of the building just past that room. It looks big enough to hold a man's weight and goes right past Chet's room. Nobody saw him fall? To my left, the alleyway opens onto a canal, but if it was late

at night, nobody would probably have noticed a body, and . . .
I shake it off. One day in Amsterdam, and I'm already se-
duced by the mystery. Enough. I go around to the front entrance and glance once again at the plaque for Chet Baker.

Hope you're having some luck, Ace.

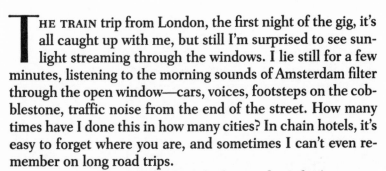

4

THE TRAIN trip from London, the first night of the gig, it's all caught up with me, but still I'm surprised to see sunlight streaming through the windows. I lie still for a few minutes, listening to the morning sounds of Amsterdam filter through the open window—cars, voices, footsteps on the cobblestone, traffic noise from the end of the street. How many times have I done this in how many cities? In chain hotels, it's easy to forget where you are, and sometimes I can't even remember on long road trips.

I get out of bed and take a look outside. I don't see any windmills or people in wooden clogs, but those voices are Dutch. Must be Amsterdam. I don't even look at the cigarettes on the nightstand but just head for the shower. Coffee and some breakfast is much on my mind as I get dressed in jeans, a sweater, and some well-worn running shoes.

I pull my door shut and see the maid's cart outside a room a couple of doors down—the Chet Baker room. The door is open, but I don't see the maid. I glance in and see the room is all made up, with no sign of luggage, so its occupant must have checked out early. I can't resist walking over to the open window and looking out. I can almost touch the drainpipe running along the side of the building. The view of the canal is even better from here. Was Chet looking out, trying to get a better look at a woman, waving at her or something else? Maybe just sitting there, heroin coursing through his veins, nodding off, oblivious to the danger.

"This is your room?" The maid is standing in the doorway, holding an armful of towels, looking at me.

"Oh no, sorry. I'm down the hall. I think my friend was staying here a few nights ago. Do you remember a very tall American with a beard?"

She shakes her head. "I have been on holiday," she says. "To London. My friend Maria might know."

"No, that's okay. I'll find him. Thank you." She nods and goes to get something from her cart, then turns back to me. "I can do your room now?"

"Oh yes, sure. I'm going to breakfast." I follow her out into the hall. She nods again and pushes the cart down to my room, opens the door, and goes inside. She peeks out again, seeing me still standing in the hallway. "You can shut the door, please?"

"Sure." But when she goes in my room, I duck back inside Ace's room and close the door behind me. I want another look around.

There's nothing out of place, and no reason there should be. It's simply a hotel room, cleaned and ready for its next occupant. No plaque that says "Chet Baker Slept Here" either. I open the drawers of the nightstand, check in the closet, the bathroom. If Ace or anybody was here, there's no evidence of it. I walk over to the window and look out again. A metal heater runs along the wall just under the window. It's early spring, but the nights are still cool, and so is the heater when I touch it. I glance down, and something catches my eye. Something white, a piece of paper or something stuck behind the radiator. I slide my hand down to see if I can reach and drag it up, and I feel something else wedged between the wall and the heater.

I manage to get hold of the edge and pull. It's a flat leather portfolio with a zipper around three sides. I'd know it anywhere; Ace always had it with him. He couldn't have forgotten it—but what's it doing here, shoved down behind the radiator? And who put it here? Inside are file folders, typed pages, handwritten notes, newspaper clippings, photos—all of Chet Baker. Ace's research.

I zip it up quickly, open the door, and check the hallway. The maid is still busy in my room. Closing the door quietly, I slip down the stairs, Ace's portfolio under my arm.

There are several coffee bars near the hotel. I choose the least crowded one and order a tall cappuccino and some kind of sweet roll. Grabbing one of the large ashtrays off the bar, I sit at a back table and open the case, turning over the pages one at a time as I wolf down the roll and sip the hot coffee. Ace has assembled quite a file on Chet Baker—news stories from American and foreign newspapers, *Downbeat, Jazz Times,* Gene Lees's *Jazzletter,* which is available only by subscription, a number of photos, and lots of typed pages with handwritten notes, phone numbers, and names added in the margins, all in Ace's neat printing. One is for the Dutch National Jazz Archives in Amsterdam.

In the pocket in the back are also a couple of snapshots of Ace himself, smiling almost smugly, standing in front of the Chet Baker plaque in front of the hotel. I wonder who took those. Maybe the front desk clerk?

I put everything back in the case, zip it up, and carry it with me to the bar to get another coffee. I sit down again, light a cigarette, and listen to the voices around me, take in the smells of cooking and coffee brewing, and wonder what the hell is going on.

There's no way Ace would leave all this stuff behind. It is

all his research, and even if there's some logical reason—and I can't think of any—he certainly wouldn't stuff it behind the radiator and just forget it when he checked out. And he did check out, according to the desk clerk. He didn't just leave one morning and not come back. His clothes were gone, so what's the deal? It just doesn't add up.

I finish my coffee and walk back to the hotel. It's quite sunny now, but there's still a nip in the air, and the streets are crowded. Across the way at Central Station, people are streaming in and out past the hundreds of bicycles. At the hotel, I check for messages and find one from Fletcher Paige for me to call him. I go back to my room, stash Ace's portfolio in my own bag, and dial the number Fletcher has left for me.

"'Lo."

"Fletcher? It's Evan Horne."

"Hey. Got any plans this afternoon?"

"No, not really. What's up?"

"Thought I'd show you around your neighborhood, get some lunch if that's cool."

"Sounds good. You want me to meet you someplace?"

"Yeah, there's a place near your hotel, not far from the police station. Just ask anybody. The New Orleans Café. 'Bout noon?"

"Okay. See you then."

I hang up and take out the portfolio again, looking through every sheet of paper in there, even in the side pockets, but there's nothing there to tell me anything. That familiar rumbling starts in my stomach as I sift through the clippings and photos and typed pages, remembering how I looked at a similar file in Las Vegas on Wardell Gray. Even that made more sense than this does. At least then, Ace was sitting across from me in the UNLV Student Union.

Fletcher is already there when I get to the New Orleans Café. It's dark inside, and there's taped jazz coming from somewhere in the back. Fletcher sits in a booth by the window, drinking coffee and reading *USA Today*. He waves me over, and I slide in opposite him. He folds the paper neatly and takes off a pair of wire-rimmed glasses.

"Hey, man, you found it." He replaces them with another pair. "Gettin' old, man. It ain't fun. One pair to read, another one just to see. But shit, I can still play."

"Just like you said."

Fletcher glances at his watch. "Wanna take a walk? We're early yet for lunch. We can come back, and I can show you around the Old Quarter."

"Sure." We get up, and Fletcher tells the bartender to hold the table, that we'll be back later.

We wind through the narrow streets. Within a couple of minutes I'm totally turned around in the maze of bars, shops, and coffeehouses, but Fletcher seems to have a destination in mind.

"You do any smoke, man?"

"Not for a long time, since I worked with Lonnie Cole. He grew his own. Always gave me a bad reaction."

"Uh-huh," Fletcher says. "Well, if you're so inclined, this is the place to do it. Any of these coffee bars, it's legal. Just go in, and they'll give you a menu. Shit from all over. One of the advantages of Amsterdam is their liberal attitude on a lot of things." We turn a corner and come into a narrow alleyway with tall windows, glass doors, and the reddish-tinged lights. It could be where I walked last night, but it's hard to tell. "Here's another one."

The girls are out in full force, perched on stools or pacing in front of the windows. In some, the drapes are drawn across. "That means they with a customer, probably some business-man on his lunch hour." Fletcher waves to a couple of the girls. They seem to know him, waving back and smiling. Seeing my look, Fletcher says, "Different kind of window shop-ping, huh? No, I don't do this scene, but I been around so long lot of folks know me. Hey, look here."

Right next to one of the girls' windows is a brick building. "Take a look," Fletcher says. Inside I can see a group of small children sitting on the floor. A woman is seated before them, a book in her hand, obviously reading a story. A little farther on, more kids are working on some art project and a teacher is roaming around the room commenting on their work.

"Hookers' kids?" I ask.

Fletcher smiles. "Nope, just a regular preschool."

"Here? In this area?"

"Yep, part of the city's urban renewal. It's mostly bars, the red-light district—you've seen that—but they want to have some normalcy too, so they put in a preschool. Ain't that a bitch." He laughs and claps his hands.

"But don't the parents object?"

"No, they know it up front. The girls were here first. They can be liberal too."

I glance at the window next to the school. A tall, willowy black girl is seated on a stool. Her hair is almost red, and she's clad in only bra and panties. She catches my eye, cups her very full breasts, and smiles. Fletcher waves and blows her a kiss.

We walk on past a beautiful old church, and Fletcher tells me it's the oldest in Amsterdam. "Some place, huh? The Old Quarter. You can get drunk, get high, get laid, and save your soul, all in walking distance." He laughs again. "This sure ain't California, man."

We continue turning corners till suddenly we're back at the New Orleans. Fletcher's booth is still vacant, his newspaper right where he left it, and menus are waiting on the table. "Now we eat," he says, sliding into the booth.

I join him. "You must be a good customer here."

Fletcher smiles slyly. "Yeah, one of the perks of living here for a while. Shit, Dexter Gordon was a write-in candidate for mayor when he lived in Copenhagen. They got a good stew you might try."

I follow Fletcher's lead. He catches the waiter's eye and signals him, putting two fingers up. The waiter nods and heads for the kitchen. The bartender brings us two draft beers. Fletcher takes a long pull of his and looks at me.

"So, what's on your mind? I can see you want to talk about something. You've been preoccupied all morning."

I nod and wonder how much to tell him, but there's nothing to lose. "How well did you know Chet Baker?"

"Uh-oh, here we go. Sam Spade on the case." He laughs. "No pun intended."

"You're a mystery fan?"

"Oh yeah, got a collection of paperbacks. Raymond Chandler, Ross MacDonald, Walter Mosley, Elmore Leonard, and some new cat, Gary Phillips. I like him because his character is named Monk. But my main man is Charles Willeford. Writes about a Miami cop named Hoke Moseley. Gotta love a guy named Hoke," Fletcher says. "Ain't got his own teeth, always owes his ex-wife money. But he's cool."

"Well, I'm not on any case, but there are a couple of things. Remember I asked you about my friend Buffington, the professor? Well, there's no sign of him. The hotel says he just checked out, and that's not like him."

"So? Lots of people check out of hotels."

"No, there's something strange about it. I saw him in London, and we agreed that if I made this gig, we'd get together. I'm sure he would have left a message for me." I pause for a moment, wondering what Fletcher thinks. "There's something else." I tell Fletcher about finding the portfolio. "He wouldn't just leave it like that, forget it when he checked out. Especially hidden as it was."

"Didn't hide it too well," Fletcher says. "You found it."

"Yeah, I know. And that bothers me. What do you think?"

Fletcher studies me across the table. "I watched you playing last night. You even look like a piano player, got that look in your eyes, the way you listen, head to the side, looking for the right chord. Piano players are like that. Always thinking, watching everything, hanging back."

"Really. You got all that?"

"Oh, yeah," Fletcher says, with a mischievous smile. "Little game I play. I see people and try to imagine them playing an instrument. I'm usually right. Piano players and bass players and drummers are different. Well, drummers are really different. But piano players, they got nothing to blow, they have to touch those keys, bringing all that metal and wood to life. They have a different look when they're comping, playing for other soloists, than when they solo. You got that look. Last night, you looked like you'd like to climb in that piano and never come out. I could see it in your eyes. You got a great touch, you listen, and you play the prettiest chords I've heard in a long time. You could give a lot of cats a hard time."

"Thanks. Coming from you, that's—"

Fletcher waves his hand, gives me a quick mock frown. "Oh, shit, I didn't say you're Bud Powell."

"Okay, but thanks anyway, it means a lot. You don't know how much I'd like to believe you're right about Ace, but I don't think so. Research is Ace's thing. That portfolio is stuffed full of information about Chet Baker. That's why he was in Amsterdam. He wouldn't just go off and forget it, any more than you'd forget your horn."

Fletcher shakes his head. "Don't matter. Unless you want back in the detective business, you just turn your friend's portfolio in to the front desk and let him claim it, or call them about it. You don't know, man. Maybe he did just forget it. Got distracted when he checked out and didn't remember till he was on a train somewhere."

What Fletcher says makes sense to a point, but I still believe Ace would have forgotten anything but his portfolio.

The waiter brings our food then, two big steaming bowls of meaty stew and a small loaf of warm bread. Fletcher was right. It's great. We eat for a few minutes in silence, both of us thinking. Finally, Fletcher makes another suggestion.

"Why don't you check with the local police, tell them the whole story?"

"I've already thought of that, but what can I tell them?

My friend checked out of the hotel. Like you, they'll just say, So what?"

Fletcher nods. "Yeah, probably. He's not exactly a missing person. Maybe he'll just show up again, and you can give him the case in person."

"I wish it was going to be that easy, but I know it's not. I almost feel like he wanted me to find it."

Fletcher puts his fork down and looks at me. "That's getting a little out there, isn't it? You said he didn't even know for sure you would be in Amsterdam, and he didn't know what hotel you'd be in, did he?"

Before I can answer, the door swings open. A tall lanky young black man in jeans, turtleneck sweater, and leather coat and sunglasses struts in, spots us, and saunters over to our booth.

"Uh-oh," Fletcher says. "Here comes Shaft."

"Fletcher Paige, what it is." He holds out his palm. Fletcher smacks it lightly without looking up. The young man just smiles and rubs his hand over his shaven head. He has one gold ring in his left ear.

"Hey, Darren. We're eating."

But Darren is oblivious. He sits down next to Fletcher and smiles at me. "You must be the piano man. Evan Horne, right?" He holds out his hand for me to shake. He lets go, then leans in, takes off his glasses, and points at me with one long slim finger. His eyes are big and round. "Oh man, you the detective cat."

"Don't go there, Darren," Fletcher says.

"Hi." I look to Fletcher. He rolls his eyes.

"Say hello to Darren. Thinks he's the hippest cat in Amsterdam."

Darren laughs. "Thinks? Man, you know it. I am the man. Well, next to Fletcher, anyway. Word is y'all were smoking last night at the Bimhuis."

"Ain't you got something to do, Darren?" Fletcher says. "You're interrupting our lunch."

Darren holds up his hands. For all his bravado, it's clear he doesn't want to offend Fletcher. He puts his glasses on again but keeps the smile intact. "That's cool, man. Yeah, I got lots to do. I might catch you tonight, dig some sounds." He stands up, waves at me. "Later."

Fletcher shakes his head. Darren waves briefly at the bartender and is gone.

"Who was that?"

"Darren Mitchell. From Newark. Came over here a few years ago and stayed. I don't really know what he does except try to act hip and bother me. Thinks he wants to be a PI. He gets his dialogue from old jazz movies. Bad old jazz movies. Used to call me Pops, but I had to put a stop to that shit. He tells anybody who will listen that when Chet was around, he used to hang out with him, score for him, that kind of shit, but he wasn't even here then, and Chet didn't hang around with nobody 'less it was a woman."

"Did you ever play with Chet?"

Fletcher finishes off his stew and signals for another beer. "Yeah, couple of times, but Chet had his own thing. Beautiful player, I'll give him that, but that dope fucked him up."

"What do you think happened?"

Fletcher nods his head. "No telling. There's all kinds of stories. He just leaned out the window too far and fell. He was pushed, or he tried climbing up that damn drainpipe and fell. Wasn't no reasoning with Chet."

"Who would push him?"

Fletcher shrugs. "Dealers, maybe. He always owed somebody money, and he always had cash. Word is he had a lotta bread from that last record date he did in Germany. Got paid and drove right here to score like he always did." He stops, shaking his head as if remembering something. "But I lean toward the falling-out-the-window story. He just nodded out and fell." Fletcher laughs then. "I saw Philly Joe Jones do that in San Francisco with Miles at the Jazz Workshop. Little small stage, drums against the wall. They were playing 'Oleo,' kickin' ass—Philly, Red Garland, Paul Chambers, Hank Mobley—when the drums just stopped. Miles turned around, and there was Philly, his head against the wall—gone, out. Miles just walked off. But Chet? He'd been trying to commit suicide for a long time. Just took him thirty years to finish it."

Fletcher lets me pay the check this time, and we get up to leave. Outside, the Old Quarter is getting busy. Fletcher looks up at the sky. Big white puffy clouds move by slowly in the deep blue sky. "Can you find your way back to the hotel okay?"

"Sure, I'm fine."

Fletcher doesn't look at me, just stares straight ahead. "Look, man, I know you worried about your friend, but there's probably an easy explanation. If I were you, I'd just let it be, you dig?"

"Yeah, you're probably right."

Now he looks at me and smiles. "All right, then, catch you tonight." He takes a few steps, then turns around. "Hey, you know 'Lush Life'?"

"Yeah, you want to do it?"

"Uh-huh, long as you let me play the verse. You know Billy Strayhorn was only sixteen when he wrote that song? Cat was a motherfucker, huh? Later."

"Hey, Fletcher," I call to him. "You ever picture Darren on an instrument?"

He stops for a moment, thinks, then turns to me. "No. Darren would be a jive-ass singer."

Fletcher Paige, on the verge of seventy, walking away, humming the first few bars of "Lush Life." I watch him till he disappears around the corner. It's a picture I want to keep in my mind.

We play "Lush Life" and more at the Bimhuis. Fletcher and I are meshing well, better than I thought possible. The bassist and drummer sense it and know enough to stay out of our way, just adding their support. The audience feels something too. They don't know what exactly, but they feel it, some kind of magic happening right before them.

On the break, I can feel the electricity surge through the crowd. Nobody is leaving, but it's hard to stay focused when people are talking to you, and they don't know what to say. It isn't just the language, either. They want to communicate, but they can't get across that gap. You like to give, and the music, the playing, is what attracts people.

I went through different stages with that. I used to feel very arrogant at one time, would hardly talk to anyone. Later, I was switched off in a different way. It's hard because sometimes you don't want to talk to anyone and there's nothing to do but kill time, wait for the next set, then get back up there and lose yourself in the music. Time on your hands, and with some people, it can start funny habits.

Playing jazz, playing it well, is something that's very hard to do, so if you drink, or smoke, or whatever at the same time, it doesn't work, at least not for me. There's an element of it that can be destructive when art takes place in clubs, and that element has claimed many musicians. The Bimhuis doesn't feel like that. For the most part, these people have come for the music, to be witness to something they can talk about tomorrow or next week or next year, so they can say, "Yeah, I was there the night Fletcher Paige and Evan Horne played in Amsterdam." Tonight they're getting their money's worth.

I come off the stand feeling up—energy keyed up and have all this time. I'm working, but everyone else is having a good time enjoying me working. Once, during the second set, Fletcher eyes me over his horn as if to say, This is where you belong, and in that moment, I know he's right. However short-lived these moments seem, they mean everything.

When we finish for the night, Fletcher and I have a last drink at the bar, avoiding as much as we can the constant well-wishers who want to come by and say hello—especially those pseudo fans who've come to be seen, to sit in the front, wear sunglasses, snap their fingers, nod their heads, hoping they'll be perceived as cool.

I sit there with Fletcher, basking in the glow, knowing I've played well. "Feels good, huh?" Fletcher says. He looks totally at peace with himself.

Leaning back, relaxed for the first time in weeks, I can't help but grin. "That it does," I say. "That it does."

But then, across the room, something makes me sit up straight, break the spell. Fletcher sees my expression and turns to see what I'm looking at, then rolls his eyes.

The resemblance is uncanny at first glance. It's the ghost of Chet Baker, as if he stepped out of the photo in the hotel lobby—this young man in jeans, white T-shirt, hair falling over his eyes. The only thing missing is his trumpet. He sits at the bar alone and stares moodily, sipping a beer. Nobody is paying any attention to him.

"That cat's around here all the time," Fletcher says. "Got some obsession with Chet. Dresses like him in his younger days. Before that, it was James Dean, the actor."

I can't take my eyes off him. "Does he play?"

"Nothing but the radio."

I nod, relaxing a bit now. "It's spooky, though."

"Yeah," Fletcher says. "Ghosts always are. C'mon, man. We got some more music to play."

On the last tune of the night, "I'm Getting Sentimental Over You," we take it at a medium tempo. But after everyone solos, Fletcher doesn't take it out. He starts on a long tag, inviting us to join him as he turns the chords inside out, challenging me to stay with him, playing like he's somewhere else than a club in Amsterdam. The bass player digs in, and the drummer finds the groove as we roll on almost to the breaking point. Then Fletcher, with only a slight nod, finds an opening, and we go out.

Over the applause, he eyes me as if he's done that tag to prove a point. It's like a drug, but I also feel another kind of pull, in another direction, a path I've been down before.

It's one I don't want to follow, not yet. But the question, as always, is how long I can avoid it.

5

AFTER BREAKFAST, I decide to check once more at the front desk for messages. Maybe Ace has called in, left a message or asked about his portfolio. "No, nothing, Mr. Horne," the clerk tells me, "but the owner is here this morning."

"Where?"

"In the bar."

"Thanks." I hurry through to the adjoining bar and find a short, stocky man drinking coffee, reading the newspaper.

"Excuse me. I'm staying here. The desk clerk said you were here. Are you the owner?"

"Yes?" He looks up at me. "Is there some problem with your room?"

"No, the room is fine. I'd just like to ask you about a friend of mine. He stayed here a few days ago." The man looks puzzled for a moment. "He might have talked to you about Chet Baker?"

"Oh, yes, a professor, Buffington, wasn't it?" He puts the newspaper aside.

"Yes, that's right. Do you have a few minutes?"

"Of course. Please, sit down. You will have some coffee?"

"Yes, thanks." He signals the bartender and turns back to me. "Your professor friend was very persuasive. He stayed in the same room as Chet Baker and asked me a lot of questions. I took some photos of him, in front of the hotel."

"Yes, I can imagine. We were supposed to meet here, but he checked out and didn't leave a message or anything. It's not like him to do that, so I just wondered if you have any idea where he might be. If he said where he was going next."

"No, I'm afraid not." The waiter sets down my coffee and another for the owner. "I'm not here much these days. I have a manager who runs the hotel."

"Thanks." I take a sip and light a cigarette. "What did you talk about with him?"

The owner shrugs. "Mostly Chet Baker. He said he was researching a book. He had a great deal of papers already, but I'm afraid I couldn't tell him anything. I wasn't here the night it happened. I'd been in the country. My manager called me, and I came back and talked with the police. I confess at the time I didn't know how famous Mr. Baker was."

"What did the police think happened?"

"That Mr. Baker was involved in drugs, was perhaps intoxicated, and fell from the window." He looks away for a moment, remembering. "It was very distressing to have that happen here at my hotel, of course, but there was nothing I could do." He smiles, remembering something. "You'd be surprised at the number of trumpet players who have come to stay in that room. Since we've had the sculpture outside, we get lots of inquiries. I thought for a while of charging extra, but that wouldn't be right." He studies me for a moment. "You are also a trumpet player?"

"No. Piano. I'm playing over at the Bimhuis, with Fletcher Paige."

"Ah yes, Fletcher Paige. He's become as famous in Amsterdam as . . . was it Weber?" He sips his coffee, then looks at me.

"Webster. Ben Webster."

"Yes, that's it. Forgive me for saying so, but somehow that doesn't seem right. All these American musicians coming to Europe, playing, living, dying here and, I suspect, forgotten in their own countries."

"No, you're quite right. It is a shame."

"And Chet Baker? He was famous in America?"

"Well, at one time he was, the early days. He had some hard times."

"Yes." I can see his mind is already elsewhere. He finishes his coffee and folds up the newspaper. "I'm sorry I can't be more help." He stands up to go. "Well, excuse me. I have work to do. Are you also staying in Amsterdam?"

"Me? I don't know yet."

"Well, if I think of anything else, I will let you know."

"Thanks. I appreciate it."

I watch him leave, sitting there for a while, the day stretched before me, wondering what to do next. Maybe after my blunt refusal of Ace's proposal in London, he simply decided to not bother catching up. But it nags at me. It's a loose end I want tied up. There are a couple of other places I can check, and I think both of them are not far from the hotel. The desk clerk marks both places on a city map and sends me on my way.

There's a truck loading cases of paper in front of the Old Quarter police station. Inside, two women sit on a wooden bench, talking quietly. One seems to be comforting the other. The small reception desk is manned by a young officer in a light blue shirt with gold epaulets on the shoulders and dark blue pants, looking through some papers. He glances up when I approach the desk.

"Ah, excuse me. I'd like to talk to someone."

He looks like he's not quite sure how to respond. "Yes?"

"Yes. It's about my friend. I think he is missing. Well, I don't know if he's missing, but—"

"A moment, please." He picks up the phone and talks briefly in Dutch with someone, then hangs up. "I'm sorry, my English is not so good. Wait, please. Someone is coming."

"Thank you." A couple of minutes later another, older officer comes out, looks at me. He's short, stocky, looks to be late fifties, and dressed in civilian clothes—dark pants, white shirt with the cuffs rolled up, and a tie loosened at the neck.

"Yes, can I help you? I'm Inspector Dekker."

"It's about my friend. He was staying at the Prins Hendrik Hotel." I can see he's trying to figure out what I want, whether I'm just a nuisance or really have a problem. "Look, can we go somewhere and talk?"

Dekker looks around, then nods. "Yes, of course. Come this way, please." I follow him down a corridor to an office not much bigger than a closet. Beyond his office, I can see the corridor opening onto a larger room with several uniformed policemen. "Sit down, please," Dekker says.

There's barely room for Dekker's desk and the chair I sit down in opposite him. His desk is cluttered with papers and files that nearly hide a telephone. Peeking out from behind a stack of heavy binders is a framed photo of a woman and a teenage boy. I look at Dekker and wonder where to start, but he beats me to it. "May I see some identification, please? Your passport."

"Oh, sure." I take out my passport and show it to him. He looks it over and glances at me a time or two.

"And why are you in Amsterdam? Tourist?"

"No, I'm a musician. I'm playing at the Bimhuis." I think I catch a slight smile, but I'm not sure. "This isn't about me, it's about my friend."

"Yes, I understand. Your friend is in trouble? What is his name, please?"

"Charles Buffington." I spell it out for him, and he writes it down. "Well, I don't know if he's in trouble or not." I explain my concerns about Ace having checked out of the hotel without leaving a message for me. He listens patiently, letting me get it all out before asking any further questions. "So, that's it. I just wondered if the police can check on it."

He nods and glances at my passport again before handing it back. "Mr. . . . Horne, is that how you pronounce it?"

"Yes."

"Your friend is a tourist, yes?"

"Yes. Well, he's doing some research here. About the musician who died in Amsterdam some years ago. Chet Baker." There's no recognition of the name in Dekker's face.

"Do you have some reason to believe something has happened to your friend?"

"Well, no, I mean I don't know. I'm just concerned."

"I understand. But perhaps your friend just left." He holds his hands up and shrugs.

"Well, I know that's possible, but it doesn't seem very like him to do something like that." I wonder for a moment if I should tell him about the portfolio, but there's nothing to wonder about. Of course I should, but I decide not to for now.

He glances at his watch. He's obviously got more important things to do than listen to me. "Since he did leave the hotel, and he owes no money and left no message, I don't see what we can do. I could perhaps suggest the American consulate. Unless your friend is officially missing, I'm afraid there's nothing much we could do for you. I'm sorry."

"What do you mean, officially missing?"

"I mean a report filed officially, but I suggest you exhaust other possibilities first."

I nod and think for a minute. Do I really want to do that? File a missing person's report? He's right, of course. Ace could have just checked out and left. Were it not for the portfolio he left—no, hid—I'd have no problem with that beyond thinking it was kind of unusual. But it's the portfolio that nags at me.

"All right. Well, thank you for your time. There are a couple of things I can check on."

He stands up. "Not at all. Please let me know the results of your investigation."

"My investigation?"

He does smile now. "The wrong word, perhaps. Pardon me."

"Oh, okay." I stand up to go. "There is one thing. The musician I mentioned that died here several years ago. Chet Baker. Do you know if the detective in charge of that case is still working here?"

"He died here in Amsterdam? When?"

"Nineteen-eighty-eight, I believe. He fell from a hotel window. At least, I think he did."

He frowns for a moment. "Ah, the Prins Hendrik. The one with the—" He pauses for a moment, searching for the right word. "The memorial sculpture on the front of the hotel, yes?"

"Yes, that's the one."

"I was not here then, but I heard about it. The officer who investigated that case has retired now."

"Oh. Do you know if he's still in Amsterdam?"

"Yes, I believe so . . . but I would have to . . . do you wish to talk with him?"

"Well, I don't know. I thought perhaps my friend might have contacted him."

"Oh, yes, I see. I will make some inquiries. Where can I reach you?"

"I'm at the Prins Hendrik also."

"Very well. I shall leave a message, then, if I find out anything."

"Thank you."

"Mr. Horne." He gives me a thoughtful look.

"Yes?"

He seems to consider, measures his words carefully. "There's a difference between disappearing and being missing. And, please, take no offense. You and your friend perhaps had a disagreement? Sometimes people simply don't want to be found." He shows me to the door. "Even friends do strange things at times."

"Yes, I guess they do."

I walk out past the desk again and stand on the front steps for a moment. Maybe Dekker was right. I guess you could call what happened in London a disagreement. Maybe Ace doesn't want to be found—but when does not wanting to be found change to officially missing?

I find the American Express office on the Rokin Damrak, not far from the Central Station, opposite the church, amid some department stores and other travel offices. I want to change some money, and I can make a call from there. I push through the glass doors and follow the signs upstairs. There's a bank of kiosks to change money, and two pay phone booths on one wall. Not much business this morning. Two students with backpacks are cashing traveler's checks, and a family of four is studying a map and talking about sight-seeing.

I change some money at one of the windows and ask about the phones. "I need to call the States. Can I use one of those phones and charge the call to my card?"

"Yes." The teller indicates the glass-enclosed booths without looking up.

I get in the booth and close the accordion door. There are signs in several languages for phone/credit card use. I start with international information for the number of UNLV in Las Vegas and copy the number down on my money change receipt. I take a deep breath and dial the number after inserting my card in the slot.

"University of Nevada, Las Vegas."

"Yes, can you connect me with the English Department, please?"

"One moment." I listen to the hums and clicks, then another voice.

"English department," a female voice says. "How can I help you?"

"Yes, can I speak to Professor Buffington, please?"

"Professor Buffington is on sabbatical. He won't be returning until next semester."

"Oh right, he did mention that. I'm a friend of his. Do you know where I could contact him?"

"No, I'm sorry, I don't. Just a minute." She puts her hand over the phone. I know she's asking somebody something, but it's too muffled for me to hear. Then she's back.

"He's in Europe, doing some research. That's the only information we have."

"Okay, well, thanks anyway."

I hang up the phone. Strike one. I dial a second number, but I don't need information for this one. At Ace's home number, I get his answering machine with a brief message that he's unavailable but to leave a message.

"Hi, Ace, it's Evan, just on the off chance you're back home. I'm in Amsterdam at the Prins Hendrik if you get this."

I feel silly leaving it, but what the hell. Strike two.

One more call, and this one I know the number for too.

"Santa Monica Police," a male voice says.

"Lieutenant Cooper, please."

"Name?"

"Evan Horne."

"One minute."

For once, when Coop comes on the line, he sounds genuinely pleased to hear from me. "Hey, Evan, how's it hanging?"

"Pretty good, Coop. How about you? How's the shoulder?"

"Fine. Got me a lot of time off." In my duet with Gillian, Cooper suffered a deep slash from her knife and was briefly hospitalized.

"Good, Coop, that's good. Glad to hear it."

"Where are you calling from? How's it going wherever you are?"

"Going good, Coop. I'm in Amsterdam."

"Amsterdam, as in Holland?"

"The same."

"Just a minute. I have to check and make sure you didn't make this a collect call."

I laugh. "No, I know you wouldn't accept that."

"So what are you doing over there?"

"Oh, it's a long story, but I'm working a club here, might connect with some other gigs as well, but that's not why I called."

"Uh-oh. I don't like the sound of that."

"Relax, it's no biggie."

"Uh-huh. I never relax when I'm talking to you. What?"

"Well, I saw Ace when I was in London. He was on the way here to do some research, and we tentatively planned to get together. But now he's already been, checked out, and gone. I just wondered if you'd heard anything from him."

"Ace? No, not a word. Not since I saw him in Las Vegas when we . . . well, you remember."

"Yes, I remember. Well, it's probably nothing. Just not like Ace to disappear like that." I hesitate again, wondering if I should tell Coop about the portfolio, but again decide against it. "He might have just ducked out somewhere. Maybe he'll show up before I leave."

"Yeah," Coop says. "Anyway, you said the plans were tentative, right?"

"Right." There are a few moments of silence. I know Coop is mulling it over. "I did hear from somebody else you know, though. Natalie."

"Really? How's she doing?"

"Seems fine. Said to tell you hello if I talked to you. Listen, man. I don't know how long you're going to be gone, but if I were you, I'd talk to her. We had a beer, kind of caught up, you know. She understands things a lot better now. Might be worth your while."

"Yeah, I know, Coop, but not yet. I'm not ready for that."

"Gotcha. Just wanted to let you know. Well, listen, you're burning up charges here. Got somewhere I can call you if I hear anything from Ace?"

I give him the hotel number. "You can probably catch me mornings, my time. We're eight hours ahead of California. Leave a message otherwise."

"Will do. You take care, huh?"

"I will, Coop, I will."

I hang up, but reluctantly. It was good to hear a familiar voice. If Ace has gone back to the States, maybe he will pass through L.A. and call Coop. Nothing would make me happier.

Otherwise, I'm going to have to tell Coop and Inspector Dekker about the portfolio Ace left behind and make it official.

Back at the hotel, I go through the portfolio again, looking through every article and piece of paper in there, trying to come up with a logical explanation as to why Ace would leave all this material behind. I don't even want to go there, but had he come across something that had made him overcautious? Was he afraid someone would find it, know what he was up to? I run over another scenario in my mind, just to try it out, see how it plays.

What if Ace had been forced to check out, been taken somewhere, against his will? And maybe his abductors—was that too strong?—had supervised his packing. They wouldn't have known about the portfolio, that it was hidden, and if that was the situation, Ace certainly wouldn't have told them. No, he would have left it right where it was, hoping that eventually somebody—the maid, the next occupant—would find it, turn it in, and raise the alert. Or was he counting on me finding it? When I suggested the possibility to Fletcher, he was right to say that's a little out there, but now I'm not so sure. In any case, I'm not prepared to give it up now. There might be a time for that later.

Looking through the material, it's clear that Ace has certainly done his homework on Chet Baker. I knew of Chet, of course, had several of his records, and knew something about his legendary career in jazz. But that's nothing like the dossier Ace has assembled. I read it all just to pass the time, hoping to find some clue that might tell me where Ace might be headed next and why he's gone off in such a rush.

Chet Baker had crisscrossed Europe since the 1950s. He'd played in, recorded in, and been arrested, jailed, and deported from several countries in Europe. He'd spent jail time in Italy—sixteen months—and left a trail a researcher like Ace would drool over. His celebrity had followed him everywhere, helped along by run-ins with the law. Ace could be in Italy, France, Scandinavia, even Spain. Chet played all those places more than once, but he'd spent a lot of time in Amsterdam, from the sound of it—no doubt because heroin was readily available, and the attitude much more liberal than elsewhere.

Chet grew up in southern California and started right at the top, auditioning for Charlie Parker in L.A., beating out every trumpet player there to make some gigs with Bird. When Parker went back to New York, he told Dizzy and Miles, "There's a little white cat on the coast who's gonna eat you up." Next to that quote is Ace's handwritten reminder to check the quote.

By then, Chet was in the pianoless quartet with Gerry Mulligan and well on the road to fame and fortune. Unfortunately for Chet, the road was littered with heroin.

He had his own group after that with pianist Russ Free-man. That was the beginning of his singing career too. Young, talented, good-looking, he seemed destined for stardom. Hollywood was interested, but drugs always waylaid the ultimate arrival. In and out of methadone programs—some official, some self-made—Chet hit bottom in San Francisco, when he was beaten up on the street in 1969.

There were several versions of that incident, and from the clippings, it wasn't clear whether it was a simple mugging or a payback by drug dealers he owed money to. Whatever the case, his teeth were damaged, and he had to learn how to play all over again with dentures. It took him over three years, but he did it, making his first comeback with a series of records that were more commercial than artistic. They didn't work, so he retreated as always to Europe, and eventually, so the critics said, was playing better than ever.

More records, reunions with Gerry Mulligan, and the legend continued. So did the drug use. It was just a part of his life that he could never fully shake. Still, people always turned out to hear him play, buy his records, and hope for more. There was a string of women, wives, kids, but nothing, it seemed, kept Chet Baker from playing jazz. Music was indeed his life, but time turned against him.

There are several photos, which I spread out on the bed, ranging from some very early days to one not long before he died—Chet sitting on a stool onstage, his trumpet nearby. He seems to be thinking, What happened? It is Dorian Gray in reverse.

I look at the two photos of Ace again. On impulse, I take one of them and slip it in my passport wallet. I put everything back in the case and zip it up. I light a cigarette and try to put myself in Ace's head. Chet's last recording, with a big band in Germany, is in my own collection—*My Favorite Songs: The Last Great Concert.* I remember from the liner notes that he had driven off right after the recording session for another gig somewhere, then back to Amsterdam with a pocketful of cash. Two weeks later, he was dead.

On one of the sheets with phone numbers and addresses, I'd come across the Dutch Jazz Archives again. Logical place for Ace to start after the hotel, digging through articles. A research library, where he'd be at home and comfortable. Somebody besides Fletcher Paige and the hotel owner must have seen him, talked to him. Ace could also still be right here in Amsterdam too, running around, excitedly talking to anyone who knew Chet Baker. Maybe that was the key to everything.

Find Chet Baker, find Ace Buffington.

6

FLETCHER PAIGE is a wonder. He plays every night with the maturity of a wily old veteran and the enthusiasm of a young kid on his first gig. This is simply one I don't want to end. The audiences are responsive, the band is cooking, and I'm learning what it's like to play with a master of what some critics have called America's classical music. And here we are, doing it in a foreign country—me, the new arrival fresh from the States, Fletcher in self-imposed exile for eighteen years.

Personally, the relationship couldn't be better. We share the same sense of humor, tell stories, talk about music, politics, even race. Jim Crow, Crow Jim, all of it. "You're too young to remember the sixties," Fletcher says, "but it went both ways. When Bobby Timmons left Cannonball Adderly, Cannon wanted to hire Victor Feldman, the white English pianist, but he knew that wouldn't go over with the other guys."

"Yes, I've heard him on records, did one with Miles, before Herbie Hancock."

"That's the one. All that free-jazz shit was going on then,

and the black militant movement. The Panthers, Black Power. Nothing wrong with that, but it got into the music. So Cannon played the rest of the band a record with Feldman, said this is who he wanted. They listened, said, yeah, he's the one. Then he told them who it was."

"Like Miles hiring Bill Evans."

"Exactly. Ornery as he was, Miles never let anything interfere with the music."

I listen to these and other stories from Fletcher's days with Count Basie, and as is so often the case, they make me wish I'd been born earlier. It feels like I've known Fletcher all my life. But when I casually ask him if he's ever thought about going back, he just shrugs it off, and my question obviously triggers old memories.

"Why should I, man?" We're talking again, just after the gig. Some of the people are lingering over stale drinks, not wanting to give it up yet. I watch Fletcher's face set as he packs up his horn. He snaps the case shut, then turns and looks sharply at me. "Why should I go back to scuffling for gigs, playing for people who don't even know who I am? Who thought I was dead." He sets the case down and lights a cigarette. Beneath that congenial exterior, the anger is still there, but this is the first time I've seen it surface.

"You know, I talked to Johnny Griffin once, asked him the same question you askin' me. Griff told me he once played Carnegie Hall and the stagehands gave him shit, and we both know why. Carnegie Hall!" He shakes his head. "No thanks, I been there, man. Don't need more of that. I like it here just fine."

There's nothing I can say to that. I just nod. "Yeah, but Dexter Gordon found it different when he went back, didn't he?"

"Well, I ain't Dexter Gordon." He breaks into a smile then. "Shit, I play better than Dex anyway. C'mon, man, let's get off this and get something to eat."

We go in Fletcher's car, an old VW that nonetheless runs well. He crosses canals, winds around the back streets of

Amsterdam until we pull up in front of a small coffeehouse nowhere near the Old Quarter. Fletcher gets out of the car. "Not here," he says, as I start for the coffeehouse. "Around the corner."

I follow him inside, where we're greeted by a striking Indonesian woman who smiles broadly when she sees Fletcher. She has straight black hair that almost reaches her waist, large eyes, and smooth dark skin. "Fletcher, you're a bad boy," she says. "Haven't come here in a long time." She hugs him and glances at me.

"Maria, say hello to my friend Evan," Fletcher says. "We're playing at the Bimhuis, and Evan is one fine piano player. And you haven't been to see me, either." He playfully shakes his finger in her face.

"Okay, okay," she says. "Too busy. You going to eat?"

"What else?" Fletcher says. "You know what I like. Same for my man too." He looks at me. "Okay with you?"

I nod. "Sure, bring it on."

"Well, you heard the man," Fletcher says. "Get those pots on."

She shows us to a back table. Despite the hour, the restaurant is busy. I catch a mix of languages from tourists and locals alike, and take in the smells of spicy food. We settle in, and Maria brings us two beers. "You'll like this, man. Best Indonesian food in Amsterdam."

The table is soon covered with an array of small dishes, saucers of condiments, stainless steel trays kept hot with a candle, and more food than both of us can get through.

"Wow," Fletcher says. "I'd almost forgotten how good this is." He raises his beer to Maria across the room, and she nods a smile back. Over coffee, we light cigarettes, and before long I catch Fletcher studying me. "Well?"

"What?"

"What have you done? You look like you got caught doing something. You didn't turn in that portfolio, did you?"

"No. I spent the morning going all through it."

"And?"

"It's a dossier on Chet Baker, all of Ace's notes. Very thorough, as I would expect of Ace, and vital to his research." I signal a waiter for some more coffee and look at Fletcher. "Look, let me try something out on you. You already think I'm going overboard on this, so I might as well go all the way."

"Go. Just don't expect me to agree with you," Fletcher says.

"Fair enough." I gather my thoughts and start again. "Suppose Ace decided to keep that case where I found it, just to keep it out of anybody's hands—the maid even, when he left the room. People do that, don't they? If they don't take it with them, most people wouldn't leave an expensive camera just lying around in plain sight. They'd put it in their suitcase or in a drawer under some clothes."

"Maybe," Fletcher says. "Least it's not immediately visible."

"Right, what I thought. Now here's the jump. Suppose somebody wanted Ace to go with them, maybe even forcibly, and went with him to the room to supervise his packing and checking out."

"Uh-oh." Fletcher stubs out his cigarette. "Go on."

"Well, that would explain why when Ace checked out, the portfolio was still there. Maybe he hoped somebody would find it—okay, maybe me—and raise the alarm, report it to the hotel, and then maybe the police if he was really in trouble." But even as I'm talking, I realize how much of a stretch I'm trying to make. Maybe Fletcher and Inspector Dekker are both right. I'm letting my imagination get away from me.

Fletcher thinks hard for a minute. "I see where you're going with this, but you're making a big jump, aren't you? 'Course, you know this Ace guy better than I do."

"I don't know, Fletcher. It just doesn't make any sense. I'm just sure Ace would never consciously leave without that portfolio, much less just forget it."

"Yeah, you're probably right about that. Have you been to the police?"

"Yep, told them about everything but finding the case. I

also called the university and Ace's home. Just got his answering machine, and the English department says he's on sabbatical. Nothing funny there. Also called up a cop friend in L.A. Didn't tell him all of it, but asked him to let me know if he hears from Ace."

Fletcher's eyebrows go up. "What did the police say?"

I shrug. "Nothing other than they would be alert, whatever that means. The guy I talked to is also checking on the guy who investigated Chet Baker's death. He's retired now, living in the country somewhere. I'm sure Ace would have looked him up."

"Uh-huh," Fletcher mumbles. "So what's your next move?"

"Hell, I don't know. I feel funny checking hospitals, again with the police. The cop told me to check with the American consulate. I suppose that might not be a bad idea, although I doubt that Ace would check in with them."

"No, probably not," Fletcher says. "All the time I've been here I've never done that."

"Tomorrow I'm going to check out the Dutch Jazz Archives. It's not far from the hotel. Maybe Ace has been there, somebody talked with him."

Fletcher nods. "Well, I can see this is bothering you. You're not going to quit till you find some answers, and in a way, I don't blame you. He is your friend. But . . . you might also find some trouble. You've found it before."

"I know, I know. Last thing I want now, but I just can't help feeling something has happened to Ace." I can't tell if Fletcher is just humoring me or really thinks I'm way off base. He considers some more, then his lips curl into a smile.

"Tell you what," Fletcher says. "You find that detective on Chet Baker's case, I'll go with you."

"Really?"

"Yeah. I'd like to hear the real story on that myself." Fletcher laughs. "Maybe I'll write a book of my own."

We drive back to the hotel, and as I get out of the car, Fletcher stops me. I lean back in the window. "Listen, man, maybe I shouldn't say this, but . . ." He looks away for a moment. "Find your friend. Maybe you'll find yourself."

Then he pulls away, leaving me to wonder what he meant.

In the morning I make my way down the Prins Hendrikkade after breakfast, about a fifteen-minute walk. It's cool, but spring is definitely here. Across the way I can see ships docked and unloading, and the usual plethora of bicycles I have to watch for at every crossing. They seem more dangerous than cars or trolleys crammed with riders. Los Angeles is such a car city, the trolleys by comparison are fascinating, crisscrossing the city, seemingly always full.

In a row of gray buildings, I check the address and find the Dutch National Jazz Archives sign. It's a few steps down, below street level. Inside, through a small room on my left, I see hundreds of books on gray metal shelves. I find a larger room and some offices off to the side. At the far end of the room, three men are sitting around a table discussing some Duke Ellington recordings. Their voices, in English, carry to my end of the room, and the discussion seems rather heated. I catch Johnny Hodges's name, then hear a voice behind me.

"Can I help you?"

I turn around. A young woman, maybe late twenties, early thirties, with short dark hair and a friendly smile, is standing behind me. Once again I'm thankful English is a second language here. "Well, I hope so. A friend of mine might have been here to do some research, on Chet Baker. An American. His name is Buffington, Charles Buffington."

She thinks for a moment. "Ah, yes. He was in a few days ago, looking through our clipping library. He had written from America for permission. It was very polite but not really necessary." She smiles again. "We're not so formal here."

"Oh, I guess Chet Baker is a pretty popular subject here."

"Yes, many people have come to visit Amsterdam because

of his death here. Did you want to see something? Are you doing research also?"

"Well, no, actually I'm a musician. I'm working at the Bimhuis, with Fletcher Paige."

"Ah, yes, he is one of our well-known citizens. Amsterdam has adopted him. And what is your instrument?"

"Piano. I came here hoping to find out something about my friend. We were supposed to meet, but he checked out of the hotel and didn't leave a forwarding address."

Her expression suddenly changes. "Are you Evan Horne?"

"Yes, why? How did you know?"

"Pleased to meet you. My name is Helen." We shake hands briefly. "A moment, please." She goes back into the office for a minute, then comes back with an envelope. "This is for you, then. Mr. Buffington left it. He said you might visit here."

I take the envelope from her, start to open it. "Did you talk to him? Did he give you this?"

"Yes. He spent the day looking at clippings and one or two videos we have, but I didn't talk to him much. He gave me the envelope when he left and said to give it to you if you came here."

This is getting more spooky by the moment. "And if I didn't come here?"

She shakes her head. "He didn't say. I'm sorry, that's all I know."

"Well, thank you anyway, Helen."

"Excuse me, please. I have some work to do, but if you want to see something, please let me know."

"Sure, thanks." I sit down at one of the tables and open the envelope. It's a handwritten note, and definitely in Ace's writing.

Dear Evan,

Well, if you're here, you're hot on the trail as I am. I didn't think you could resist. Wonderful facility here and

they treat you well. Have the girl show you the other sculpture. It's really something. Sorry I missed you at the hotel,
but the search is on.

Best, Ace

I read it several times, but nothing hits me. Was this after
he checked out of the hotel? And how or why did he think I'd
come here looking for him unless he knew I'd find the portfolio and see his notes. I sit for a few minutes rereading his
note, thinking, wondering about the trail Ace has left, but I'm
just more puzzled. I am curious as to what Ace looked at,
though, so I go looking for Helen in her office.

"Sorry to bother you again. Could I see the material my
friend looked at? And he mentioned another sculpture—is it
different from the one at the hotel?"

She gets up from her desk and smiles again. "Yes. Come,
I'll show you." She takes me around the corner, and there in
the hallway is a human figure made from what looks like tree
branches. There's an old trumpet wedged in as well. "That's
Chet Baker's trumpet," she says.

"You're kidding." The shine has faded, and it's all oxidized.
"His family never claimed it?"

"No, no one did. This was outside for a while, behind the
hotel, but it couldn't be secured, and the hotel thought it was
not appropriate to be displayed."

"Yes, I can imagine they wouldn't." I can't take my eyes off
it. It wouldn't have lasted five minutes in New York. I keep
looking back as she takes me into another room crowded with
gray metal shelves—books, cardboard holders for file folders
and magazines, and several shelves of videotapes.

She pulls one holder out and two videotapes. "He looked
at this collection of files, but I'm afraid most are in Dutch. He
also looked at these two videos."

I look at the titles. One is a commercial copy of Bruce
Weber's film on Chet, *Let's Get Lost*. I'd seen it many times at

video stores. On the other box, the title *Chet Baker: The Final Days* is written with a black marker pen.

"And this one?"

"It was done by a Dutch documentary filmmaker. The interviews are in English or translated. There's also an interview with the policeman who investigated his death."

I don't remember hearing about any such film. "I would like to take a look if it's possible."

"Certainly." She takes the tape off the shelf and shows me to a small room set up with a VCR and a television. "Take your time. I'll be in my office if you need something." She puts the video in the player and turns on the television.

"Thanks."

I sit down at the machine and hit the play button. The narrator's voice—it's a woman—startles me at first. It's very cold, objective, even harsh.

"Chet Baker, trumpet player and singer, died in Amsterdam, the thirteenth of May, 1988. His death was caused by falling or jumping from a hotel window. Chet Baker was fifty-eight."

I rewind and watch it again. Cold, hard facts, nothing else. Then there's a black-and-white photo of Chet, lying on his side in the alleyway, as the narrator continues.

"His face was covered with blood. At first, the police think it is a drug addict aged about thirty. In the hotel room, the papers of a fifty-eight-year-old American named C. H. Baker are found, so they assume it is a junkie who has robbed a tourist."

I press the pause button on the black-and-white photo, freezing the frame, and feel those familiar stirrings, looking over the edge of a dark, deep hole, but not quite able to step back. For a moment I'm right there, in that photo, looking at Chet's body, glancing up to the window of his room. But there are no clues, nothing to tell the real story. Not Chetty or Chet of the golden-tone horn. Just a dead junkie, his face covered in blood, discovered in an alley in a foreign country.

The rest of the film is fascinating, and I wonder why it's

never been shown in the States. Seems like a natural for PBS. There are interviews with, among others, Russ Freeman, Chet's longtime pianist, the photographer William Claxton, record producers, friends, and a Rotterdam pianist, recounting a night when Chet just wandered in a club and asked to sit in. There's also a segment with Chet and bassist Red Mitchell sitting at a piano together, talking, reminiscing, playing a couple of tunes: Red friendly, smiling; Chet holding his trumpet, watching Red warily play the chords on "My Romance."

The story is told chronologically from May 7, five days before Chet died. The interview with a policeman who describes the scene and gives his opinion in no uncertain terms still leaves it very vague and inconclusive.

"We believe," the detective says, "that Mr. Baker, under the influence of drugs, simply fell out of the window of his hotel. He was found at approximately three in the morning. There was no conspiracy, no sign of foul play, and his room was locked from the inside. Perhaps he thought he could fly," the sergeant says, but he isn't smiling. There's even a brief glimpse of an Interpol memo, recounting, I suppose, Chet's scrapes with the law in various countries.

I fast-forward through the tape, skipping over the many musical segments at various points in Chet's career, seeing the physical changes that occurred over the years. I stop now and then for some of the interviews. When I have more time, I'd like to watch the entire film. I stop the tape and lean back, thinking about the detective's comments. I'd have to check the locks on the doors again at the hotel, but if the door was self-locking, anyone could just close it behind them—or, if they were really worried about being seen, lock the door, then shinny down that infamous drainpipe—but it's not even mentioned. None of this, I remind myself, tells me anything about Ace's whereabouts. And even though I said I wouldn't help Ace, here I am, already speculating, getting hooked on the story.

I rewind the tape, hit the eject button, and put it back in

its box. Flipping through the file of clips, I find only two in English. I take those out and go back to the office. I knock and stick my head in.

"Helen?" She's on the phone. She looks up, holds up one finger, talks for a minute or so, then hangs up.

"Thanks for your time," I say. "Just one more thing. Can I get copies of these two articles?"

"Of course." She takes them from me and goes off to another room. She comes back in a few minutes and hands me the copies. "I'll refile these," she says. "I hope you found what you were looking for."

"We'll see," I say. "I don't suppose I could borrow that tape, check it out for a couple of days?"

"No." She shakes her head. "That is not permitted. You can see it anytime, but we don't let material out of the building."

"I understand. Well, thanks, Helen. You've been very helpful." I start for the door, then turn back. "You can do me one last favor."

"Yes?"

"If my friend comes back, tell him I was here."

I walk back to the hotel, replaying those film images in my mind. The interview with the detective sticks out the most. He seemed emphatic that Chet Baker's death was an accident, a fall from the window, possibly under the influence of drugs. Given Chet's history, that seems more than possible. But Chet thinking he could fly? I don't think so. Chet could fly, but only with a trumpet to his lips.

At the hotel I pause for a moment, looking again at the sculpture. Only you know for sure, Chet. And you're not talking. When I go inside, two men at the front desk turn toward me. One is the policeman I talked to at the station, Inspector Dekker. "Ah, Mr. Horne," he says. "We were just looking for you."

I notice then that the other man is carrying a plastic bag. "Yes. Anything wrong?"

"This is Sergeant Vledder." He nods toward the other man. "I'm not sure." He pauses and looks around. "Perhaps we could go to your room and talk?"

"Yes, sure." I don't like the sound of this, and I'm already starting to regret my visit to the police station. As we ride up in the elevator to my room, I keep eyeing the bag in the other policeman's hand. I unlock my door and invite them in. The maid has already done the room. I glance at the closet, thinking about Ace's portfolio in there.

"So what's this about?"

Dekker motions to Vledder for the bag, opens it, and pulls out a dark brown suede jacket. "I wonder if you recognize this or have seen it before." He holds it up. It's large, and I know immediately it could fit Ace. I try to picture it on him. "Where did you find it?"

"You do recognize it." He watches me closely. "It could be your friend's jacket?"

"Well, I'm not sure. It seems to be the right size. He's a big man."

"This was found in one of the coffeehouses, in a booth. It was turned in to the proprietor by a customer, and he called the police."

"What makes you think it's my friend's?" But even as I say it, I know it's Ace's jacket.

"These." He reaches into the inside pocket of the coat and takes out several business cards, with a rubber band around them. He shows me one. It has the red University of Nevada logo, "Charles Buffington, Ph.D., Department of English," and Ace's office number.

I sit down on the bed and look at the card, stalling, not wanting to consider what this might mean. "Isn't it unusual for this to happen? Why was it turned in?"

"It's hard to say. The coat is obviously an expensive one.

The owner is possibly looking for a reward. Or perhaps he is just being honest. It does happen occasionally. Even in Amsterdam."

"Of course. I didn't mean—"

"It's quite all right. You do recognize the business cards."

"Yes, they are my friend's." I look at the coat and cards again. "Any ideas?"

"No, I'm afraid not, except—" He glances at his partner. "It was found at one of the brown houses, where marijuana may be legally consumed. Is it possible your friend perhaps indulged?"

I laugh. "Ace? No, I don't think so. Two glasses of wine is about all he could take."

"Ace? Not Charles."

"Ace is his nickname. He plays a lot of tennis."

"Oh, I see." Dekker and Vledder exchange glances and some words in Dutch. Dekker shakes his head, then turns back to me. "Is there anything else you can tell us, Mr. Horne?"

Now is the time to show Dekker the portfolio—make up a story about why I didn't tell him earlier, give it up, and let the police handle everything. This is Ace's jacket, his business cards. But of course I don't do any of that. And I don't even know why.

"Like what?"

Dekker smiles patiently. "You would know that better than me, Mr. Horne. Surely your friend would miss his coat sometime. This is not conclusive, but the coat suggests that he may still be in Amsterdam."

"Yes, I see what you mean. I wish I could tell you something more, but I can't think of anything."

7

A T THE Bimhuis, halfway through the second set, I'm reminded of something else from the film. We've just finished a raucous blues and need something of a breather
to cool down. Fletcher is standing by me at the piano.

"Man, that was smoking," he says, nodding his approval at
the drummer, who is mopping his face and grinning. "You got
a ballad up your sleeve?"

"Do you know 'Green Dolphin Street'?" I ask Fletcher. He
looks surprised. It's one of those jam session staples, always
part of Miles's early book. Everybody knows it, has played it
countless times, but it's still a beautiful, haunting song.

"Yeah, I know it." He smiles then, guessing what I'm
thinking. "Like a ballad tempo?" The tune is usually played at
medium tempo or even faster, with the first and third eight
measures given a Latin flavor.

"Almost, just easy," I say, reviewing the chord progression
in my head.

Fletcher smiles. "I got an idea." He goes over to the drummer and bassist, says something to them. They nod and leave

the stand. Fletcher comes back. "Just you and me on this, okay?"

"Sure." Without any more discussion, I start a rubato introduction, letting the minor chords do the work through one out-of-tempo chorus. Then I start a vamp, in tempo, just beyond ballad speed. Fletcher slips in like he's parting a curtain, and just suddenly there, sliding into the melody, singing with his horn, catching everybody off guard with long, elegant lines, at times almost like cries, floating and lingering like billowy clouds in the air even after they're gone. He plays three choruses that ought to be recorded, so saxophonists everywhere can hear just how this tune can and should be played.

I follow, and my hands just seem to take over. Playing with good musicians sharpens your focus, makes things happen sometimes that you're not aware you could do. I feel Fletcher's presence beside me, and without looking up, I know he's smiling. After two choruses, he joins me and we do some interplay, counter lines as if they'd been written for us and rehearsed for weeks, playing off the other's ideas, changing them, quoting them back, or starting anew. Then we take it out as quietly as we'd begun, as if the tune disappeared in a mist.

We look at each other as the final notes fade to just an echo on the piano and air from Fletcher's tenor. There's what seems like a long, perfect moment of complete silence when we finish, as if the audience doesn't want to break the spell. Only when I take my hands off the piano does loud applause arrive. I look up, almost surprised to see people there.

"Hey," Fletcher says. "We better quit while we're ahead." He takes off his horn and sets it on its stand. "Let's go outside. Got something to talk to you about."

We get through the crowd to the exit. It may be old stuff to Fletcher, but I'm still tingling. Outside we both light cigarettes and stroll down the block. "Just didn't feel like talking to anyone yet," he says. "Those kind of moments don't happen often."

"Yeah, I know. I could go home right now and feel good about the whole night."

Fletcher nods. "What made you think of 'Green Dolphin'?" he asks me.

"I saw a film today, at the Jazz Archives, about Chet's last days. Done by Dutch television. Thought I'd see if Ace had been there."

"He was there, huh?"

"Yeah. Even left a note for me. In the film, there's an interview with a pianist in Rotterdam. He was playing at the Dizzy Café. Said Chet just wandered in, came up to the bandstand, asked if he could play. They did two tunes. One of them was 'Green Dolphin Street.'"

Fletcher nods. "Yeah, he used to do that."

"The pianist said he thought it might have been the last tune Chet played. Just seemed right to do it." We stop and turn around, start heading back toward the Bimhuis. "Kind of sad, huh?" Fletcher doesn't say anything, just keeps walking slowly, head down. "What did you want to talk to me about?"

"You're not in any hurry to get out of here, are you? Amsterdam, I mean."

"No, why?"

"Well, as good as this gig has been, it ends this weekend, but this guy I know called me. He's opening a new place. Small club, wants me to think about a duo." Fletcher turns and looks at me. "You up for that? Won't be a lot of bread, but he's cool. We can play what we like. Might be a long-term thing."

"Are you serious? Yeah, I'm up for it. When does it start?"

Fletcher smiles. "Cool. Maybe as early as next week. We could make like Kenny Barron and Stan Getz. I just heard something new with Herbie Hancock and Wayne Shorter doing something similar. Just pure music, piano and horn. I got some things written too we could try. Maybe do some rehearsing at my place. I got an old upright piano."

Fletcher's excitement is contagious, and I'm elated of

course at the thought of continuing to play with him. "You have a deal, Fletch."

He smiles again. "Well, it's partly economic. You know club owners. This guy likes the idea of only having to pay two musicians. We ain't going to get rich, but we'll have some fun. We'll just split fifty-fifty."

"You know how to make a million dollars playing jazz?"

Fletcher laughs. "Yeah, start with two million. C'mon, man, we got another set to do, then you can tell me about that film and the note from your friend."

After the gig, Fletcher and I sit in a small bar sipping brandy—another of his haunts. Everywhere we go he's greeted like an old friend, almost a celebrity, and if there were justice in the world it would be the same in America. It's easy to see why he has chosen to stay in Europe, why so many did. And now maybe I'm considering it myself. I'm still wired from playing. We tried another duet number toward the end, this time on "My Foolish Heart."

"I think I'm going to like this duo idea. It's really going to happen, you think?" I ask Fletcher. He looks decidedly cool, his tie loosened, relaxed in his chair.

"Oh yeah, baby. I'm going to make it happen now for sure. You and me, we got something going." He sets his glass down and looks at me. "So you gonna tell me about the note from your friend?"

"Okay." I'd been holding off, not wanting to destroy the musical mood. "He left it with this girl who works at the archives." I tell him what it said.

"Hot on the trail? Your friend does know you, maybe better than you do—or was he just guessing?"

I'd thought a lot about it since this afternoon. Did Ace know me that well? Or was he just guessing, hoping? I was creating all kinds of scenarios. The best case would be Ace, checking back with the archives, discovering I had picked up the note and suddenly reappearing, saying, "Gotcha, huh, Evan?" I'd be annoyed, but at least I'd know Ace was okay.

"He just knows my history. He's been part of it. And I have to admit the film was fascinating." I take another sip of my brandy. "You know what was the saddest part of that film? There was one interview with a recording engineer, talking about a session Chet had done for him. The sounds he was making, blowing the spit out of his horn, were leaking through on the piano solo, so he put Chet in a booth. Just like any studio isolation booth. Glass, so you can see, a door, headphones."

"Uh-huh," Fletcher says. "I've been in a couple." He laughs.

"Sorry. Anyway, Chet wasn't sure at first, but then he told this guy he liked it, called it the room. Said it was cozy and he'd never had his own room, let alone a house. Wanted to know if he could rent it." I see Fletcher shaking his head, listening. "Well, the guy, I guess, thought Chet was just putting him on. Told him, sure, Chet. You come back, do another record, and you can rent it for a lot of money." I lean forward, put out my cigarette, and down the rest of my brandy. "But you know what, Fletcher? I think Chet was serious."

Fletcher nods. "Cat was just a nomad, what do you call it, a troubadour. Those last years over here, he just went from place to place with a bag and his trumpet. Playing where he could, where anybody wanted him. He stayed in rooms—hotels, friends' homes—anywhere he could. Playing was all he had. You know about San Francisco? Some guys kicked his ass, knocked his teeth out?"

"Yes, that story has made the rounds. Russ Freeman talked about it in the film, and Chet too. Said it took him over three years to be able to play with false teeth."

"Uh-huh. That should tell you how badly he wanted, needed, to play."

I shrug. "Yeah, I know all about that." I hold out my right hand and flex it. Not a trace of pain. Before my accident, I'd always taken my hands for granted.

Fletcher looks at it. "Still give you trouble sometimes?"

"Yeah, once in a while, but nothing I can't deal with."

"You're lucky." Fletcher stands up and stretches. "Well, I'm older than you. I need some sleep. C'mon, I'll drop you at the hotel."

"Wait, there's something else."

"Oh, shit, do I want to hear this?"

"The police came by the hotel today. They found Ace's jacket, with some of his business cards in the pocket."

"Damn." Fletcher puts his hands over his eyes, rubs them. "I need another drink." He signals the waiter and sits down again. "You want one?" I wave him off.

Fletcher turns back to me. "You don't have to tell me. I know you didn't tell them you got his case, right?"

"It just didn't seem the right time."

"And here I am, sitting here drinking with a fool. Man, when will be the right time? You need to take that case over to the police in the morning. Get it out of your hands, you dig?"

"Yeah, I know I should. I just—"

"Can't let it go?"

"No, not yet."

Fletcher just shakes his head. "Now I know how you got into that other shit with Wardell, those Clifford Brown tapes." He looks at me again. "You crazy, man, you know that, don't you?"

"I don't know. I know it must seem like it."

Fletcher downs his drink and stands up. "Well, that's all I can handle tonight. Let's go."

"No, that's okay. It's out of your way. I'll just take a taxi. I might have another drink."

Fletcher studies me for a moment, then touches my shoulder. "Okay. Catch you tomorrow." He starts off, then turns. "I sure hope your friend shows up before we start that other gig. I want you focused."

"Don't worry."

"I hope I don't have to. Later."

I sit for a few minutes but decide against another drink.

Outside, I get my bearings, head for a main street, and find a taxi fairly easily. I get out at the hotel and stand for a moment, looking at the sculpture of Chet. It's like a magnet now. I walk up to the corner, deciding what to do, waving off a couple of taxis that slow down.

I know I won't sleep. Nothing has been resolved about Ace. What else can I do? I've been to the police, talked to anyone who's seen him—and nothing. He's just vanished. I'm already beating myself up for turning him down so quickly, and the picture of him sitting in that London pub is still with me.

Finally I decide to take a walk around the Old Quarter, maybe get a snack. The tourists and curious are out in full force despite the hour. Music blares from several bars; loud voices, many of them drunk or on the way, echo around the cobblestone alleyways bathed in a mix of bright blinking neon and amber streetlights.

I pass one of the coffee shops and stop on a whim. Maybe this is what I need. Why not? It's been a long time. Dark green curtains cover most of the windows, and the door is heavy wood with an opaque glass window. I go in and find it's not noisy like a bar, but subdued in a kind of laid-back solitude—marble tables, young waitresses serving lattes, and the unmistakable pungent aroma everywhere. There is some laughter from a number of booths, but it's not the loud, boisterous bar kind of sound. The music too is subtle, quietly oozing out of the sound system. As my eyes adjust, I find an empty booth and slide in the side facing the door.

I order a coffee from the young waitress, and she directs me to the small bar on the side of the room to place my other order. It feels weird to look at a marijuana menu. The descriptions are complete with strength, properties, and source of origin. There are various forms of Thai sticks, Maui Wowie, Moroccan hash, and scores of others I never heard of, including skunk weed, the local offering. Before I change my mind, I order a medium strength from Humboldt County in northern California. Might as well support the home team.

While I'm waiting, I notice a man enter, glance at me quickly, and head toward the bar. He looks vaguely familiar, but I can't place him, and he doesn't talk to me. I turn my attention to the other patrons awhile, then, when it's ready, I make my buy, return to my table, and light up, sucking in the sweet smoke, holding it as long as I can. Involuntarily, I look over my shoulder. Relax. It's all legal and aboveboard. This is Amsterdam.

A young couple in a nearby booth watches me and smiles. If we had glasses, we would hold them up in a toast. I take another long hit and feel it steal through my body quickly—too quickly. Maybe I've underestimated medium strength.

I lean back, still hearing the music, the muted conversation, but suddenly everything is hazy, out of focus, spinning. The hanging lamps over each table seem to sway and leave light contrails in their wake. I put my hands on the table to steady myself, even though I'm not moving at all. I close my eyes for a moment, but that seems to make it worse. Way too strong, and so long since I've smoked anything stronger than a menthol cigarette, I rationalize. I panic, feeling like I'm falling, watching myself grab the table edge to steady again. I lean back against the seat, try to focus, but everything is in a haze and still spinning. Got to get outside, get some air.

I wait for a few minutes, get up, and start for the door. It seems so far away, like I'll never make it. I know people are watching me, pointing. The waiter comes, takes my elbow to steady me. "You are all right?" he asks.

"Yeah, I'm . . . okay . . . thanks . . . just want to get outside."

He opens the door. I step out, feel the cool night air wash over me. I lean against the building for a moment, try to stop the spinning. I don't know how long I stand like that, but I know whatever I've smoked is nothing like anything I've had before. I look up the street. The neon lights from bars and restaurants are blurry, moving, yet fascinating, distracting. I must get to the hotel, lie down. I try some tentative steps but feel like I need something to hang on to. I stay close to the edge of the sidewalk, against the buildings, only vaguely aware of people passing me, looking, laughing, pointing.

I'm lost, can't find my bearings, but finally I spot the blue Police Station sign. Hotel is just around the corner from that, if only I can make it. Two cops are standing on the front steps, but they give me only passing notice. I get past them and turn onto the alleyway behind the Prins Hendrik Hotel. The canal, the main street, is just ahead of me, but I have to stop again, lean against the building. I close my eyes, try to stop the spinning. It seems to have slowed some, but still the feeling is out of my control. I lean my head back against the bricks. When I open my eyes, I can see the window of my room. The block-long street is deserted, but then suddenly out of nowhere, to my right, someone has appeared, standing in the middle of the alleyway, gazing at me.

I close my eyes, squeezing them shut, then blink them open, but he's still there. Oh, my God, this stuff is strong, whatever it is. I've never hallucinated like this, but I'm seeing him, that smooth young face, hair falling over his forehead.

The lips curl up slightly, and Chet Baker smiles at me.

I close my eyes again, try to erase the vision, but he's still there, gazing now up at the drainpipe running up the building toward the room he fell from. He looks at me again, smiles. I want to say something, but I can't speak. He raises his hand now, points to the drainpipe, smiles again, then looks at me questioningly.

Is that it? Is that how it happened after all? No, no, I'm not seeing Chet Baker. I'm very high, stoned out of control, but I'm leaning against a building. There's no one there, I tell myself. Now I look at the drainpipe, then back to the figure. His head moves slightly in a nod, then he turns and walks away. I call out, hear my own voice say, "Chet, wait." But he's gone, faded away. There's no one there.

What did he want me to see? What did he want me to do? I make my way across the alleyway till I'm right in front of the drainpipe. I reach out and touch it. It's very solid, securely fastened to the building. I grip it with both hands, the metal cold, slightly damp to my touch. Yes, it could be done, couldn't it? Chet, where did you go? I need you to tell me. The spinning has decreased somewhat, and I feel good holding on to the pipe, secure, letting it be my anchor. I slide my hands up the pipe until they're over my head and start to pull myself up.

I get my feet on the building, feeling for traction on the bricks, and begin to shinny up the pipe, but looking up, it seems a long way to the second floor. I hang on tightly, try to lock my knees around it, like a sailor on a mast. Don't look down. I try a few more inches, but my hands keep slipping. I look down, and now the street seems a long way away. The spinning starts again, and I cling to the pipe. How will I get down? I can't move either way. My hands slip more, then slide off entirely. I feel myself falling backward. How far? Only a few feet? It seems to take forever, like slow motion.

Finally my feet hit the cobblestones. My body is so limp I just crumple and topple over backward, feel my head hitting the stone with what feels like an explosion going off. I close my eyes again, but the spinning continues. When I open them, I look up at the night sky, hear sounds, but I can't move, just want to lie there till everything stops. I turn my head to the right, and he's there again.

Chet Baker, gazing at me, nodding, a slight smile on his lips. All I can think is, Where's his trumpet?

I close my eyes once again and give in to the feeling of restfulness and peace.

April 29, 1988

Chet is racing through Germany, racing through time, on the autobahn, loving it, driving the Alfa as fast as he wants. He likes it, driving alone. He smiles, suddenly flashing on Russ Freeman riding with him in L.A., not even looking out the window as he careened around corners, pushed the car and Russ's patience to their limits. Russ, getting out of the car, saying he would take a taxi back. All those years ago.

Racing through time. His mind wanders back to an earlier time in Los Angeles, summer of 1952. Just out of the army on a general discharge, gigging with Vido Musso for a while, then with Stan Getz. Arriving home one day, he finds a telegram from Dick Bock of Pacific Jazz Records. Charlie Parker is auditioning trumpet players for some dates in California. He has to be there at three o'clock.

Rushing over, a little late, but he hears Bird even as he gets out of his car. In the darkened Tiffany club, he can barely see after the glare from the sun. Eventually he makes out Bird on the bandstand, racing through a blues. Finally, when his eyes become accustomed to the dark interior, he looks around, sees nearly every trumpet player in Los Angeles, some he knows have more experience, some can read anything.

Then there's a break. Someone goes to the bandstand, whispers to Bird. He steps to the microphone. Charlie Parker calls his name. "Is Chet Baker here?"

"I'm here, Bird."

"Would you come up and play something with me, please?"

Chet, feeling self-conscious, gets to the bandstand, taking out his horn, fingering the valves, everybody in the club watching. Twenty-two years old, looking at Bird, Charlie Parker. They play two tunes: "The Song Is You," and then a blues of Bird's called "Cheryl." Chet's relieved that he knows both tunes.

He doesn't have to wonder for long how he played. As soon as they finish, Bird leans into the mike again. "Thank you all for coming," he says. "The auditions are over."

They do two weeks at the Tiffany—every night with Bird, but after the breakneck tempo of the first tune each set, the rest is easy, and Bird treats Chet like a son, putting down anybody and everybody who tries to offer him drugs.

Between sets, Chet drives Bird to a taco stand, watches him wolf down taquitos with green chili sauce. During the day, they drive out to the beach. Bird stands on a cliff, staring out to sea, watching the waves break on the rocks. Chet wonders what Bird is thinking about.

More gigs follow. For Billy Berg at the 54 Ballroom on Central Avenue. Then on to San Francisco, Seattle, and Vancouver, a tour that includes Dave Brubeck and Ella Fitzgerald. Then back to San Francisco at the Say When club. Bird, falling asleep with a cigarette in his hotel room, sets his mattress on fire. Chet, waking up, sees somebody throw it out on the street, and the band gets fired, not for that, but because Bird tries to collect money for muscular dystrophy without the owner's approval. Then Bird is gone, back to New York. Long after, Chet would hear Bird bragged about him to Miles and Dizzy.

Chet smiling now, shaking his head, remembering, racing through time.

He downshifts going into a curve, then floors the accelerator, feeling the power of the Alfa push him back in his seat. Paris not far now. Then he can relax for a while, play in one of the cave clubs.

Just cool out till the next gig and spend some of this money, take a run up to Amsterdam, get the feeling back.

8

"MAN, YOU are one crazy motherfucker!"

I hear the voice, but it doesn't sound like Chet Baker now. I open my eyes. I'm still lying down, but it's not a cold, hard cobblestone alleyway I feel under me. It's soft, a bed, and the voice is not Chet Baker. It's Fletcher Paige.

The spinning has stopped now, and gradually Fletcher's face comes into focus. He's staring at me hard. Another man, all in white, is just behind him. A doctor? There's white everywhere, and a pale green curtain surrounding the bed.

"You with it now, man?" Fletcher says.

I squeeze my eyes shut, then open them again. "Yeah, I think so." I try to sit up, but I'm still shaky.

"What the fuck were you trying to do? You been wailing about Chet Baker for over an hour. I don't know what you smoked, but whatever it was, fucked you up good. Damn!" Fletcher wheels around, then turns back, looks down at me again.

I sit up and swing my legs over the edge of the bed. So far, so good. "I did see Chet Baker," I say, then know immediately how silly that sounds. It's all coming back now, finding my way back to the hotel, the alleyway, trying to climb up the drainpipe, falling.

"You didn't see shit," Fletcher says, like he's angry. The doctor puts his hand on Fletcher's arm to calm him down. Fletcher looks at him and nods, lowers his voice. "You tried to climb up that drainpipe at your hotel, believin' that dumb story that Chet tried that, fell, and killed himself."

"No, it wasn't like that. It was, I don't know, weird, like a bad dream."

Fletcher laughs, and now I see the anger dissolve to relief on his face. "Yeah, you got that right. You were out cold on the street. You're lucky Darren prowls around down there. He found you, brought you here, and called me. That boy finally did something right. He ain't telling me everything. There's something else going down, but I'll find out what it is, you can believe that."

The doctor, who's been watching and listening to this exchange, steps forward now. "Mr. Horne? Is that right?"

"Yes."

"It appears you are not seriously injured, but I will need you to complete some paperwork before we release you." He glances at Fletcher. "You have ingested a great deal of a very strong drug. It is very dangerous in such amounts."

I touch the back of my head then, feel a bandage and a bump underneath it.

"A small head wound," the doctor says. "Not serious."

I feel the doctor's scrutiny and disapproval, the concern on his face; to him, I'm just some dumb American tourist, getting off on smoking dope legally in a foreign country.

"Yes, I guess I did."

"You must be more cautious," he says. "Hashish is very potent."

I look at Fletcher and shake my head. "Yes, I will be. Thank you, doctor."

He pulls the curtain aside, and I can see the rest of the

ward, with some of the other beds occupied. Some people are asleep, some are awake, watching, stirring around.

"Come on, man," Fletcher says. "Let's get you out of here. I'll take care of him," he says to the doctor. "Here, man, get your shoes on."

I am still dressed. I get into my shoes and test my balance when I stand up. A little shaky, but I'm able to navigate. My stomach muscles are sore, feel like I've been punched hard.

"Yeah, you lost it all," Fletcher says. "Best thing." I lean on Fletcher and walk to the reception desk.

I don't even remember that. I stop at the desk of the small clinic, complete the forms, and then go with Fletcher outside to his car.

"Hey, thanks for coming over," I say. "I can make it now." I get in the car and put my head back on the seat. Fletcher comes around, gets in, and starts the car.

"Uh-huh," Fletcher says. "Well, you comin' home with me, not to that hotel. Don't want you seein' Chet again."

I'm too tired, too weak, and too shaky to argue.

When I open my eyes, the first thing I see is Chet Baker again, but this time in a photo. There's a woman with him. Both of them are smiling, sitting on a wall of some kind. It's black and white and not very good quality—taken several years before his death, by the look of it. This is the older Chet, the youthful good looks already gone now.

The clock on the nightstand tells me I've been asleep for several hours. I swing my legs over and sit on the edge of the bed. How could I have been so stupid? I get out of bed, pull on my clothes, and look around. Fletcher's place, but this is a woman's bedroom. There are other photos, combs, brushes, perfume bottles on the dresser, and the open closet is filled with dresses.

I go in the bathroom, splash cold water on my face, and look in the mirror. Not so good, but I do feel better than I look. My stomach muscles are still sore, but if that's all, I can count myself lucky. How far did I climb up that drainpipe? I must have been totally out of it to do that. And hallucinating, thinking I saw Chet Baker. Or maybe it was that impersonator I'd seen. I certainly hope so. I've got Chet Baker on the brain.

I hear music coming from somewhere in the house—a tenor saxophone down the hall, some old recording. I listen for a moment, then follow the sound. Fletcher is sitting at a table, reading a paperback book with a bright yellow cover. *New Hope for the Dead.* He looks up, puts the book aside. "Well, finally," he says.

"Lester Young?" That smooth, breathy tenor sound is unmistakable.

"Yep, my daily dose of Prez," he says. He holds up the book. "And Hoke Moseley. A good pair to start the day with. You back with us now?"

"Yeah, I think so." I sit down opposite him at a large table in front of the window.

Fletcher looks at me and chuckles, shaking his head from side to side. "First time I smoked shit, in Kansas City, I'd just joined Basie—hit me hard too, but nothing like that. Man, you were out!"

"Tell me. It was really weird." I fumble for my cigarettes.

"You can smoke. Just open the window, okay? Margo don't allow smoking in here."

"Margo?"

"Yeah, Margo Highland. This is her place. I rent from her, watch it, take care of shit when she's gone."

"Who is she?"

Fletcher studies me. "Let me get us some coffee, then I'll tell you all about her, and you can fill me in on last night. You do want to talk about it, right?"

"Yeah, maybe I better, to make sure it was a dream."

"Oh, it was a dream all right, a smoke dream. I'll be right back." Fletcher is laughing as he heads for the kitchen. I hear him mumble, "Shit, the boy had reefer madness."

I look around the large living room, furnished with over-stuffed chairs, bookcases, and some smaller tables, probably oak. Some prints dot the walls, and over a shelf unit with the television and sound system is a collection of photos. Even from where I sit, I can see Fletcher is in one with the same woman as the photo in the bedroom.

The view from the window is a narrow street on a canal with cars parked diagonally on the canal side. At the end, there's a bridge curving up over the canal, and more bicycles chained to the guardrails. Across the street, on the other side of the canal, are some small shops and a bakery. People are going in and out, carrying loaves of bread wrapped in white paper. Suddenly I'm very hungry.

Fletcher comes back with a French press coffeepot and a plate of croissants. There's butter and a pot of thick jam. "I know you need these," he says, putting them on the table. He pours us both coffee and watches me wolf down two of the croissants and half a cup of coffee. He refills my cup and leans back, watching me with a sly smile.

"Is that Margo in the photo, with Chet in the bedroom?"

"Uh-huh. They were good friends, and she recorded with him once, I think."

"How come you never told me about her? Where is she now?"

Fletcher shrugs. "It never came up. She's got a place in California, north of San Francisco. When Chet was out there, he used to stay with her." Fletcher gazes out the window. "She probably knows more about Chet than anybody." He turns back to me. "Anyway, let's hear about your night of reefer madness." He laughs again. "I'm sorry, man, I can't help it."

Margo Highland. The name rings a bell. From one of the pages in Ace's portfolio. I tell Fletcher about going to the Old Quarter, to the coffee shop, and ordering the smoke.

"You remember the name of the place?"

"No, but I think I'd know it if I saw it again."

"Okay. Then what?"

"I remember feeling so dizzy after just a couple of hits, everything was spinning."

"What'd you do, order the strongest shit they got?"

"No, I don't think so. I know it was supposed to be medium strength."

Fletcher looks away for a moment. "Okay, we'll come back to that. Then what?"

"I don't know. I just wanted to get out of there, back to the hotel, where I could lie down, stop the spinning. I made it to the street behind the hotel, and that's when—"

"You saw Chet Baker." Fletcher rolls his eyes.

"Okay, I know it sounds crazy."

"Well, shit, it is crazy! Motherfucker's been dead eleven years. It was probably that kid impersonator you saw."

"Yeah, must have been. I wasn't thinking at the time." I hope it was. I'd feel a lot better than if it was a full-blown hallucination. "It just seemed so real. He was standing there in the alleyway, smiling at me, pointing to the window of his room, the drainpipe."

Fletcher shakes his head. "And you thought you'd try it out, that he, whoever the fuck that was, wanted you to."

"Yes. I know, I know, I was loaded."

"Man, you must have been flying."

"Yeah, I guess I was. I've never smoked anything like that, never experienced that kind of . . . being so disoriented."

"Uh-huh, and I know you bought that story that Chet forgot his key, tried to climb up that drainpipe, fell off, cracked his crazy head, and died right there in the street."

"That seems to be a theory."

"Did they talk about it in that film?"

"No. It wasn't even mentioned."

"Uh-huh. Did it ever occur to you that the reason they didn't is for that to be true, somebody had to see it happen, see him trying to climb up?"

That stops me. No, it hadn't, now that I think about it. It just sounded like a workable theory.

"And if that's true," Fletcher continues, "wouldn't who-ever saw it go to him, get him some help?"

"Yeah, of course they would." But I stop then, thinking of something else. "Unless."

"Unless what?"

"Unless whoever saw it happen didn't want to help him. Or maybe got scared and ran off."

"Oh, man." Fletcher rolls his eyes, but the phone rings be-fore he can say anything else. He goes into another room to answer it, and I think about what he said. My next comment would have been, Unless somebody made it happen.

Fletcher comes back and sits down again. "That was Dar-ren, said to ask you if you remembered the name of the place. He could check it out."

"No, I don't. I remember green curtains on the windows, but that's about all."

"Yeah, that's what I told Darren. He's got some connec-tions, maybe take you around, see if you can find it."

"Why?"

"Because what you had in you wasn't what you ordered."

"But why—"

Fletcher puts his hand up. "That's what we want to know, and maybe Darren can find out. I told you he wants to be a PI. He'll love it."

I shrug. "Okay."

"I got another idea too," Fletcher says. "Your hotel runs out when the Bimhuis gig ends Saturday, right?"

"Yeah, I guess it does. That was the deal I had with Wal-ter Offen."

"And you gonna need a place to stay if we do that duo gig. So, how about moving in here? There's a piano, we can re-hearse, hang out, you know."

I hadn't even thought beyond Saturday. "Well, yeah, sounds good to me. What about Margo? She wouldn't mind?"

Fletcher shakes his head. "No telling how long she'll be gone. She's got family in California. She takes off every once in a while to visit with them. It'll be cool. I'll let her know."

"Great, I'd like that."

Fletcher grins. "Yeah, you'll love it more when you taste my cooking." His grin fades then. He points his finger at me.

"You need to get out of that hotel. You've seen enough ghosts."

In daylight, the alleyway behind the Prins Hendrik Hotel seems innocuous. Just a convenient shortcut through to the Old Quarter from the main drag. Standing across from the back of the hotel, I look at the spot where I fell, where Chet Baker fell eleven years before. But last night it held different qualities for me. I look to my left, where I saw the hash-induced apparition of Chet Baker, and yes, that's all it was, I keep telling myself. Everything seems clear in the daytime, but it's hard to get that image out of my mind. Nothing is ever what it should be.

A famous jazz musician falls, jumps, or is pushed from his hotel room. Nobody knows how or why. It's tragic, but it should stay that way, a mystery. Instead, here I am, eleven years later, looking for my missing friend, having all kinds of doubts about myself and Chet Baker's death.

"Hey, piano man." It's Darren, coming up behind me. Still the leather jacket, the shaved dark mahogany head, and of course, the sunglasses. Fletcher is right. He does look intimidating, but the broad smile and outstretched hand are friendly and change everything.

"Hey. Guess I need to thank you for last night."

"No need, my man, no need." He spreads his hands. "I was here, and you were there." He points to the ground. "Fate, my man, fate." He smiles broadly again.

Was it? Something else flashes through my mind, but I try to dismiss it. "Well, anyway, thanks again."

Darren nods and looks up at the hotel window. "If I had been here in 'eighty-eight—well, that's another story. So, Fletcher tells me you might recognize that café."

"Maybe," I say.

"Let's walk."

We circle through the Old Quarter. There are a couple of false alarms as I try to remember where I walked, but in less than ten minutes, we're standing in front of it. "That's it," I say.

Darren looks, takes off his shades. "You sure?"

"Yes. I recognize the poster in the window." And now I take in the name. Mellow Yellow.

"Okay. You wait here. I got to have words."

I watch Darren go inside, light a cigarette, and scan the passing faces of tourists and locals strolling by. I don't have to wait long. In a few minutes the door opens, and Darren motions me over.

I follow him inside to the bar. Way in the back, a man sits in one of the booths. I don't recognize him, but he nods as we approach.

"Hello," he says, half rising and extending his hand. "I'm very sorry about last night. Darren has told me what happened. I would never have done that otherwise." He seems genuinely apologetic and concerned, so I don't want to push it.

"Done what?" I ask.

Darren slides in next to the man. I can't see his eyes for the shades, but he keeps his head straight ahead and goes into his other voice. "Man says your order was switched to Moroccan hash by some dude who paid the difference. Said he was your friend."

"Who?" I ask the bartender.

He shrugs, his eyes dart around, and I know he's lying. "I don't know. He just pointed you out, and then was gone." I remember now the man coming in the bar right after me, but I still don't know who he is or if he even had anything to do with the switch.

Darren takes off his shades and looks at me. He raises his eyebrows. "Is that cool?"

"Yeah, thanks."

Outside, Darren and I walk through the Quarter, back toward the hotel. "Looks like you got an anonymous friend," Darren says.

"Yeah. Wonder who it is?"

"You best find out. Maybe I'll find out for you." He looks up the street, sees something, then motions to me. "Come on, I want you to meet someone."

I follow him toward a woman who is talking to a man with his back to me. He turns when he sees the woman look over his shoulder. His face makes me stop in my tracks. He's still dressed in jeans, T-shirt, and a leather jacket, and his dark hair is falling over his forehead. It's daylight, but this is Chet Baker, the impersonator from the Bimhuis.

Darren sees my expression and laughs. "He won't hurt you, man." I walk closer. The resemblance is uncanny even in the light of day, but it's clearly not Chet. "This here's Philippe."

I put out my hand. Philippe's hands are jammed in his pockets. He hesitates, then shakes with me, but says nothing. Darren seems entertained by the whole thing.

"Las Vegas has Elvis impersonators. Amsterdam has Chet Baker impersonators, but just this one." Philippe gives Darren an uneasy look, nods to me, and starts to walk off. I watch him for a moment, feeling a rush of relief.

"He was there last night?" I ask Darren.

"Yeah. He saw you, got scared, went for help, and ran into me. Least you know you didn't see no ghost, right?"

Saved by Chet Baker's ghost. "Yes."

"Well, later, man." Darren puts his glasses back on and heads around the corner.

Fletcher has vouched for Darren, but is it too much of a

coincidence that he was in the alleyway right after I fell, and this Philippe guy too?

I'm still thinking that as I head back to the hotel.

There are no policemen waiting for me, but there is a message from one—Inspector Dekker. I'm almost afraid to call, but if it was bad news about Ace, Dekker would come in person. After being switched around for a couple of minutes, I finally get him.

"Inspector, it's Evan Horne."

"Oh yes, Mr. Horne. I have some news."

"About my friend?" I grip the phone tighter, trying to read Dekker's tone.

"No, I'm afraid not, but I have contacted the investigating officer on Chet Baker's death. You inquired about him."

I sigh and light a cigarette. "Oh, yes. What does he say?"

"He said for you to call him, but he's leaving town soon, so it will have to be this week."

"Fine." Dekker gives me the number, and I copy it down. "Thank you very much, Inspector."

"Not at all."

I learn from the desk clerk that the number is for a small town about thirty miles from Amsterdam. I take another deep breath and have the call put through. It answers on the third ring.

"Allo."

"Mr. Engels? My name is Evan Horne. I spoke with Inspector Dekker, and he said he'd talked to you, said it was all right to call."

"Yes, we spoke. This is about the Chet Baker business, yes? It was a long time ago, Mr. Horne."

"Yes, I know. I'm sorry to bother you, but I'm trying to find my friend. He is gathering research for a book. I thought he might have talked to you."

There's a bit of a pause before Engels answers. "Yes, I spoke with a Professor Buffington. Is that your friend?"

"Yes. When was that?"

"Some days ago." Engels chuckles. "He is very inquisitive, your friend."

"Yes, I'm sure he was. Mr. Engels, is it possible I could meet with you? If it's convenient, I could come to you." There's another pause as Engels thinks it over. Two Americans in the space of a few days might be too much for him.

"Very well. I will give you directions." I write everything down and repeat it back to him to make sure I've got it right.

"Would tomorrow be okay?"

"Yes, tomorrow is fine. There is a small pub near my home. Call me from there, and I will meet you. At noon. That is convenient for you?"

"Yes, that's fine. Thank you. I'll see you then."

"Good-bye, Mr. Horne."

I hang up the phone. Well, at least three people have seen Ace—Fletcher, Helen at the archives, and policeman Engels. I have a feeling about Engels; I'm counting on him to have some answers. I take out the portfolio and go through Ace's research material once again, looking for a mention of Margo Highland.

I find some of Ace's notes with phone numbers and addresses. Halfway down one page is a handwritten note, a name underlined: Margo Highland—Chet's friend? Northern California.

No address or phone number, but a source Ace obviously hoped to check out, and one I can learn more about from Fletcher. I also think about the film I saw at the Jazz Archives. If I know Ace and his methods, once he saw that film, he'd want to go back and check out those locations Chet visited during his final days.

Thinking about it in that light, Ace could be in Rotterdam, checking out the Dizzy Café or the Thelonious jazz club, talking to the musicians who worked with Chet if they are still around. It's worth a shot, but it still doesn't explain the jacket, or the portfolio. The longer I have that without telling the police, the more it bothers me. I know if something breaks, Dekker will give me hell.

Damn you, Ace, why didn't you leave a message? Where in the hell are you?

9

A NIGHT OFF and more sleep revive me. I do a little wandering, just kind of soaking up Amsterdam on a long walk past Dam Square, through a major shopping district. There are goods from all over the world, a variety of restaurants, and on one of the main canals, glass-enclosed ferries that tour the waterways of the city. Back at the hotel, I take a nap, eat a late dinner nearby, catch an English film on TV, and crash early—the exciting, glamorous life of a musician on the road.

When I wake up, I feel close to normal. I shower and dress quickly and head for the hotel bar for coffee and a croissant. I want to get out of there early and meet Engels on time, but I would like to get by the Jazz Archives and look at the film again first.

There's no time to call Fletcher, even though he wanted to go. I decided to rent a car for this little country trip. The desk clerk at the hotel helps me arrange it with the rental company; they promise to have the car ready and delivered to the hotel when I get back from the archives.

Outside, it's busy Amsterdam as usual as I walk down the Henrikkade to the Jazz Archives building. Cars, trolleys, huge buses, pedestrians, and bicycles elsewhere, and riders of all ages and dress. Many are old ladies, with loaves of bread sticking up out of the baskets on the handlebars.

Inside the archives, I find Helen again in her office, but today there's something in her manner and expression that throws me. She's polite, asks if she can help, but her smile and manner are chilly.

"Hi, Helen. I'd like to see that film again, please."

She looks puzzled. "You didn't see it yesterday?"

"Yesterday? No, I wasn't here. Why?"

"Oh, there's been a mistake, then." She frowns, looks embarrassed.

"What do you mean?"

"I was off yesterday, but I was told someone came to look at the film. It was temporarily misplaced, and my supervisor blamed me. It took me all morning to find it." She gives me a relieved smile. "I'm glad it was not you."

Misplaced or hidden? "You don't know who it was?"

"No—a foreigner, though. I just assumed they meant you. I apologize."

"No need to. So, can you trust me today? I'll personally hand it back when I'm finished."

"Yes, of course."

She takes me back to the film room and brings me the tape. "Perhaps you should bring it back to me. That way we can be sure.

"No problem."

I load the tape in the player and wonder who else is interested. I make some notes on the hotel stationery I've brought with me, noting the dates from May 7 to the early morning of the thirteenth, when Chet was found. I run the segment with the Engels interview a couple of times to see if I've missed anything. Engels seems efficient, sure of his facts, but uncomfortable in front of the camera. He does seem definite about there being nobody else involved, no crime.

There's nothing else I need, but I stop the tape during one segment where Chet was interviewed sometime in 1987. His hair is long, and he wears tinted glasses and holds a glass of beer. He looks bad, maybe even high, but his crinkled face brightens when he talks about Diane, a woman with him at that time.

"She's a gift any man could appreciate," he says. "Nineteen-eighty-eight doesn't have to be better. If it's as good as 1987, that would be fine." Well, it was for four months.

I fast-forward to the end and check the credits, but there are no names I recognize. I rewind the tape and take it back to Helen. "Here you are," I say. "And thanks again."

She takes the tape. "I am sorry for thinking it was you yesterday. Please come back anytime. I'll be glad to help in any way I can. No luck on your friend yet?"

"No, not yet. Oh, you can do me one more favor." I write the hotel number on some paper and give it to her. "If somebody else comes looking for the tape, would you call me?"

"Yes, of course." She takes the paper and puts it in a desk drawer.

"Thanks. I hope to see you again."

"Yes, I also."

At the hotel, the desk clerk turns over the keys to a Volkswagen Golf and shows me where it's parked. I check Engels's directions again and wind my way through the maze of one-way streets out of Amsterdam to the expressway. The exits are well marked, and I get on the right road easily enough and head southwest toward Keukenhof. The exit for the smaller two-lane road comes up about twenty miles later. According to the directions Engels gave me, this road should take me to Noordwijk.

The landscape is as flat as Texas, dotted with small canals and pools of water. The traffic is light, but there are bicycles here too—kids, women, maybe housewives on shopping trips, and touring bicyclists loaded down with backpacks and bike bags weaving through dunes teaming with bird life.

I check the directions again and start looking for the canal crossing. At the entrance, there's a wooden gate, like a corral, and a bell to ring. A man in a gray sleeveless parka comes out and waves me forward. The ferry is nothing more than a large raft that would hold maybe two cars at most. Cables stretch across the canal to the other side, where I can see some homes and more flatlands.

I drive on. The attendant secures the gate and begins to crank the cable attached to a large wheel. There's no room to get out of the car as we're slowly pulled to the other side. Except for the wake of the raftlike ferry, the water in the canal is still. At the other side, he opens a similar gate and takes my money, and I drive off. People on this side of the canal must go to work this way every day. It's a long way from rush hour in Los Angeles on the 405 Freeway.

Following the curving road, I pass through a residential area with small, solid brick homes, and then, with another turn, the road empties into a square. There's a small shop, like a convenience store, a church, and a low redbrick restaurant-bar. I park in the empty lot and go inside. The telephone is in the entryway. Engels answers on the second ring.

"Mr. Engels, it's Evan Horne."

"Ah yes, you are here. Wait there. I will come soon." He hangs up, and I look around the bar. A woman perched on a stool behind the bar is reading the newspaper. Nobody else is around. She glances up at me. I order a coffee and take a table near the window that looks out over the square. The ashtrays are all clean, but obviously there for a reason. I have a cigarette going when she brings my coffee and sets it down.

"Thank you," I say. "I'm waiting for a friend." She nods and goes off, hoping, I imagine, that my friend speaks Dutch.

In five minutes or less, I see Engels coming across the square toward the restaurant. He walks briskly, waves at someone coming out of the convenience store, then turns up the walk. Inside he speaks with the woman and points at me, then comes over.

"Mr. Horne."

"Yes, thank you for coming." He's not as old as I imagined, and I realize that the film I saw him in was made fairly recently.

He points to the menu. "You would like some lunch, perhaps? I am hungry myself."

"Maybe a sandwich, but please, my treat."

He smiles. "As you wish." The woman comes back, bringing him a draft beer. They have a quick conference about the menu. "A beer for you?" he asks me.

"Yes, sounds good." She disappears again.

"There is good soup here, and she makes the sandwiches herself. So, you had no trouble finding this place."

"No, your directions were very good. Quite a change from Amsterdam out there. I enjoyed the canal crossing."

"Yes," he says. "It's not for impatient commuters. I like it here very much, but occasionally I miss the city. When I do, I go in and stroll around the Old Quarter."

"That's where I'm staying. At the Prins Hendrik Hotel."

"Yes, I am not surprised. I'm told it has become an attraction for musicians and jazz people when they come to Amsterdam."

"Well, in the jazz world, Chet Baker was famous."

"Yes, I didn't realize how much so until later," Engels says. "At the time it looked to be a simple investigation, an accident, but of course it was not. Once he was identified, the police station was flooded with calls from around the world."

"I saw you in the film, where you are interviewed. Do you remember anything else about that night?"

He sips his beer and glances out the window. "Ah, I was very nervous. No, I'm afraid not. The report came in of a man being found in the street. Somebody called from a bar but wouldn't identify himself. I was called over. We found Mr. Baker's passport and other papers in his room, his baggage, and his trumpet. It was out of its case, lying on the floor. There was also a considerable amount of heroin and cocaine on the table."

"Speedball," I say.

"What?"

"That's the slang for heroin and cocaine mix." My imagination spins off. Chet had his fix; maybe playing a little, he decides to sit on the windowsill, check out the scene. Or did someone knock on the door? Did he lay down his trumpet on the floor to answer? The conspiracy theories won't go away.

Engels continues. "Someone, I forget who, contacted his agent, and he came over. He didn't even know Mr. Baker was in Amsterdam. Apparently he had arrived in the afternoon, and the hotels he had stayed in before were all full. The agent, Peter Huijits, explained to me who Mr. Baker was." Engels looks back at me. "They had been expecting him. He was scheduled to play that evening, in a concert."

"Yes, with Archie Shepp."

"I'm sorry," Engels says. "I don't know the name."

The woman returns with our order, two bowls of steaming lentil soup and meat and cheese sandwiches on toasted bread. When she leaves, I say, "Another famous musician."

"Yes," Engels says. "I assume so. Forgive me, I am not such a big jazz fan."

We eat in silence for a few minutes, then Engels continues. "A shame about Baker," he says. "Not just his death but his addiction. When I checked with Interpol, he had a history in Europe. Sixteen months' imprisonment in Italy, many other arrests."

I nod as I finish half of the sandwich. "Yes, his drug problems were as well known as his music. But as many people have said, he did it to himself."

I know Engels's memory couldn't be this good if Ace hadn't reminded him.

"So, about my friend, Professor Buffington. You also talked with him?"

"Yes, but not here. I was in Amsterdam and suggested we meet there to save him a trip. We had coffee. He took many notes." Engels smiles, remembering. "He is, I believe, intense? Yes?"

"Very. And when was that? Last week?"

"Yes, Thursday, I think. We talked for about an hour."

The day before I arrived in Amsterdam. "Did he say what his plans were? Where he was going next? Anything like that?"

"No, I don't recall. Just that he was continuing to research Mrs. Baker's time here."

"Did he mention my name at all?"

Engels looks surprised. "No. I had not heard of you until Inspector Dekker called."

That also strikes me as strange. But to talk to a cop, Ace didn't need me. "Do you remember if he had a leather case with him, like a portfolio, zipper on three sides?"

"Yes," Engels says, nodding. "He had it open when we talked, referred to some papers. Why do you ask?"

I finish my sandwich, push the plate aside, and take out my cigarettes. "Do you mind?"

"No, please."

I light a cigarette and look at Engels. "Can I tell you something in confidence? I mean, I know you're retired now."

"What? There is something else to our visit, yes?"

I lay it all out for him then, about Ace and our tentative plans to meet, the bar turning over his jacket, the business cards, and what I consider very unlikely behavior for Ace. I also tell him about talking with Dekker. Then I sit back and watch Engels's reaction.

He's quiet for a few minutes. He has his policeman face on now, digesting what I've told him, sorting through it. He holds my gaze then.

"But," he says, "you have left something out."

I nod and smile. "I guess you were a good detective."

Engels shrugs but isn't distracted by the compliment. "Your friend's actions probably have some logical explanation, but on the other hand . . ." His voice trails off, and his scrutiny is more intense now. He likes answers too.

I jump in with both feet then, thinking worst case is I'll have to tell Dekker as well. I tell Engels about finding the portfolio and the way it seems to have been hidden.

Quiet again, he gazes out the window, then turns back to me. "You did not tell Inspector Dekker about this discovery?"

"No."

He nods again. "Very well, if Dekker asks me anything, I shall have to tell him. If he does not . . ." He spreads his hands in front of him.

"Thank you, but I plan to tell Dekker about finding the case."

"Good," Engels says. "I think it is necessary. There is something obviously strange about your friend leaving the portfolio behind, hidden, as you say. Policemen are suspicious by nature," Engels adds, "but here there is cause, I think."

It's a relief to hear him say that, that I'm not imagining things. Something is very wrong.

"Yes, I think you're right. I just don't know what to do from this point."

Engels looks at his watch. "I'm sorry, but I do have to go." He signals the woman for the bill, and when she comes, he helps me sort out the necessary money to pay it.

"My advice is to tell Dekker everything so the police can make an official missing person case. I think there is grounds, from what you tell me. Leave it to them, Mr. Horne."

We get up and walk outside to my car. "Well, thank you for your time," I say. We shake hands. "And I appreciate your advice."

"You can find your way back?"

"Yes, I think so." I get into the car. Engels stands there for a moment and looks up at the sky.

"Anything else?" I ask.

"No," Engels says, "I was thinking. It is nice to be not a policeman any longer."

* * *

Driving back to Amsterdam, I'm so lost in thought I almost miss the exit for city center. I follow the signs for Central Station and manage to squeeze into a parking place near the hotel. The parking meters are at the end of the block. I put in enough coins for two hours, get a ticket, then go back to the car and leave it on the dashboard. Only one message at the front desk. The clerk hands it to me. "I did not understand," he says.

I look at the slip of paper. "No Ace," it says. "Coop."

"Oh, this is fine. Thank you," I tell the clerk. I go up to my room and call Fletcher, tell him about my visit with Engels.

"Damn," he says. "I wanted to go too."

"I know, just wasn't time to set it up. He's going out of town tomorrow. Anything new?"

"Just had an e-mail from Margo, told her about you, that you were going to stay awhile. Everything is cool," Fletcher says.

"Good. I've had enough of hotels for a while."

"Well, Mister Nappy is knockin' on my door," Fletcher says. I can hear him yawning. "I'll see you tonight. The guy with the duo gig is coming by, so we might talk after we play pretty for him."

"All right, Fletch, see you then."

I hang up, open the closet to get out the portfolio to take to the police. I stop and look again, moving things aside, but I come up empty.

The portfolio is gone.

I stand there for a few moments, thinking I've put it someplace but knowing I'm not going to find it. It's not here.

I look around the room but don't see that anything has been disturbed.

Now I do have to talk to Dekker.

"We go to my office, Mr. Horne, please." He seems agitated, which I interpret to mean he's already talked to Engels. I follow him down the hall, dreading this conversation. Dekker has been patient with me and tried to be helpful. Now I am going to have to confess I've been withholding information and lying to him. He isn't going to like it.

We go into his office, and he motions me to sit down as he takes his seat behind his cluttered desk. "I'm glad you called. I was going to contact you," he says. His expression is a grim frown, not angry but like he's got bad news. I try to play it out.

"Oh? I've been gone most of the day, visiting with Detective Engels."

"It's not about that," Dekker says curtly. "I'm afraid I have some bad news." He's no longer a patient policeman, humoring a tourist's concerns about a missing friend. I know he'll be studying my every reaction.

"What?"

He opens one of the large file drawers near his desk and reaches inside. And there it is—Ace's leather portfolio. Dekker holds it out, drops it on his desk, and looks at me. I don't have to feign surprise as it lands with a thud.

"This is your friend's case, is it not? The one you described to me?" I nod and reach for it. I unzip it and look inside. None of the papers or files seem missing at first glance. I set it back down and risk a glance at Dekker.

"I don't understand. Where—"

Dekker cuts me off. "It was found last night and delivered to me."

"Not another coffee shop. Who found it?"

I lean back in the chair. He doesn't have to tell me a thing. He can just say it's not my concern, go back to my piano playing, he'll take it from here, and no matter how much I argue the point, he would be adamant that it's police business now. I sit back, waiting for his answer, but he surprises me.

Dekker studies me for a moment, rubbing his hand along his cheek, feeling the stubble that's clearly visible. "I've worked the Old Quarter for many years, Mr. Horne. I know many of the red-light girls. Sometimes they provide information and favors. The girls are strictly regulated, and most don't do anything to jeopardize their permits, so they cooperate with the police whenever they can."

"It wasn't my friend, I take it."

"No," Dekker says. "Unlike you, the women of the Quarter do not withhold information. The man she described who might have left it was not your friend. She was sure of that. It could have been one of several customers. She found it later, under the bed, so she can't say for sure who it was."

Dekker leans forward. "I'm afraid now this is more serious than we initially thought. Your friend checks out of his hotel without leaving word; we find his jacket, his business cards, and now his portfolio, which I take to be much more important than a jacket."

"Yes, absolutely. I can't imagine Ace letting it out of his sight."

"Exactly," Dekker says. "Do you understand what I'm saying? Is there anything else you can tell me? We have to treat this now officially as a missing person case, and consider the possibility that something has happened to your friend."

I'm dying to light a cigarette, my mind racing. I promised Engels I'd tell Dekker I had the case, and now there's no way out. "Yes, there is something you're not going to like."

Dekker leans back, waiting, as if he already expects something. I tell him about finding the portfolio in Ace's room, keeping it, but assuring him I had come to tell him just that after my promise to Engels.

"That's why I came over now," I say.

Dekker is frowning at me. He looks up, shakes his head, and sighs. "I knew there was something the other day when I showed you the jacket. I asked you then, and you seemed to hesitate. My partner thought so too, but I didn't persist. Perhaps I should have. . . . Now," he spreads his hands, "you may have delayed finding out what has happened to your friend, and something certainly has."

"Yes, I know, and I apologize for not telling you sooner. I just didn't think it would come to this."

"Yes, well, it has," Dekker says. "I'm sure you've speculated considerably as to why the portfolio was in his room after he'd checked out. What about your room? Was anything else missing?"

"No. I didn't realize it was gone until just before I came here. Whoever took it was obviously looking for the case and nothing else. They must have had a key. The room was locked when I got back."

"Do you have any idea?"

I shake my head. "None. I just don't understand what's going on."

"It would seem that whoever was in your room expected it to be there, no?" Dekker's head snaps up. "Perhaps because it was not in the room where your friend stayed. Was that not also the room Mr. Baker fell from?"

"Yes, it was." I lapse into silence, spinning out possibilities. Who else knew I was there?

"Mr. Horne, have you considered that this has something to do with Mr. Baker's death? Your friend was here to do research. He's missing; his portfolio is missing, then found. I've looked through it. There's nothing in there but newspaper clippings, photos, and notes on Chet Baker."

"Yes, I know, I read through most of it."

Dekker looks like he wishes he'd never heard of me or Chet Baker or Ace. He leans forward again and clasps his hands in front of him on the desk. "I want to be very clear about this, Mr. Horne. If you think of anything else, I want to know. We're going to have to work together to find out what happened to your friend."

He shuffles through some papers and comes up with the photo of Ace taken in front of the hotel. "This was also in the portfolio, as you obviously know. This is your friend, correct?"

"Yes, that's him. The owner of the hotel took it. I talked to him the other day."

Dekker nods. "Remember what I said, Mr. Horne."

"Understood." I stand up to go. "And again, I'm sorry for not telling you about the case before."

"Not nearly so sorry as I am," Dekker says. "That's what you need to think about, Mr. Horne. How and why it got there in the first place. When we know that, perhaps we will know where your friend is and what happened to him."

The Bimhuis is overflowing for our last night. I can hear the bar chatter even as I mount the stairs. It's three deep with people calling out drink orders, laughing, talking, and I have to push through a horde of people blocking the entrance to the main area of the club. Here too, the tiers of seats are full, and on the walkway around the top, people are talking in groups, occasionally glancing down at the stage, looking at their watches.

I find Fletcher at the piano bench on the unlit stage, his horn around his neck, playing some chords.

"A new arrangement?"

"Hey," he says and flashes me a smile. "No, just working something out. How ya doin'?"

"Okay."

"Uh-huh. Well, I'll hear about that later. The guy I told you about, Eric Hagen, will be in tonight to check us out, so we're going to play a couple of extra duo things, okay?"

"Sure. I'm getting to like it." It's been a new experience for me, playing without the net of bass and drums, but Fletcher has made it easy. His timing is so good. I'm not sure it would work with anyone else, but Fletcher and I have a connection I can't quite explain, like we're reading each other's minds. I flash to the film again.

There was a brief segment of Chet and Stan Getz, on an otherwise empty stage, just the two of them playing, the drum kit and bass, lying on its side, clearly visible in the background,

as if the other two musicians had been sent home early. Chet
and Stan, playing, listening, responding, each commenting on
the other's lines. Matching phrases, repeating them, counter-
ing them. A musical conversation on Gerry Mulligan's tune
"Line for Lyons." I understand it better now and realize that's
the level Fletcher and I are approaching.

"Cool," he says. "Let's open with the whole band for a
couple, settle these restless natives down." He stands up and
adjusts the horn on the chain around his neck. "And don't
forget, you checking out of the ghost hotel tomorrow."

I laugh. "No, I haven't forgotten."

I look around the club. The audience is settling in now,
saving seats for friends, getting drinks, and the whole place is
blue with smoke. Ah, the jazz clubs of old are alive and well
in Europe.

Walter Offen appears out of the crowd as the houselights
go down and the stage is suddenly bathed in a warm red glow.
"It is time, yes?" he says.

"Hey, we're just waiting for you. Let's do it," Fletcher says.

I want to say something to the bassist and drummer but
decide to wait for now. Walter makes the introductory announcement, and we go to work on a medium blues. Fletcher
eases into it teasingly, hinting at what's to come. He leans
back as the spot hits him, the horn, held a little to the side,
gleaming in the light. I can picture him back with Count
Basie, standing in front of that roaring band at Newport, taking chorus after chorus before nodding his head toward me,
and slowly backing away.

My entire first chorus is lost in the shouts of the audience. I cruise through two more and think about Wynton
Kelly with Miles, swaggering through "Freddie Freeloader,"
or Victor Fieldman on "Basin Street Blues," with Ron Carter
and Frank Butler right behind him like a pair of bodyguards.
Swing hard, and nobody gets hurt. I let it build gradually, feel
the bass and drums catch my mood, comping with my left
hand and stringing out single-note runs. On the last two, I

start with two-handed block chords and feel Fletcher rocking beside me until I turn it over to the bassist.

Fletcher grins at the audience and points at me as if to say, Well? What about that? He leans in next to me and says, "You keep playin' that good, I'm gonna quit letting you solo." It's better than any review I could ever get.

We come back and trade choruses several times around, let the drummer have his say for a couple of choruses, then finally take it out. We could stop right there for the night, and it would be fine with me. We're a hard act to follow.

The audience breathes a collective sigh of satisfaction and quiets down. "My man is here," Fletcher says. "How about 'Sophisticated Lady'?"

I nod and play an intro, then listen to Fletcher breathe life into the verse. When he begins the melody, I stay out of his way and just feed him the richest, fattest chords I can find. He takes my breath away with his lines, and my only regret is I have to follow him. I give a nod to Duke Ellington and realize again how much I love playing ballads. We continue with a line Fletcher wrote, another blues we play almost entirely in counterpoint, and end the set with "My Foolish Heart," which makes me wonder how Bill Evans and Chet Baker would have sounded together.

Fletcher calls my name, and I stand up for a quick bow, but the show is his. "We have one more set here at the Bimhuis," he says on the microphone. "We hope you stay around."

A tall, thin man about forty climbs up on the stage and comes toward Fletcher. He has a crew cut and lightly tinted glasses. Fletcher takes him by the elbow and brings him over to the piano. He smiles at me and extends his hand. "You two are wonderful together," he says. "Just wonderful. I am Eric Hagen."

We shake, and Fletcher beams behind him. "Hello," I say. "Glad you enjoyed the music."

"Oh, yes, very much. Please, we must talk." We go into a

small room behind the stage to avoid the crowds. It's cluttered with instrument cases and several cartons of wine and beer stacked against the wall. Fletcher shuts the door, putting the din of the club behind us.

"So, Fletcher has told you of my proposition?"

"Yes," I say. "It sounds very interesting."

"My club is small, nothing like this, but I'm sure you'll enjoy it. I have a very fine piano also." He looks to Fletcher for confirmation.

"I stopped by the other afternoon," Fletcher says. "Pretty cool."

"So," Hagen continues, "I would like to start next weekend, as a sort of trial, then we will talk more about a long-term arrangement." He looks at us both.

"I'm for it," Fletcher says.

"Me too."

Hagen grins at us both. "Excellent. Fletcher, I will call you on Monday, then, and we will make the final arrangements. I'm sorry I cannot stay longer this evening. It was very nice to meet you, Evan. I look forward to next week, then."

After he goes out, Fletcher and I look at each other for a moment, and then both of us laugh and slap hands. "I told you you'd like Amsterdam," he says.

Yes, and now I have some time.

10

SUNDAY MORNING breaks quietly. After the excitement of closing night and the confirmation of the new gig, I don't sleep as long as I thought I would, but it's just as well. I want to get checked out of this hotel and over to my new digs with Fletcher. I shower and dress, pack my bag, then take one last look around the room, a ritual I've performed before in countless hotels on the road. Nothing left behind unless I want it left.

Ace, I remind myself once more, would have done the same if he'd departed the Prins Hendrik Hotel under normal circumstances. Ace wanted that portfolio left behind, and he wanted me to find it.

I take a final look out the window to the street below, the canal bridge at the end, bustling with people and traffic and inevitable bicycles. I won't see this view again.

At the front desk, the clerk tallies the charges for me from the bar, and I pay for the extra phone calls. Everything else has been prepaid by Walter Offen. Nothing left to do but call Fletcher from the lobby phone.

"Hey, Fletch, you up and ready for your new boarder?"

"Yeah, if I have to be," Fletcher says sleepily. "You coming over now?"

"Yeah, I'm going to grab some coffee and get a taxi."

"Okay. At the hotel? I'll pick you up."

"Next to the hotel, a few doors down, is a coffee place. I'll be in there or out front."

"Gotcha. Be there in about an hour."

"See you then," I say and hang up the phone.

Outside, I study once again the sculpture of Chet and the list of donors. Something clicks in my mind as I read the donor list of names, individuals, record companies. I wonder how much it cost. Who commissioned it? Who was the artist? I get a pad and pen out of my bag and quickly jot down all the names, then wander down to the coffee shop.

I order coffee and a croissant while I try to decide what to do next, making a mental note to let Dekker know where I'm staying in case there's some news. But I'm resigned to the idea that if anything develops, it will be of my own doing. Dekker may now officially make Ace a missing person and have the alert out, but the Old Quarter precinct is a busy one. A "possibly" missing tourist won't be a high priority.

I sip the coffee and try to put myself in Ace's mind. After viewing the film at the archives, I'm convinced, Ace would backtrack Chet's final days, starting with the Thelonious in Rotterdam, then work back to Amsterdam and the afternoon of May 12. Even with the information in the film, there were some gaps in time, and those gaps are what Ace would be looking to fill.

Where was Chet, and what was he doing then? May 11 and 12, a couple of days and nights—why didn't anyone know where he was? But what if somebody did know, and Ace found them, along with more than he could handle? If I could find that out, I might get closer to finding Ace. Dekker wasn't going to do it, and he didn't know anything about Chet Baker, musicians, or musicians' friends, or what it was like for a junkie to be desperately looking for a fix. If Chet hadn't come to Amsterdam until May 12, and he was last seen in Rotterdam, then he had to have had some contact there. That's who I have to find.

I put out my cigarette, finish my coffee, and glance out the window for Fletcher's car. For a minute it all sounds plausible. On the other hand, this could all be nothing but Ace's forgetfulness—losing his jacket, leaving the portfolio in the hotel. It is possible, but I'm not convinced. The jacket maybe, but not the portfolio. And now that it's been taken from my room, too many more questions are bothering me. My gut feeling is too strong.

Something has happened to Ace, or somebody is orchestrating his every move.

I look out the window again and see Fletcher's car pull up. I grab my bag and go out to meet him. Fletcher is curiously quiet as we make the short drive to his place. He wedges his car into a space dangerously close to the canal, between a small truck and a Mercedes. The parking is diagonal on the canal, parallel along the curb on the opposite side. There's just enough room for a car to get down the narrow one-way street.

"Good thing Margo has a permit," Fletcher says, getting out of the car. We hear a tinkling bell, and both of us jump back between two cars. "Damn, all these years, and I still can't get used to these bicycles."

I grin at him as we walk back up the street to Margo's flat and my temporary home for who knows how long. "You ought to get one," I say. "Take a photo and send it to *Downbeat*."

"Yeah, yeah," Fletcher says. "You just play the piano."

Inside, Fletcher hands me a key off the hall table. "That's an extra," he says.

I'm to be in Margo's room, where I woke up the day after what Fletcher called my reefer madness night. I make a little space in the closet for the few clothes I have with me and leave the small items in my bag. Fletcher stands in the doorway, watching me. "You do travel light," he says.

I shrug. "Yeah, well, I didn't know if I was coming over for two weeks or two months. I can always pick up some things later if I need to—or I've got stuff in storage in L.A. I can send for if I stay longer."

"Well, make yourself at home. I'm going to practice. I try to get in a couple of hours every day. If you feel like it later, you can try out the piano."

I look at Fletcher. "Thanks for everything, man. I appreciate it."

"No problem. I like the company, and you won't see no ghosts here." He wanders off to his room, and in a couple of minutes I hear his saxophone, running scales, playing exercises, while I check out the rest of the apartment.

I wonder about Fletcher and his self-imposed exile. Like so many musicians who have chosen to stay in Europe, Fletcher is more welcome here than in his own country, but ironically he's still playing American music.

An apartment in Amsterdam is nothing like my old place in Venice Beach. I feel a twinge of nostalgia thinking about the beach, the long walks, the smell of the ocean. Here, it's heavy wood furniture, large throw rugs on the wooden floors, and high ceilings. Sunlight streams in through the tall windows, their heavy drapes thrown open now. The kitchen must have been remodeled at one time. It's decked out with fairly modern appliances and a well-stocked refrigerator. I'll have to work something out with Fletcher on the food, especially if his cooking lives up to his promise.

In one corner of the living room is an upright piano. Some handwritten music sheets rest on the stand—probably tunes Fletcher's working on. The upholstered wooden stool is the kind that's raised and lowered by spinning the seat. I get it adjusted to my liking and sit down. The notes ring out loud and clear, surprisingly well in tune despite the dampness from the canal that must affect the piano. I run through some chords, play some scales, just warming up easily, and continue to marvel at my hand being so pain free.

I'm aware of Fletcher playing in the other room, but it's

not enough to distract me. Once I catch a few moments of silence; then he resumes, playing on the tune I'm trying. An hour later, I'm used to the action of the piano and getting to like it. Then I sense Fletcher standing behind me, listening.

"Not bad, huh?"

I stop and turn around. "No, not at all. You have it tuned?"

"Uh-huh, a couple of times. How about some lunch?"

"Sounds good to me."

I follow Fletcher into the kitchen and watch him at work. "Got some chicken left over from yesterday and some of my dirty rice. Sound okay?"

"Whatever, I'm easy."

Fletcher nods and gets the rice going. "There's a bottle of white wine in the fridge. Why don't you open that, and we'll have us a little taste. You can tell me about your visit with the *po*-lice," he says, emphasizing the first syllable. He opens a drawer and hands me a corkscrew.

I watch Fletcher bustle around the kitchen, as at home here as he is on the bandstand. He gets the chicken simmering in a big cast-iron skillet and the rice in a saucepan. The room fills with the aroma of garlic and something I can't make out. He slices several pieces of bread off a large loaf, turns down the chicken, and checks the rice. Everything under control.

"Looks like you've done this a time or two before."

He laughs. "Yeah, everybody cooked in my family, and on the road with Basie, sometimes we'd get a location gig and set up shop. Try to find motels with kitchens. Some of the guys brought their own pans with them."

"Must have been some good times."

He smiles, remembering. "Oh, yeah. I got on after he reformed the band. Late fifties, early sixties. Just missed Joe Williams. Lot of good music, good times, good food, and yes, plenty of women." He claps his hands together and does a little dance. "Don't get me started on that. One thing I don't miss, though, is that bus. No, baby." He checks everything again and turns the heat down. "Why don't you pick out some music?

Then we'll eat. Margo has a lot of stuff, and some of mine is mixed in there."

I take my wine and go into the living room. On shelves under the stereo is a large selection of compact discs and a sizable number of LPs. And yes, there is a turntable. I look through them and pick out an early Chet Baker, the band with Russ Freeman on piano, just as Fletcher comes through with two hot plates of chicken and rice.

"Now, how did I know you were going to play one of those?" he says, sitting the plates on the table. "Come and get it."

We sit down and dig in. After a few bites I tell Fletcher if he ever quits playing he could always open a restaurant. "This is fantastic. What's on the chicken?"

He nods, obviously pleased. "Don't ask. That's my grand-mother's recipe, and the secret stays with me, white boy."

When we finish, Fletcher opens the window, and we each have a cigarette with the rest of the wine, and listen to Chet Baker. I tell Fletcher about Russ Freeman's comments in the film, how Chet really didn't know harmony. "He said all Chet wanted to know was the first note, and he just took it from there. He must have had a phenomenal ear."

"Yeah," Fletcher says. "You could put changes in front of him, and they didn't mean nothing. I heard guys try to fool him and tell him wrong keys. Shit, it was them who got in trouble. Chet just played, man. I don't think he even knew how he did it. Sang the same way. Let me show you something."

He goes over to the stereo shelf and searches through some videotapes, finds what he's looking for, slides the cassette into the machine, and turns on the television. "Margo got this. It was made at Ronnie Scott's club in London about a year before he died."

There's an opening shot of Chet sitting on a stool, just star-ing at his trumpet, as if he's gathering strength to play, or de-ciding whether to even pick it up. The camera stays with him for what seems like a long time before he turns to the piano player and they begin. No drums, just Chet, piano, and bass.

The song is "Just Friends," an easy loping tempo, but Chet is clearly struggling, although the pianist feeds him one luscious chord after another. He manages a couple of choruses, then listens to the piano and bass, head down. Then he sings. It's not that young boy voice anymore. It's deepened, become rougher, but has more emotion. He strains here too, as if he's not going to make it, but somehow he does, wrapping his voice around the familiar standard, making you pull for him in the process. He scats one chorus too, the phrasing sounding exactly like his trumpet playing, as if to say, I can't do it with the horn anymore, but this is what it would sound like if I could. There's no showy technique, no vibrato to his voice at all. He ends on a very hip little flurry of notes and smiles. But he looks so tired. He follows with a couple of ballads and a tricky little bop blues line of Kenny Dorham's he plays in unison with the pianist.

Chet Baker playing and singing pure jazz. It's not playing with soul—it is his soul.

We listen to a few more, then Fletcher gets up and stops the tape. "That's the best stuff," he says. "Couple of pop singers come on with him. Don't know what they were doing there. Trying to sell records, I guess. That Kenny G character still selling a lot?"

"Oh, yeah. Millions."

Fletcher says, "He's the anti-Bird, but I guess he's getting to some folks."

"Chet's playing really gets to you, doesn't it? It does me, anyway."

"Uh-huh, and his thing is as secret as my grandmother's chicken recipe."

I think for a moment, the film images and sound still in my mind. "He'd be what, about your age, if he'd lived, right?"

Fletcher nods. "Yeah, I guess so."

"Wonder what he'd be doing now?"

"Same thing." Fletcher shrugs. "Playing jazz and scoring dope. Somebody asked him once, What's the worst thing about drugs? Know what he said?"

"What?"

"The price."

I shake my head. "I wonder if he just meant money. To play like that. What a waste."

"Got a lot of folks. Got hold of Chet early and wouldn't let go. Everybody else from those times either cleaned up or died." Fletcher gets up and stretches. "Well, since you enjoyed my cooking so much, I know you won't mind doing the dishes. I'll make some coffee."

We get the kitchen cleared up and go back to the living room. He picks the music this time: Miles at Lincoln Center in 1964 with George Coleman on tenor. They're doing that band's version of "All of You." Near the end of Coleman's solo, Fletcher puts up his hand. "Check this out."

They've doubled the tempo from the original ballad start by then. Coleman plays a flurry of sixteenth notes, then slides into the vamp that started the whole thing and sets up Herbie Hancock's solo.

"Damn," Fletcher says. "That just kills me. Left Herbie Hancock something to think about." After Herbie, Miles comes back, all forlorn and mournful, like a little kid wanting to be let into the room. "Okay, I'm done," Fletcher says. He turns down the stereo. "Now tell me about the police."

I recap my visit with Detective Engels, and my surprise that Dekker already had the portfolio before I could tell him I had it.

"Damn," Fletcher says, "this is getting weird."

"Yeah, they're treating it officially as a missing person case now, but that doesn't mean much. If Ace is going to be found, I think I'm going to have to do it." Fletcher doesn't say anything for a moment. I pause and look at him. "What?"

"I was just thinking. Maybe I'm out of line here, but . . . but, I know this is your friend, but aren't you maybe taking it too far? Shouldn't you just let the police handle it from here?"

"Yes, you're probably right, and given what's happened before, I should know better. Ace is my friend, but it's more than that. After my accident, I didn't play much at all. I couldn't. I lost my confidence. I thought for a while I'd never play again. And then Ace arranged this gig for me. He pulled some strings with the music department at UNLV—the department supplied piano students—got me in on it as a guest. It was a dumb gig, at a shopping mall in Las Vegas, but it got me playing again." I look at Fletcher. "I owe him, Fletch. I have to find him."

Fletcher nods. "Yeah, I can see that. I just wanted to know where you're coming from. I still say just let the police handle it, but I know people have told you that before and it didn't do any good, so I'm not going to bother trying to convince you otherwise. So what's your plan?"

"Try to do what I think Ace would have done. Retrace Chet's last few days. They have it in the film, part of it, at least. He was at the Thelonious in Rotterdam on May 7, and three nights later, he dropped in and played a couple of tunes at the Dizzy Café with the band there."

Fletcher nods. "I know them both."

"If I talk to people there, I can at least find out if Ace has been to Rotterdam." I tell Fletcher about my suspicion that Chet had some other contact there for drugs. "It was two days before he showed up in Amsterdam again on the twelfth. He would have been hurting. I don't know what else to do. You have any ideas?"

Fletcher gets up and begins to pace around. "It's been years, but there was a guy in Rotterdam. He used to put guys up for a promoter down there. I even stayed with him once. I think he had some drug connections too."

"You remember his name?"

Fletcher shakes his head. "Block or Blove or Stove, one of the few Dutch names that wasn't van-something. I don't know, I can't remember. It was a long time ago. Anyway, let's take a ride down there. Maybe it will jog my memory."

"Us?"

"Oh, yeah. I want in too." I think then about Pappy Dean, Cal Hughes, Natalie, Coop. Fletcher catches my change of expression. "What?"

"It's not that I don't want or couldn't use some help, but well, in the past, I've gotten other people involved in a way I didn't mean to. This thing with Ace could be nothing, or I could stumble onto something I shouldn't, and that could be trouble. I don't want to jam you up because of my meddling."

Fletch laughs. "Is that all? Hell, man, don't worry about me. I grew up in Harlem. I know all about that shit. You might need someone to watch your back, and I'm the man. Besides, I told you. I read Hoke Moseley books."

I can see it won't do any good to try and convince Fletcher it's not a good idea, any more than he could persuade me to let the police handle it. Who can resist Fletcher Paige?

"Okay, Hoke. Let's do it."

"Hey," Fletcher says. "I do understand where you're coming from. Ace is lucky to have you for a friend. I just hope he appreciates it."

Monday morning, while Fletcher is still sleeping, I call Inspector Dekker to let him know where I am and to see if anything has developed.

"I'm glad you called, Mr. Horne. I wanted to talk with you. I called the hotel and was told you had checked out."

"Yes, I'm staying with a friend. You have some news?"

"No, it's something else. Could you come down to the station this morning? There is something I want you to do."

"Yes, of course."

What now, if it's not about Ace? When I get to the station, I'm ushered back to Dekker's office very quickly. His door is open, and he motions me inside to a chair. "Thank you for coming so promptly, Mr. Horne." Ace's portfolio is on his desk.

"You mentioned wanting me to do something."

"Yes," Dekker says. He taps the portfolio. "I assume while this was in your possession you went through the articles and notes, yes?"

I shrug. "Well, yes, I'm afraid I did."

"I'm not criticizing, Mr. Horne. It would be natural for anyone to do. You were looking for some clue as to Mr. Buffington's whereabouts. What I would like you to do now is look through it again, see if anything is missing, or perhaps more important, if there's something there that shouldn't be."

"I don't understand."

Dekker looks at me like a teacher impatient with a slow student. "Do you know anything about literature, Mr. Horne?"

The question catches me by surprise, and I wonder where this is going. "Well, I took classes in college. I read a lot, I suppose."

"Hemingway?"

"Well, yes, some. Why do you ask?"

Dekker settles back in his chair. "Do you know the story about Hemingway's suitcase, the lost stories?"

The question vaguely rings a bell, but nothing more. "I'm not sure I do."

Dekker seems almost happy with my response. Now he can recite the story. "Hemingway was in Switzerland. He had left a number of stories he was working on in his apartment in Paris. His wife was to join him. On her own initiative, she took along the stories when she packed, thinking he would want to work on them during their vacation. But at the train station in Paris, she set the suitcase down for a moment, and it was stolen. She searched frantically, but it was gone. Then she had to confess her mistake to Hemingway when she arrived. At the time, he took the news fairly calmly, at least according to some biographers. More than a dozen stories in various stages of development were lost. He tried to re-create them but eventually abandoned the idea. Only one was saved; it had fallen behind the dresser in their Paris apartment and wasn't in the suitcase."

Dekker pauses, almost dramatically, to let this sink in. "The suitcase was never found, and of course there has been much speculation about its disappearance. Remember, at that time Ernest Hemingway was not famous, merely a struggling young writer. Some say the thief would find some clothes, and some paper with typing on them. The stories would mean nothing to him. The thief perhaps took what he wanted and threw away the rest, or left the suitcase for someone else to find. In any event, it was never found. Another theory is that the suitcase is long forgotten, still in someone's attic in Paris. Can you imagine what a literary find that would be? The lost stories of Ernest Hemingway." Dekker shakes his head in wonder.

"Inspector Dekker, you're a romantic."

"Hmmm. Yes, perhaps." He allows himself a smile.

"But I don't—"

He taps the portfolio. "It strikes me that your friend's portfolio is similar, only it's not lost—and it raises a number of questions beyond who is responsible. Why abandon it? Did the thief—we'll call him that for now—want it returned and hope nobody noticed something was missing; or was something added to the contents, perhaps accidentally; or was it something he hoped someone would find? Do you follow me, Mr. Horne?"

Dekker looks as self-satisfied as if he's spent the weekend working out this scenario, and now he has an audience. It doesn't make sense to me, but I go along with him.

"Yes, I think I see what you mean. Should I look through it now, here?"

"Please," Dekker says, "and take your time. I will show you to a room where you can have some privacy and even smoke if you like."

"Fine. Show me the way."

Dekker takes the portfolio and walks me down the hall. The room is small and bare—gray walls, a linoleum floor, probably an interrogation room. There's only a small table and two chairs. "I will be in my office. Please tell me when you've finished." Dekker sets the portfolio on the table and walks out.

I light a cigarette and get to work. Unzipping the portfolio, I take everything out and set it aside. Turning over each sheet, I skim the articles and note pages two or three times, careful to make sure nothing is stuck together. I know most of the material already, but three or four cigarettes later, I'm totally absorbed with the articles and read more carefully, learning more and more about Chet Baker but nothing else.

After over an hour, nothing strikes me as missing that was there when I first found the case at the hotel. More important, I don't see anything new. It all looks familiar.

I check the portfolio one last time. There's an inside pocket in the back, where I'd found the photos of Ace. Dekker has one; I have the other, so I didn't bother much with it before. But now, there is something. I feel around, and my hand touches a small slip of paper. It's some kind of printed receipt in Dutch. It's hard to make out, as the ribbon on the register must have been nearly worn out. I check the pocket again, but there's nothing else. As I'm about ready to go look for Dekker, he comes back in the room.

"Good timing," I say.

Dekker's expression, however, is different now—not so much angry as irritated about something. "Have you found something?"

"Just this." I hand him the receipt. He sits down slowly in the chair opposite me and studies it, nodding. "What is it?"

Dekker holds it closer, trying to make out the faint printing. "It's from a photocopy store here in Amsterdam, in Dam Square." He flips through the stack of articles. "From the amount, I would say the entire contents were copied." He looks up at me then, as if I have the answer.

I shrug. "No idea."

"Yes, it is puzzling," he says. He puts all the articles back in the portfolio but holds out the receipt and places it on top. He folds his hands and looks at me in the way he must look at a suspect when he wants a confession.

"I just talked to a Lieutenant Cooper with the Santa Monica Police. He too was concerned that you had checked out of the hotel."

"Yes, I meant to tell him. We're old friends, from school."

"So it would seem," Dekker says. "Lieutenant Cooper tells

me in the past you have been involved in a number of investigations, one even assisting the FBI. I'm impressed, Mr. Horne."

Oh, here we go. The warning lecture. "Well, my part was rather minor, as I'm sure Cooper told you."

Dekker's eyebrows rise slightly. "Minor? I don't think so. I certainly would not characterize the apprehension of a serial killer as minor." He sets the paper down and continues. "Be that as it may, Mr. Horne, I feel it is necessary to tell you that the Amsterdam police will not tolerate interference in any way. I would also remind you that you are not familiar with Amsterdam, and your American passport does not make you immune from Dutch law. So please, Mr. Horne, curb your tendencies to—go off on your own, as Detective Cooper put it, I believe. I understand your concern for your friend's whereabouts, but leave it to us. If you have any ideas or thoughts on the matter, I will be happy to consider them, but that's all."

"Yes, of course."

"Good. Lieutenant Cooper said I might have to emphasize that to you."

"I bet he did." Dekker lets that one go. I give him Fletcher's number and promise to be good. "I may run down to Rotterdam for a couple of days, but I'll stay in touch with you."

"Oh?"

"Yes, there are two jazz clubs I'd like to check out, for potential work. Nothing to do with my friend."

"Yes," says Dekker, but I can see he only half buys it. "Enjoy your trip."

I go over to the American Express office to change some money and decide to call Coop at home, even if I do wake him up with the time difference.

"What?" is his friendly answer.

"Hey, Coop, what are you doing up so late?"

"Watching a movie. I understand you've already ingratiated yourself with the Amsterdam police. That didn't take long."

"That's a pretty big word for a cop to use. Did you have to give Dekker my whole résumé?"

Coop laughs. "Yeah, I enjoyed that part. Just wanted to let them know what they're up against." His tone changes just as quickly. "No sign of Ace, I take it."

"No, nothing. I suppose Dekker filled you in."

"Yeah, sounds kind of weird. I'd watch myself with Dekker, though. Remember where you are."

"Yeah, he gave me the stay-out-of-things-unless-you're-asked lecture. I can't figure it, Coop. This is not like Ace at all, and I'm beginning to wonder just what's happening. His portfolio was stolen from my hotel room and then turned up with Dekker, everything intact."

"No, he didn't tell me about that."

I fill Coop in. He listens, then says, "I won't even tell you I told you so. Somebody besides Ace wanted it, didn't find what they were looking for, and dumped it. Anyway, sport, got a new number where I can reach you?"

"Yes." I give him Fletcher's number. "He's a musician I've been working with."

"Okay," Coop says. "Go easy. Oh, ran into somebody you know."

"Yeah? Natalie again?"

"No, haven't seen her. I had to go to a weekend seminar put on by the FBI. Andie Lawrence. She asked about you—quite a lot, I might add—but I just told her you were still in Europe."

"Good."

"She's with the San Francisco bureau now."

"Am I supposed to take note of that?"

"No, just letting you know."

"All right, Coop. Thanks. Go back to your movie. What are you watching?"

"*The French Connection.* Already there," Coop says.

I hang up the phone and walk outside. The streets are, as usual, full of shoppers and tourists as I walk up toward Dam Square, where several boulevards converge. I pick out an empty bench in the main square and just enjoy the passing parade for a while, thinking about Ace's portfolio.

Who knew about it besides Ace, and why did it turn up again with nothing missing? Across the square, the name from the receipt on a store flashes at me like neon. Inside, it's busy and noisy and looks like any Kinko's. There's a group of self-service machines, a counter, and several clerks behind it manning the larger copiers. I get in line for service, wondering if clerks pay any attention to what they copy.

The young man who helps me has on a white shirt and blue name tag with "Jerrod" on it. He's confused by my request and gets somebody else to help. It's a long shot, but I describe the pages that were copied to the second man.

"Do you remember the man who had the copying done? It's important."

The clerk thinks a minute. "Ah yes, Chet Baker. I remember now. We talked about his music. I too am a fan, and of course, Baker died here."

"Yes, that's right. These were typed pages he had copied. What did the man look like?"

"Hmm . . . very tall, he had a beard, I think. And yes, American."

"Wait a minute." I take out my passport case and show him the photo of Ace. "Is this him?"

The clerk takes the photo and looks at it. "Yes, this is the man."

"Do you remember when this was?"

The clerk shrugs. "Only a few days, perhaps. No more than a week."

I nod. "Thanks, thanks very much."

"Not at all."

I go outside in the busy square again, traffic and people buzzing all around me, but only hearing that voice in my head, asking another question: Why would Ace need to copy the entire contents of his portfolio?

11

I T'S A little too quiet when I get back to the flat. No music playing, no sound of Fletcher's saxophone. Nothing. I close the door and listen for a moment. "Fletch, you in?"

"In here," he calls from his room. I breathe a sigh of relief and walk down the hall. His horn is set aside, lying on the neatly made bed. He's in jeans, T-shirt, and sandals, holding something up to a high-intensity light at his desk with one hand. In his other hand is a small knife. He pauses for a moment to push his glasses up. I look around his room for the first time.

"Be with you in a minute," he says. He glances over for a second, looking at me over the top of his glasses, then turns back to what he's working on. "I'm a neatnik, huh?"

He is. Not only is the bed made, everything seems to have a place. Books in low cases along one wall, and I know without looking they're in alphabetical order by author. There are a few strays stacked neatly on the nightstand by size. The pictures on the wall, the posters of jazz festivals, are arranged symmetrically. The closet door is open to several suits, hangers spaced evenly.

"Getting these how I like them too," he says without looking at me. I see now he has a saxophone reed in his hand, shaving the edge carefully with a small knife. He blows on it, checks it again. "Want to hand me my horn?" I get it and bring it over. He puts the reed in the mouthpiece and tightens it in place. He blows a few notes, his eyes open, listening, then runs through the first few bars of "Body and Soul" before he puts the horn down. "Yeah, that's it. Don't know why they can't make them like that out of the box." He looks at me now. "Hey, man, you been out early." He pads out of his room and lights a cigarette.

"Yeah, I called the police. Dekker wanted me to come down and go through Ace's portfolio again." Fletcher looks at me through a cloud of smoke and laughs. "What?"

"I was just thinking. *You* called the police."

"Okay, okay. He wanted me to see if anything was missing or if something had been added." I watch the smoke curl over his head. "What happened to the smoking rule?"

He shrugs and looks for the ashtray. "Hell, Margo ain't here. We can always air the place out. Anyway, this thing has me keyed up. Find anything?"

"Just a receipt for some photocopying. Everything in the portfolio was copied. I checked at the store, showed the guy the photo. He remembered all right. It was Ace."

Fletcher sits down and looks at me. "Let me see the photo of Ace. I didn't know you had one."

"Yeah, guess I forgot to tell you." I take it out and show Fletcher. He studies it for a moment.

"Yeah, that's the guy I talked to all right. Just wanted to make sure. This was in the portfolio?"

"Yes, there were a couple. I . . . okay, I kept this one."

Fletcher nods knowingly. "Why would he copy everything?"

"My question exactly."

Fletcher is still squinting at the photo. "We're missing something here," he says, "but damn if I can figure what it is." He hands it back to me.

"I know. Nothing about this makes any sense."

Fletcher goes to the window, pulls the drapes apart, and turns the crank to open the window. Cool air rushes into the room. "Want some coffee? I was just gettin' ready to."

"Yeah, sounds good." We walk back to the kitchen. Fletcher puts on the kettle to boil water, gets coffee out of a canister, and spoons some into a French press. "You ever been married, Fletcher?"

"Oh, yeah. Twice. My second wife and I split about ten years ago, but we'd been separated a long time before that."

"Kids?"

Fletcher grins. "Yeah, one daughter. Prettiest thing you ever seen. She's married, made me a granddaddy a few years ago. Lives in Portland. She's a lawyer."

"Hmmm. My ex-girlfriend is about to become a lawyer."

"Ex?" He cocks his head to the side. "You ain't got no ladies waitin' for you back home?"

"Well, one maybe. I talked to my cop friend this morning. He says the FBI agent I worked with in L.A. is asking about me."

Fletcher gets two mugs out of the cabinet. He pours the hot water just short of boiling into the glass press and takes everything to the table. We sit down, and he lets the coffee sit for a minute before pouring it into the mugs. I add cream and sugar to mine.

"FBI, huh?" He stirs in sugar for his coffee. "FBI girlfriend, cop friend, ex gonna be a lawyer. Man, you the most law-enforcement-involved piano player I ever knew. Lucky you don't do anything illegal."

"Well, nothing much happened with Andie. It could have, though. We were kind of thrown together, made a trip to San Francisco and spent the night. She was pretty up front about things, let me know how it was, how it could be, but I was still involved with the ex-girlfriend."

Fletcher grins. "And let me guess. This FBI agent is a fine lady, and the girlfriend got jealous, right?"

"Something like that."

"Oh, I know that song, man." He shakes his head slowly from side to side. "Women sure can mess you up. Slow as a Shirley Horn ballad, but it happens." He looks at me again. "Is the ex really an ex, or are you still deciding that?"

"I think so. When I was working with the FBI, I couldn't tell her what I was doing, and she took all the time I spent with the agent the wrong way. Even later, when I could explain things, maybe too much damage was already done."

"Yeah, it happens," Fletcher says. "Sounds like you got some decisions to make. You haven't talked to either of them since you left home?"

"No. Natalie, she's the ex, is still in L.A. Andie, the FBI agent, is in San Francisco."

Fletcher grins. "Well, maybe you should invite one of them over for a visit."

"Yeah, that's just what I need now."

"Well, like Prez said, 'Man does not live by jazz alone.'"

"Lester Young said that?"

"Oh, I don't know. Sounds like something he'd say. He did say, 'Stan Getz the money for playin' me.'"

"So you're a philosopher too, huh?"

"No, just an observer of the human condition." Fletcher sips his coffee and looks at me. "So, got any plans?"

I'd thought it through on the way back to the flat. The best course seemed to be to check out Rotterdam, the clubs there, see if Ace had been there, then work our way back to Amsterdam. "I want to go to the Dizzy Café and the Thelonious. You still want to come?"

"Yeah. We can drive or take a train. There's several every day, but might be good to have the car, so we can get around while we're there."

"What I was thinking."

"When?"

"Let's go today, later this afternoon." I'm anxious to get going, do something. I hate waiting around, not hearing anything.

"Cool," Fletcher says. "You want to play some first?"

"Sure." We take our coffee and go back to the living room. Fletcher gets his horn, and I walk over to the piano and warm up a little. Fletcher takes some sheet music from on the piano. "Let's try this. New one of mine."

It's called "Canal Bridge Stroll." I look over the chord changes and try them out. "What's the tempo?"

Fletcher closes his eyes, moves his head up and down, walks in place for a minute. "About here. Play that first four bars, and then I'll come in."

I play the setup, then follow Fletcher's line, following the chords on the sheet. We clash a couple of times, back up, and start again until it makes sense. "You want to play with those chords, go ahead."

"Okay." I try some substitutions, do a little reharmonizing, and it starts to jell.

"Yeah, that's it," Fletcher says.

We work on it for a half hour or so until we're both satisfied, then try some tunes we've already played. The interplay is even better now as we follow each other's thoughts, mixing lines, playing off each other. With no drummer or bassist to follow, it's just him and me, getting into one another's head, a kind of musical telepathy. The more we do it, the better it gets.

"We need a couple of bebop tunes. You know 'Billie's Bounce'?"

"Yeah." We take it fairly up, and we both know we'll add it to the repertoire.

"I like that," Fletcher says. "Got us plenty of music to play."

"Yes, we do."

"Now all we have to do is keep you focused. Let me make some calls. Then we can pack a bag, have some lunch, and head out."

"You think this is a good idea?" I'm already having reservations, but at the same time, I can't just let it go. I know I won't rest till I find out where Ace is and what happened to him.

Fletcher pauses a moment. "Now, don't take this the wrong way. If we're looking for your friend, I understand that. I'd do the same. But if you get hung up on Chet Baker and what happened to him, we might go on a detour, go down the wrong road."

"I don't think so, Fletch. I think they're the same road."

After lunch, we each pack enough for an overnight stay, throw the bags in Fletcher's car, and head south on the A4 Expressway for Rotterdam. I let my mind wander, thinking about Chet Baker making this same drive over eleven years ago for his gig at the Thelonious, weak, hurting, and unaware he's going to find only a handful of customers, not even enough to get paid. How did that feel? Is that what set him off to wander the streets, lose his car, and hustle back to Amsterdam to fix?

"Got it figured out?" Fletcher asks. He's a careful driver, both hands on the wheel, shaking his head as car after car passes us. He's found a music station on the radio, and it plays softly in the background.

"What? This trip?"

"Why your friend would copy all that shit in his portfolio?"

"Oh, I've got a wild theory or two." I look out the window, watching the green fields flash by; I still haven't seen a windmill.

"When don't you?" Fletcher laughs and looks at me. "I'm just keeping your feet on the ground."

"Okay, okay."

"Well? What is it?" Fletcher keeps his eyes on the road but turns down the radio.

I shift in my seat, light a cigarette, and crack the window a couple of inches. "Well, let's suppose he did leave the port-folio, hoping I'd find it. Then, he knows I did, but wants to keep on with his research and needs his notes and the articles. So he steals it back, copies all the papers, and then makes sure it turns up again."

Fletcher is already frowning. "And just leaves it somewhere, hoping somebody will find it, turn it in to the police, and they'll call you and give it back?" Fletcher laughs. "Man, your imagination is something else."

"Well, I told you it was a wild theory. I don't think he consciously left it to be recovered. I think it was stolen, something he hadn't counted on."

"Well, that's slightly better," Fletcher says. He frowns again. "Tell me again why he wanted you to have it in the first place."

"Because he wanted me to help him research Chet Baker. I turned him down flat in London, but he knows from past experience I would follow the leads in that material. You know, go to the archives, check out musicians, see the film. I'm sure he thought the temptation would be too great."

Fletcher looks at me again. "Yeah, just like you're doing. He was right."

Maybe he was. I'd thought about it a lot. If I'm honest, I have to admit my fascination with solving mysteries. Dekker's story about Hemingway's suitcase opened the flow for a lot of juices. But when the mysteries deal with jazz musicians, the pull is even stronger, especially when I discover not many people have bothered to solve them. So far, Chet Baker's death is unsolved, on record as an accident because nobody could come up with anything better.

"Yeah, maybe he is. Don't you wonder what really happened to Chet?"

Fletcher shrugs. "I'd be interested, but not enough to want to do all this research and spend all this time on it." He laughs out loud then.

"What?"

"I was just thinking about what some guy in Maynard Ferguson's band told me. They were on the bus, going to some gig. Maynard was going to take a nap and said, 'Don't wake me up unless they find Glen Miller.'" He holds out his palm for me to slap.

I laugh too. From what I've heard about him, that sounds like Maynard. Glen Miller's plane was never found after it went down somewhere in the English Channel.

Fletcher turns up the radio again. I put out my cigarette and lean back on the seat and close my eyes. "Well, remember what Maynard said." I drift off, and before I know it, Fletcher is shaking me.

"No Glen Miller, but we're in Rotterdam."

We check in to a hotel Fletcher knows from previous visits. It's small, clean, and spartan, but the price is right for two singles, and we're not going to be spending much time in the room. We grab something to eat, and Fletcher makes a couple of calls from the restaurant. I'm finishing coffee and a cigarette when he comes back.

"The Thelonious is closed, but the owner was there." He shakes his head. "Tried to get me to come down cheap for a weekend. Anyway, he hasn't talked to anyone asking questions about Chet Baker."

I put out my cigarette, feeling really disappointed. "So, any other ideas?"

"We can try Dizzy's. They're open, but no guarantee we'll find anything there either."

"Worth a shot, I guess." I didn't really expect to find the pianist from the film after all this time. I pay the check, and we go outside.

"Let's walk," Fletcher says. "I need some exercise." He laughs. "Maybe we'll find Chet's car."

Fletcher leads the way. It's about a fifteen-minute walk to the small club. A trio is playing a lackluster set of standards to a handful of people in the room. "Shit, wish I'd brought my horn," Fletcher says. "Might shake these guys up."

We go to the bar and order a couple of beers. The bartender recognizes Fletcher, and they have a brief reunion before he introduces me. "This is one bad piano player," Fletcher says. "Evan Horne."

I shake hands with Jan and, after the pleasantries are over, ask him about Ace, showing him the photo. He looks at it, shakes his head. "No, nobody like that," he says. "Chet Baker. Haven't thought about him in years." Fletcher gives me an I-told-you-so look.

"Well, thanks for your time," I say, then remember the pianist from the film. "He was in a band called Bad Circuits." But this draws another blank.

"Oh no, he moved, to Paris I think. Some time ago."

"Well, we tried," Fletcher says. He suddenly sits upright and smiles. "Stove. The guy's name I was trying to think of. It was Stove."

The bartender looks at Fletcher and stops drying the glass in his hand. "Yes, I remember him. He sometimes helped the promoter who booked Chet. Some musicians used to stay with him. Woody Shaw, and an alto player, I think. Yes, Woody Shaw."

"That's the one," Fletcher says.

"Yes," Jan says. He puts the glass down as gears mesh in his head. "Now I remember. He was with Chet that night. He and another man—Blok, I think his name is. He still comes in here sometimes. He has a small secondhand record shop near here." He takes out a pen and paper and writes down the address. "He lives over his shop."

"Thanks, thanks very much," I say and drop some money on the bar.

"Send him to me," the bartender says. "He still owes me money."

We give the address to a taxi driver, and make the ten-minute ride in silence. I feel my excitement growing with every turn. I tip the taxi double for the short ride, and we get out. The shop is closed, but there are lights on upstairs and a night bell and intercom near the front door of the shop.

I press the button and wait. A voice comes through the intercom shortly. "Allo."

"Mr. Blok? I would like to talk with you, please. About Chet Baker."

"The shop is closed. Come tomorrow. Chet Baker is dead."

Fletcher rolls his eyes and pushes the intercom button himself. "We know that, man. Just come down here a minute. This is Fletcher Paige."

"Fletcher Paige?"

"Yes, c'mon, man."

"A moment, please."

A couple of minutes later, we see the light go on in the store and the shade go up on the door. A thin man in a sweater and pants peers out at us. His face flashes in recognition at Fletcher, and he opens the door. He's all over Fletcher, inviting us in, offering us coffee, which we refuse, then locking the door and pulling down the shade once more.

We go to the back of the small shop. Most of the space is taken up with bins of vinyl LPs. I glance at the tabs and see the names of jazz greats, from Louis Armstrong to Miles Davis, printed in black marker pen.

"Look," Blok says, stopping at the P's. He shuffles through some albums, pulls out one of Fletcher, and hands it to him.

"Damn," Fletcher says, looking at it. He turns it over and looks at the liner notes. "Sweden. Forgot I did this one."

Blok holds out a pen. "Please."

Fletcher signs it and hands it back. Blok takes it back to an old desk with a cash register and props it up against the register. "This will sell quickly," Blok says. "Come, we talk."

He takes us back to a small office that was probably once a closet. "You play with Fletcher?" he asks me. In the harsh light, his face is lined, ravaged by time and probably a lot of drugs.

"Yes, at the Bimhuis in Amsterdam."

"Ah yes, I have heard." He asks Fletcher some more questions. It takes a while to get him focused, but finally I take him back to that night in 1988. "Yes, I was with Chet and Stove, at the Dizzy Café. Chet was not good. He did not play well." He puts his hands out and shrugs. "He needs . . ."

"Yeah, we know what he needed," Fletcher says. "Did he have a connection here?"

Blok eyes Fletcher warily. "It was not me, but . . . I tried, but . . ."

"Did Chet stay with Stove, at his house?"

"Yes. I was there, I saw him. He slept and slept, but then he left and went back to Amsterdam the next day. He was very impatient."

That at least explains the time gap, but doesn't put us any closer to Ace's whereabouts, and I don't even bother asking Blok if he's seen Ace. "Who would Chet see in Amsterdam? For drugs, I mean? Did he have somebody?"

Blok looks around, as if the police will break down the door any moment. "It was a long time ago, a different life for me. Now I have my shop." He stops, sees us waiting for more. "Sometimes he can get methadone from a doctor. Heroin?" He spreads his hands and shrugs. "Van Gogh, per-haps—"

"Van Gogh?" I look at Fletcher.

"Oh, shit," Fletcher says. "We don't mean no damn painter."

Blok laughs. "No," he says, "a different van Gogh. If he is still alive."

"How do we find this van Gogh?"

"You must ask. Someone will know." We spend another ten minutes with Blok but, getting no further, finally thank him and leave.

"Well, what now?" Fletcher asks as we walk back to our hotel.

"You think van Gogh is a waste of time?" I'm disap-pointed, but it's a name, and we have nothing else to go on.

"I think he just wanted to get rid of us. Van Gogh, my ass.

We can ask around, but maybe it's time to give this up. Have you thought about that? Nobody could say you haven't given it your best shot."

I have, of course, and Fletcher is right. What more can I do? What more could anybody do? I reported Ace's disappearance to the police. They have Ace's photo, his portfolio, his jacket. It's really up to them now. Chasing down a onetime drug connection named van Gogh in Amsterdam seems like a bad joke. But those questions won't go away. It still doesn't feel right somehow, and Ace is still missing.

"Yeah, I guess. Not much else I can do anyway."

We stop for a beer at a bar next to the hotel, thinking our separate thoughts. Fletcher, though, rekindles the fire. "Hey," he says. "I just thought of something. There's a guy in Amsterdam. Chet used to stay with him a lot. He's a trumpet player too. Maybe Ace stumbled across him."

"Who?"

"What was his name?" Fletcher thinks for a moment, then snaps his fingers. "Hekkema, Evert Hekkema. Knew Chet real well."

I remember then. "Oh yes, he was interviewed in the film. He sold Chet a car."

Fletcher looks at me. "Maybe I should see that film. Might give me some more ideas, jog my memory."

"Cool. When we get back."

"Hey, I didn't tell you. I'm going to be in a film too, about us jazz cats living and working in Europe."

"Really?"

"Yeah, they called me a few weeks ago. Don't pay shit, but what the hell. I'll talk."

"Where is this going to be?"

"Maybe on our gig, some at the house. Don't be surprised if a camera crew shows up." Fletcher laughs. "Well, I'm tired, man. Don't forget I'm old. Let's head back to the hotel."

"I'm with you."

"I got these," Fletcher says, taking out some money for the beers. "Hang on a minute. I want to make a call."

While Fletcher is gone, I run over everything again in my mind, still haunted by the thought that something has happened to Ace. He should have been here. He wouldn't have seen that film and passed on these two obvious sources on Chet Baker. It just isn't right.

When Fletcher comes back, his expression has changed completely. "Just checked my messages at home."

"Yeah? What is it?"

"A call for you from that policeman, Dekker. They found something on your friend."

The drive back to Amsterdam seems to take forever. Fletcher drives, plays music, and keeps trying to convince me that it isn't over yet, that Dekker's call might not be anything. I haven't slept much. Every time I close my eyes, I see myself identifying Ace's body. By the time Amsterdam comes into view, I'm impatient to get to the flat and call Dekker. But even that doesn't work out. Fletcher exits the expressway, and we make our way slowly into the city center.

The traffic is heavy, and we get stuck in Dam Square in a gridlock of pedestrians, cars, and trolleys. Then, as the light turns green, something catches my eye. Fletcher is halfway across the intersection, behind a bus belching black smoke.

"Stop the car!" I yell.

"What?"

"Stop the car!" Fletcher brakes. I throw open the door and start running across the wide boulevard, dodging cars and people still trying to cross against the light. I try to keep my eye on the trolley just pulling out. I'm running, pushing people aside, but I know I'm not going to catch it. The trolley is halfway down the block when I get to the stop and feel the stares of people waiting for the next one.

I turn and see Fletcher pull to the curb. He jumps out of the car and runs over. "What the fuck is wrong with you? What are you doing?"

I shake my head. "I think I saw Ace on that trolley."

"Inspector Dekker, please." I wait a minute while I'm switched around, then Dekker comes on the line.

"Inspector, it's Evan Horne."

"Ah, Mr. Horne. How was Rotterdam?" He's almost cheerful. No ominous tone as if he's about to tell me some bad news. I almost slip and tell him, Not very helpful, but I think he knows I was there looking for more than work.

"Fine. What's the news about my friend?"

He catches the concern in my voice. "Oh, I'm sorry, I didn't mean to alarm you. It's nothing like that, but it is very strange. In fact, it's good news."

I grip the phone in frustration. "What?"

"We canvassed some hotels that cater to or advertise for tourists."

"Yes?"

"It seems your friend Mr. Buffington stayed at another hotel. The Canal House. Very nice and very expensive."

"What? When? Is he still there?"

"No, no, it was just for a few days. He checked out already."

"Well, what did the hotel say? Did they have any information?"

"No, other than he was a quiet guest, paid his bill, checked out, and left."

"And they're sure it was Ace?"

"Yes, quite sure. I sent someone over with his photo. They identified him positively." I hold the phone for a moment, thinking. "Mr. Horne?"

"Yes, sorry. So what does this mean?"

"I'm afraid it simply means your friend is not missing. As I mentioned before, he apparently just doesn't want to be found."

"So you're not going to do anything else?"

"What would you like me to do, Mr. Horne?"

Good question, but I can't think of a thing. "Look, can we talk about this some more? I can come down to the station."

Dekker's sigh is audible. I can picture him frowning in exasperation. "If you wish, but I don't see what that would accomplish. I cannot devote any more time or personnel to this matter."

"Yes, I understand. I'll be down in the morning."

"Good-bye, Mr. Horne."

I hang up and turn to Fletcher.

"He says Ace has been around all the time. At another hotel."

Fletcher frowns. "Well, man, you know him. Maybe there's something going on he doesn't want you to know about. Hell, maybe he's got a woman. You've done all you can."

Before I can answer, the phone rings. Fletcher picks it up. From his smile and tone, it's obviously for him. I go into the bedroom, put away my things, and sit down on the bed to think about everything. Ace is making me angry now. No matter what he's into, he could have let me know. He must have known I'd be looking for him. I fall back on the bed and stare at the ceiling, going over things. It's not that I don't believe Dekker. I just want to see for myself. I turn and see Fletcher in the doorway, all smiles now.

"Remember the documentary film I told you I was going to be in?"

"Yeah, it's still on?"

"That was the woman running it. They're here in town. They want to shoot some of it tomorrow. Okay with you?"

"Hey, it's your film."

"Yeah, but they want to have some of me playing. I told them about our duo gig. They can shoot us right here, if you're okay with that."

"Sure, Fletch. Whatever you want is fine with me."

"Cool. Well, I'm going to do some practicing and pick out some clothes for my film debut. What's up with you?"

"I think I'm going to check out a hotel."

The Canal House Hotel is a restored eighteenth-century building on one of those cobblestone streets facing a canal. At least that's what it says on the postcard as I wait in reception for the owner. As it turns out, she's American. She's pleasant enough but can offer me no more than Dekker already found out.

"No, Mr. Buffington stayed three nights. He checked out yesterday."

I show her the photo. "And this was him?"

She looks quickly. "Yes. I told the police the same. Is he in some kind of trouble?"

"No—well, he may be when I catch up with him," I say, smiling. "We just got some wires crossed, I guess. Anyway, thanks for your trouble."

"No problem."

I go outside in the bright sunlight that glints off the water and stand on the front steps, watching small boats float by on the canal. It still doesn't sit right with me; that unsettled feeling won't go away. Unless I hear it from Ace himself, I know I can't let go of it. Then I think of something else, walk up to the corner, and grab a taxi.

"Do you know the American consulate?"

"Yes," the driver says, pushing down the flag on the meter.

The ride takes us across town, and he drops me along Meuseumplein and points to a building nestled in among some large Gothic buildings. "That way," he says, pointing across the street.

I pay him and get out to walk over. This part of town reminds me I haven't done much sightseeing since I've been in Amsterdam. I've never been much for museums, but maybe it's time to let go and explore van Gogh's hometown.

The consulate is not much help. No one named Buffington has checked in with them in the past week or two, or asked for any help. "Sometimes tourists lose their passport or traveler's checks, that kind of thing. We recommend that people check in with us, but most don't do it until it's too late," a clerk tells me.

"Well, thanks anyway."

"I hope you find your friend," she says.

So that's it. Again I find myself wondering why I'm going through all this. Nothing left now but to talk one more time with Dekker in the morning. Do it early and get it over with. Back at the flat, I find a note from Fletcher that he's gone to dinner with the film crew. I grab something to eat at a small family restaurant nearby and go for a long walk along the canals.

I stop for coffee at a small café and take a window table. Across the street is a bookstore with the name Alibi in neon lights. They're about to close, but the friendly owner helps me find a Charles Willeford book. A used copy in good condition.

"I'll take it," I say, and hope Fletcher doesn't already have it.

I take a long hot shower, listen to some music, and by ten I've exhausted myself. I fall into bed with my Hoke Moseley purchase. I get far enough into the story to read about Hoke getting beaten up and having his badge, gun, even his false teeth, stolen. Even that didn't happen to Chet Baker.

That's when I fall asleep.

Dekker isn't too happy to see me; his expression betrays that he had hoped I wouldn't show up. I tell him about visiting the consulate and the Canal House Hotel.

"I have to admire your persistence. It would seem to me, Mr. Horne, that you've done everything possible, and I'm afraid I have also. With your friend at another hotel, he is obviously not a missing person."

"Yes, I suppose so. I just think it's strange he changed hotels, and I'm still concerned about the jacket and the portfolio."

"I think it's easily explained. If you do find your friend, tell him we will hold them here for him. We have no reason to keep them."

"But what about your Hemingway's suitcase theory? Don't you find it odd that he would copy everything in the portfolio?"

Dekker smiles. "Mr. Horne, I'm sure you know the expression 'absentminded professor.' Perhaps your friend foresaw just such a loss and made the copies for that reason. Perhaps after he lost his jacket."

I sigh and shrug. "Yes, I'd thought of that. I guess you're right."

"Well, I'm very busy this morning. Enjoy the rest of your stay in Amsterdam." Dekker is already on his feet, ushering me toward the door.

"Thanks again, Inspector. Sorry to bother you so much."

Okay, Ace, you're on your own after this one last errand. I check my watch. Still time to drop by the archives before getting back for Fletcher's film. I swing by the Prinz Hendrik Hotel and take another look at the Chet Baker plaque, the list of donors, looking for the answer to one more question.

At the Jazz Archives, Helen is at her desk as usual. She smiles at me when I walk in, much happier to see me than Dekker was. "Ah," she says. "Hello. Come to see the film again?"

"No, but I do want to ask you about something else."

"Of course."

"The plaque over at the hotel. Is there some kind of official list of the donors and how much they contributed?"

Helen looks troubled and doesn't answer right away. She glances around nervously. "The donor list is right there with the plaque, but the contributions . . . I don't know. That's confidential information. Some were made in cash, some in certified checks. Some were bank transfers."

"Bank transfers?"

"Yes."

I lower my voice. "Helen, this is very important. A friend of mine is possibly in trouble, and I'm trying to find him. I don't want to get you in trouble, and I'll understand if you don't want to help, but—"

"Oh." She puts her hand over her mouth and looks around again.

"Please, I need to see that list. One of the names might help a great deal."

She glances toward a file cabinet near her desk.

I follow her gaze and take a shot. "Can I suggest something? If that file happened to be on your desk, it wouldn't be your fault if I happened to see it, would it?"

She considers for a moment and looks around again. "No, I suppose not." She smiles then. "This is kind of exciting, isn't it?"

"Well, it could be, I guess. What do you say?"

Her answer is to go to the file cabinet and open a drawer. She flips through some folders, then takes one out and places it on her desk. When she speaks, I realize how quietly our voices have been when she suddenly raises hers.

"If you'll wait here, I'll see if I can find that book you requested."

"Oh, thank you very much," I say just as loudly. I sit down as soon as she leaves the room and open the file.

The contributions range from individuals for as small as $100 to much more from some record companies. I run my finger down the list, noting the names and the amounts, and then stop. One entry might as well be in bold type. The amount sticks out beyond the rest, but there is no name, just a notation that it was a bank transfer and the words "See attached file." I look through the rest of the folder, but there is nothing but receipts for the cash donations and canceled checks. No attached file. I close the folder and sit back, waiting for Helen to return. No need to push her further. I'm beginning to think I know who that anonymous donor is.

Helen returns then and hands me a book. "I think this is what you were looking for," she says. It's a copy of Duke Ellington's book *Music Is My Mistress*.

"Thanks," I say. "I'll leave it in the reading room when I'm finished. You've been very helpful."

"I hope you found what you want," she says, her voice quieter now.

"Yes, thank you." I start to leave, then on impulse, something else occurs to me, something Fletcher remarked on earlier. "Just one more question." I take out the photo of Ace to show her. "This is the man you talked to? Professor Buffington?"

She takes the photo from me and looks at it, but her face clouds over. "Yes, but later, there was a different man. He was Dutch."

All the alarms go off then. "Are you sure?"

"Yes," Helen says. She holds the photo. "Your friend only came once."

Instinct, gut feeling, whatever it is, I know something isn't right. My mind is racing as I walk back to the flat, going over the description Helen gave me of the man who claimed to be Ace. As I cross a street, I stop suddenly, remembering why the description sounded familiar. I hear a bell just in time to jump out of the way of a bicycle and get a litany of curses in Dutch for my carelessness.

The man at the train station, with the umbrella and raincoat, who was so helpful. I didn't think anything about it at the time, but now it was connecting. He didn't have a raincoat at the coffee shop, but now I'm sure he was the one I saw there too. Helen had said he'd presented a letter of introduction to use the archives, and she'd said it hadn't been necessary. The archives were open to anyone, but this guy, whoever he was, wasn't taking any chances.

Why impersonate Ace? What did he want? Just to see the Chet Baker film? Why? I think I know now, and it's still running through my mind when I get back to the flat.

In the living room Fletcher is sitting in one of the easy chairs, a bright light shining on him and a reflector on a stand to the side. Opposite him is a young woman with dark short hair and large eyes. She has a pad and pen on her lap. Behind her a large burly man in jeans and plaid shirt points a camera at the two of them.

Fletcher looks at me and smiles. "Here's my man," he says. "We're just doing some sound and light checking. Say hello to Elaine Blakemore." Elaine is also in jeans and a pink T-shirt. She has a light meter around her neck. She's maybe thirty and very pretty.

"Hi," I say. "Evan Horne. Sorry, didn't mean to interrupt."

"Not at all," she says, getting up to shake hands. The accent is very British. "Fletcher has been telling me about you, your collaboration." She looks at me closely, as if she's trying to place me, then suddenly her face brightens into a smile. "Hang on, I heard you interviewed on Colin Mansfield's show in London. Mike Bailey did a piece on you. You're *that* Evan Horne?"

"Afraid so."

"I meant to get down to Ronnie Scott's to hear you. Could we talk? I have several questions for you myself."

"Well, maybe later. I don't want to be in the way here."

"Oh, yes. We do want to get some footage of you playing with Fletcher. I hope that's all right."

"Sure, whatever you need. I'll just watch for now."

"Okay." She turns to the cameraman. "Are we okay, Kevin?"

"Yeah, luv," Kevin says. "I'll shoot over your shoulder for now. We can do some reaction shots later."

Elaine checks her light meter and looks at her pad. "Right, shall we have a go then?"

I mime *I'll be back* to Fletcher. He nods and turns his attention to Elaine as she begins her questions. I want to talk to Fletcher, but it'll have to wait.

I go into my room and dig out the list of donors for the plaque, reading them again, trying to unstick that thing in my mind, but it doesn't come to me. When I go back to the living room, they're deep into it. Elaine has done her homework. She leads Fletcher through the questions with ease, and he's very relaxed. I sit down out of camera range and just watch the proceedings unfold.

"I'm going to ask you some other questions," she says. "You just talk. I'll add them in with voice-over later, okay?"

"Sure," Fletcher says.

"First, then. Tell me about your decision to make Amsterdam your home."

Fletcher looks every bit the part of an expatriate artist. He's in tan slacks, a dark sports coat over a light turtleneck sweater. "I came over on a tour with Count Basie, and like a lot of the guys over the years, I just stayed. I liked the way I was treated here. I liked the people, the lifestyle, getting away from all that hustling in New York. I already had friends here—Art Farmer, Kenny Drew, Kenny Clarke—you know, they were all here, scattered around Europe and doing fine. I guess I was drawn to Amsterdam because of Ben Webster. Johnny Griffin had been here a while too."

"Was some part of your decisision racially motivated?" Elaine asks.

"I think there were a variety of reasons, but yes, that's part of it. There's a better acceptance of your talent as a jazz musician. Europeans look at jazz as an art form. There's less pressure in terms of competition, and people here are serious listeners. They exchange tapes with friends, talk about the music. Hell, they know more about me than I do. They're really involved. I can go anywhere in the world, play jazz, and not be a stranger. I thought, Hey, why not live here?

"But yes, there is a racial factor, too. I've been here seventeen years and never had a bad racial experience. No one has been rude, no one has ignored me as people will do in America if they don't want to serve you or sell you a ticket. There has never been the slightest trouble with hotels or restaurants, except maybe some slight surliness in London." Fletcher laughs then. "Guess you'll have to cut that, huh?"

"No," Elaine says. "Go on, please."

"A couple of times I've been through small villages or towns. People tend to stare then, but not in a bad way. Maybe like you would if it's a car you've never seen before. It's always something of a shock to go home—and I've been back a few times—because nothing has really changed. The same hang-ups are there. The way it is now, I can play at some small club in Europe and be recognized. In a similar American town, nobody outside the jazz world would know me."

"And that's important to you?" Elaine asks.

Fletcher stares right back at her. "Of course it is. I'm an American, playing American music, and I'm a black man too. It's funny, but somehow it's easier doing all that in foreign countries. But hey, what are you going to do? That's the way it is."

Elaine nods and turns to Kevin. "Okay, let's stop a minute."

Fletcher looks at me and smiles. "How am I doin'?"

"Looks good to me, Fletch. Is this for the BBC?" I ask Elaine.

"Yes, hopefully. We have a small grant and hope we can sell it. It might even get to America if we're lucky."

Fletcher gets up and stretches. "You want us to do some playing?"

"Yes," Elaine says. "Let's keep it casual, as if you're rehearsing."

Fletcher laughs. "That won't be hard, because that's what we're doing. Let me get my horn." He goes off to his room.

"So," Elaine says, "I assume you're here for a different reason than Fletcher."

"Mostly by accident," I say. "I came here to play the Bimhuis, and the promoter put us together."

Elaine's eyebrow rise slightly. "Oh, Fletcher told me you

were doing a little . . . investigating? He said your friend had disappeared, something to do with Chet Baker? I imagine you couldn't resist that?"

I shake my head. "I could, and would have otherwise. But let's not go into that now, okay?"

"Sorry. I didn't mean to pry."

"It's not that, it's just—"

"All right, man, let's get it on for this lovely lady. Show her how we work out all these complicated arrangements." Fletcher winks at Elaine and blows a few notes. I know he's already had his daily workout.

I sit down at the piano and warm up a little. "What should we play?"

"How about something Ben recorded?" Fletcher says. "'The Touch of Your Lips'?" He gives Elaine such a big smile that she blushes.

"Just play a bit," Kevin says, "so I can get a sound check."

"Yes," Elaine says. "I'd like to keep this as casual as possible. You can stop and start, talk it over if you want. We can always edit the footage later."

"About right here," Fletcher says, snapping his fingers. He counts us off, and in four bars, Fletcher makes me think I'm playing for Ben Webster. When he solos, it's even more pronounced as he emulates Webster's breathy tone perfectly. We start playing lines off each other and get so caught up in the tune, we don't stop. When we go out, Fletcher turns toward Elaine and the camera and raises his eyebrows. "That's jazz," he says.

"God," Elaine says. "I hope you got all that, Kevin."

Keven turns off the camera. "Oh yeah, every note."

May 7, 1988, Rotterdam

The Thelonious jazz club. The poster in the window reads, "Tonight Only—Chet Baker."

The turnout is light, but for once Chet is early, talking with the rhythm section, thinking he's ready to play. The three musicians listen to him, watch him warily, sneak glances at one another. Seeing his condition, they know it will be a long night. The promoter has already told them earlier that paid attendance is less than twenty people. They want to play, but they want to get paid, even if it is Chet Baker. Nobody needs to tell them Chet is not well.

Before the first set, he wanders outside, feeling the itch, trying to get himself together. The promoter follows him out. "I'm sorry, there should have been more advertising," he says.

"How many?" Chet asks him.

The promoter scrapes his feet on the pavement and looks down. "Seventeen." He looks up then, watches Chet nod, seemingly unmoved. "You are okay?"

Chet shrugs, gives him a sheepish smile, knowing he's not fooling him. "Yeah, I'm fine." But he's not fine, not even okay. He feels the gnawing inside him, the awful pain beginning to eat away at him. He just wants this gig to be over now.

Later, back inside the club, it isn't happening, but it has nothing to do with the small crowd. He tries, struggles through tunes he's played hundreds of times, but tonight he doesn't make it. His playing is lackluster, the solos short. He leaves it mostly to the rhythm section to carry him through the evening. He's not aware of the wave of disappointment from the audience, and worse, the disillusion of the rhythm section. There's nothing he can do about it. It just isn't happening, not tonight. Not like this.

Finally, after an even worse second set, he gives up. There are fewer people now, and the ones that stick around are more interested in themselves than the music. Chet nods to the rhythm section, packs up his horn, and leaves them to work it out with the promoter. He knows he won't even get paid.

Outside in the Rotterdam night, he walks the streets, looking for his car. He circles around, aimlessly searching, but he can't remember where he parked it. After an hour of this, he finds himself in front of the police station. He goes inside to report it stolen, and calls his agent.

"I can't find my car," Chet tells him.

"Do you have the keys?" It's happened before. Chet always loses his car keys.

Chet pats his pockets. "No, guess I lost them too."

He hears the agent's audible sigh. "All right, I will take care of it," the agent says. "What about the gig?"

"It didn't go too well, not many people," Chet says quietly. "I'm not feeling too good."

The agent already knows. "What are you going to do?"

Chet looks around the police station. "Think I'll run up to Amsterdam."

The agent knows what that means. "Very well, call me, Chet. Don't forget, the date with Archie Shepp is on the twelfth."

Chet says, "Sure." He hangs up the phone.

Outside, he walks the streets again, but even if he found the car now, he doesn't have the keys. He decides what he told the agent is the best thing—take the night train to Amsterdam. Maybe he can get some methadone.

He makes his way to Central Station, pushes through the crowd up to the window, and buys a ticket. He waits on the platform, leaning against a pillar, his trumpet under his arm— a quiet man, older than his age, internationally famous but unrecognized, unnoticed except for the occasional public nod from somebody who meets his eyes. Amsterdam, he thinks. He'll be all right there. He has people to call, friends to see. He just needs to score, get straight, then get his car back.

He boards the train, slumps in a seat, and hugs the trumpet case to him. His eyes close. He isn't even aware when the train pulls out of the station.

12

'M A pushover for minor keys, minor chords, minor blues. Always have been. When I was a kid, and didn't yet know the difference between sharp or flat, much less major and minor, I'd hear a song on the radio or television, and if it had that certain sound, I'd feel some kind of shiver, a chill, and I liked the feeling. I began to listen for it, learned to recognize it. Later, when I did know the difference, I devoured minor chords and tunes. As my listening expanded, and I began to discover the nuances and secrets of jazz, I was drawn to those players and composers for whom minor keys and blues-drenched creations were a way of life.

Horace Silver's "Señor Blues" and "Cape Verdean Blues"; Herbie Hancock's "Dolphin Dance" and "Maiden Voyage"; Miles's mournful sound on "All Blues"; and the dark modal lines of "So What." Those became my theme songs, my life sound track. Then there was Bill Evans, who could make everything he played sound like it was in minor keys, a sound that was so hauntingly sad, it didn't make any difference whether it was a ballad from a Broadway show or "Milestones."

Once, walking home from school, I heard music coming from somewhere. I followed the sound until I found the house and stood listening under an open window, mesmerized by the saxophone. When it finished, I knocked on the door and asked a surprised man—he probably thought I was selling magazines—the name of the song. "'All or Nothing at All.' John Coltrane," he said.

That was my musical path. It had chosen me. I accepted it without the slightest doubt, and knew there was no turning back. I was drawn to the minor sound, that quality arising from a particular cluster of notes that could create and sustain a mood, conjure up visions of mist, darkness, deserted streets in predawn light. I was hooked on poignancy, melancholy, haunting sounds, and melodies that struck me not as depressing but rather as tranquil and comforting.

So-called happy music had just the opposite effect, and has always turned me off. Those Broadway shows and old movie musicals like *Oklahoma!* and *Carousel* and *Mame,* or *Hello Dolly!,* made no sense to me at all. I felt embarrassed listening to Howard Keel or Gordon MacRae or Robert Goulet, belting out tunes on mountaintops, everybody smiling, laughing, dancing. They left me totally cold and disconnected, and the sentimental ballads, sung with soulful looks toward the sky, seemed phony, manipulative. They still do. Andrew Lloyd Webber and Burt Bacharach? Well, I won't even go there.

Chet Baker knew about poignancy, melancholy, especially with ballads. If ever a musician was destined to play in minor keys, it was Chet Baker. Wringing out every last drop of emotion possible with so little effort, he could make you feel what he was revealing was so personal, so secret, you felt guilty for overhearing it. In one of Ace's articles, I'd read that on a good night, with Chet Baker's playing, there was no barrier between instrument and emotions. The author was right.

Sitting in the darkness now, listening to Chet wrap his voice around "My Funny Valentine," I could picture him ambling up to the microphone in that German studio, two weeks before he died, and casually plucking nerve endings, then stepping back, putting the horn to his lips, and playing life. Then, just as casually, he would get in his Alfa and drive to Paris without a second thought.

"You listening to that junkie music again?" Fletcher says. I'm so lost in the music, I didn't even hear him come in. He turns on a light and stands peering at me. "You all right?" His face is creased in a frown, and he looks tired as he drops in a chair near me.

"Yeah, just in one of my minor moods, I guess. Been listening to these records." I look at my watch and realize it's been over three hours since I first sat down. I'd started with some of Fletcher's own recordings. Some were vinyl, some CDs, mostly from European companies. He sees the covers and cases on the floor.

"You been checking me out, huh?"

"Yeah, some great stuff, Fletch. Found another tune we need to do. 'Chelsea Bridge.'"

"Oh yeah, almost forgot about that one. I did that in Copenhagen. Too bad, though. Can't get most of these in the States. That's why everybody thinks I'm dead." He laughs, but there's sadness on his face.

I wonder that Fletcher seems to handle it so well. Here is an important tenor player in jazz with the best credentials, a dozen or more recordings that American audiences know nothing about. Fletcher Paige, living, working, and recording and going unnoticed in his native land.

"Where you been?" After the afternoon's filming with Elaine and Kevin, they'd all gone off to do some shooting at the Bimhuis. I stayed home.

"Dinner with Elaine and Kevin. He left early, but I talked a lot with her. Nice lady." Fletcher smiles broadly and shakes his head. "Man, if I was twenty-five years younger."

"Uh-huh." I can see the twinkle in his eyes.

He shrugs. "Don't matter anyway. I think she's interested in you."

I get up and stretch. "Yeah, I bet. She wants to hear about me being a detective."

"Well, hell, nothing wrong with that, is there?" Fletcher asks. "Makes you more mysterious. Hey, thanks for the book."

"You're welcome. Thank you for the temporary home."

"Well, she'll be in town for a few days. Pretty lady like that might get your mind off this other shit." Fletcher takes off his coat and sits down opposite me. He folds his hands and looks at me. "You're letting this get to you, man. I can see that look."

I've known Fletcher for less than a month, and he already knows me so well. It doesn't happen often, for some people maybe never. But once in a while you meet someone, connect so well and so quickly it's scary. I feel that with Fletcher, musically and personally.

"Well, I have been doing a lot of thinking." I get up, switch off the stereo, and sit down again. "What if that *was* Ace on the trolley the other day? Why would he do that, still be here and avoid me, not make any contact at all? While we were playing at the Bimhuis, I think Ace was right here in Amsterdam all the time."

Fletcher shakes his head. "First, maybe that wasn't Ace, maybe you just wanted it to be."

"I know, I know, but I've been thinking about something else."

"Oh shit, here we go," Fletcher says. He takes out cigarettes and lights one. "Well, let's hear it, but make it quick. I'm tired, man. I want to go to bed."

I get up and walk around the room. "You've never met Ace. He's a major fan, a collector, but he's also an academic, a historian. He's naive about a lot of the jazz scene, the musicians. He's a big, blustery guy. Subtlety is not his strength. So he comes to Amsterdam and announces to one and all he's researching Chet Baker, visiting the archives, talking to anyone he can, making himself very visible."

"Well, no reason he shouldn't, is there? He isn't doing anything wrong."

"No, but suppose with all this visibility, he attracts the wrong kind of attention?"

"Wrong people? What do you mean?"

"Besides music, what was the only other important thing in Chet Baker's life? Drugs, right? And I don't imagine drug dealers in Amsterdam are any different than anywhere else."

Fletcher leans back in his chair and closes his eyes. "No. Maybe worse. There's an underground scene here that's pretty bad."

"Exactly. Suppose Chet got on the wrong side of this element. He did in San Francisco when he was beaten up. Look what happened then."

Fletcher's eyes blink open. "Yeah, man, but that was years ago. We're talkin', what, eleven years since he died. That's old news."

I keep pacing, fitting pieces together in my mind. There's only one reason Ace would avoid me, not make any contact. I think someone was keeping him from doing it. "What goes with drugs? Money. No matter who the buyer is, right?"

Fletcher chuckles. "Yeah, a dealer wouldn't care if it was Chet Baker or Chet Atkins or Chet whoever. They might run a tab for a regular customer like Chet, but eventually they always want their bread."

"Of course." I stop pacing now and sit down. "What if Chet owed one of these dealers money, maybe a lot of money?"

Fletcher looks at me. "And when he didn't pay up, they killed him? Pushed him out of the window? Set an example?"

"I'm not saying that, not yet. What if he did fall? What if it was an accident, just like the police said, but it happened before this dealer could do anything about collecting his money?" I let the question hang there while Fletcher thinks it through. Then it's his turn to get up and pace around.

"And all this time, this dealer who got stiffed still wants his bread? Is that what you're saying?"

"If it was a lot of money, why not? One of the stories about Wardell Gray's death was that a dealer followed him to Las Vegas and killed him for $900."

"Damn," Fletcher says, shaking his head. "I hate the way you make sense sometimes."

"Maybe this dealer's got a long memory. Maybe Ace's poking around triggered some new interest in old things." Fletcher's pained expression is something I want to avoid. He's shaking his head like I'm crazy. He stops and sits down again while I continue. "I know Ace. If he thought he could talk to Chet's drug connection, he would, get something extra for his book. He wouldn't know what he was walking into."

"But why would this dealer think Ace knows anything about money owed by Chet Baker from eleven years ago? And that's if Chet owed money. We don't know that he did."

"Chet spent money on cars and dope, and this dealer, whoever he is, had to know that, especially if he was Chet's main connection. In one of those articles in Ace's portfolio, somebody talked about Chet's income the last year or so before he died."

I have Fletcher's full attention now. "Yeah?"

"They said it was probably over $200,000 a year."

"Damn!"

"Exactly. So what happened to it? What about the years before? And that's the same question the dealer would want answered if he were owed money. Maybe with Ace dredging up things again, he thought there might be a connection, maybe that Ace knew something about it." Fletcher is thinking about it now, stroking his chin. It worked for me, but I wanted to hear it from Fletcher. "C'mon, Hoke, talk to me. What do you think?"

"So Ace walks into this all innocent, thinking he's getting an exclusive interview with Chet Baker's connection, and the dealer forces him to really go after it, thinking his money might be around someplace, and after all this time he might still get it?"

"Well, I admit there are some flaws in this theory, but according to several accounts, the two days before Chet was found dead, he just disappeared. No one even knew he was at the Prins Hendrik Hotel. He was supposed to be picked up at another hotel to play a concert with Archie Shepp the night of the twelfth, but he never showed. The dealer might have let him run up his tab, thinking he would collect after the concerts."

"And then Chet went and got himself dead," Fletcher says. He leans back and considers some more. "That would explain why you haven't seen Ace. He got more than he bargained for, and the dealer is using him to make sure he covers all the bases looking for that money." Fletcher pauses again. "I don't know, man, it all sounds kind of crazy, and there are a lot of holes in this. Maybe Chet did just spend all that money."

"Yeah, I know, but if the dealer was that upset, he'd want to make sure. I'm betting this dealer held a grudge for a long time. There is something else, though. Two things actually."

"What?"

"I went back to the archives, showed the girl there Ace's photo. She said there was a second man. She described a man that I met at the train station the day I arrived. He was very helpful in finding the Prins Hendrik Hotel. Too helpful. It was almost like he knew I was coming."

Fletcher is shaking his head, not believing what he's hearing.

"And on that plaque at the hotel, there's a list of donors. One of the biggest contributors was anonymous. I checked that at the archives. Now, it might have been just some major fan who preferred not to be listed. But what if it was someone who had access to Chet's money, somebody he really trusted, somebody who held money for him till he needed it, and—"

"Oh, Lord," Fletcher says. He rubs his hands over his face. "What?"

"I forgot to tell you. I got hold of that trumpet player that sold Chet a car, the one Chet stayed with a lot when he was in Amsterdam. He didn't talk to Ace, but he told me once, Chet came by and left a shopping bag with over $15,000 in it. Just wanted him to hold it for a few days." I sit down and watch Fletcher, see there's something else. "I know somebody else like that."

"Who, Fletcher?"

"You're sitting in her apartment."

For the next two hours I pump Fletcher about Margo Highland. According to what she told Fletcher, she was never romantically involved with Chet, but they went way back, to Margo's time as a singer. She might have made it big, but she got into booze, and by the time that was over, so was her chance. Chet had helped her, encouraged her, even recorded with her once. She had a small studio in her home in California, but that's one recording that had never turned up anywhere. A number of times when Chet was in the Bay Area, playing the major jazz spots, or visiting his mother in San Jose, he'd roam north of San Francisco, stay at Margo's, and work small clubs near Guerneville, or play the Russian River Jazz Festival.

When Margo came to Europe and settled in Amsterdam, they renewed their friendship. "Margo kind of took care of him sometimes," Fletcher tells me. He shakes his head. "At least that's what she said. She was another one who tried to save him, but he didn't want to be saved. She took his death very hard, but it was more than just a grieving friend, now that I think about it. She wouldn't talk about it, though. All she said was, 'If only I'd been there,' like she could have done something about it. She was out of town when it happened, called me, asked me all about it. She didn't come back, though, just stayed in California. I think she might have even gone to the funeral."

I remember Russ Freeman talking about the service in the film, and there was another account in Gene Lee's *Jazzletter*. It was held in Inglewood, where Chet had spent so much time. I wonder if Margo Highland was among the mourners.

"When did you meet Margo?"

"Oh, couple of years before Chet died. She had some money, did some traveling after a bad marriage. You know how that shit goes. She liked Amsterdam and just decided to make it a second home, took on this place. She's a very cool lady. Helped me a lot. First time I stayed here, I was just kind of house-sitting for her while she took care of some business in California." Fletcher looks up at me. "Nothing was going on with us. We were and are just friends, in case you're wondering."

"I wasn't."

"Okay, I just want to be straight about that."

"You think it's possible she kept money for Chet? Opened a bank account for him, or invested it, and nobody knows about it?"

"Hell, man, anything is possible where Chet is concerned. Margo knows about money, knows what to do with it, and Chet wasn't big on paperwork, from what I hear."

I nod, flashing on another scene from the film, a record producer trying to get Chet to sign a contract. He said Chet didn't think it was necessary—a handshake would do fine—but finally agreed to a signature. When the producer tried to give Chet a copy, Chet brushed it off, saying there wasn't any point, he'd just lose it somewhere.

I feel Fletcher watching me. "I'm afraid to ask, but what are you thinking about doing?"

"We have to find this van Gogh guy we heard about in Rotterdam."

"Yeah, I knew that was coming, but how are you going to do that?"

"I'm going to need to talk to Darren."

I know I'm now standing on the edge of that chasm I talked about with Rosemary Hammond, looking over the edge, contemplating one more step, maybe one too many. I can't see to the bottom. It's dark down there, but I can't help moving closer, like somebody looking off the top of a tall building and feeling the impulse to jump.

Fletcher and I argue for almost an hour. He gives me a lot of reasons for dropping things right where they are, and some of them are good ones. But in the end, he sees it's no use and finally gives up. "All right, man, I'll call Darren, but you talk to any drug dealers, you on your own," he says.

"Fair enough. I wouldn't want it any other way." He looks at me as if he's been trying to get me to give up drugs and failed. He sighs, then gets up to call Darren and tracks him down on his cell phone.

Fletch makes some coffee while we wait, but it doesn't take Darren long to arrive. I don't think he's been invited here much, if ever, and I wonder about their relationship, whether there's more to it than Fletcher's told me. Darren saunters in with his usual ultracool demeanor, but I sense something else under that facade, as if he feels privileged and honored to have been summoned by Fletcher.

"All right, fellas," he says. "I'm on the case." In his requisite leather jacket and dark glasses, he glances around casually.

"Sit down, Darren. Take off those stupid glasses and drop that Shaft routine," Fletcher says. "We got some serious shit to talk about." Darren does as he's told. He drops into a chair and flicks a glance at me. "This is between the three of us, understand?"

Darren nods and suddenly looks like he wishes he hadn't come.

"Evan needs to connect with a dealer."

I have to give him credit. Darren looks genuinely astounded. He looks from Fletcher to me and back again to see if we're joking. When he sees we're not, he says, "A drug dealer?"

Fletcher sighs. "No, a used car dealer. Of course a drug dealer."

Darren stares at me again. "You into drugs, man? You look too cool for that. I never would have—"

"Darren, shut the fuck up and listen. He *is* too cool for that, and so am I. He wants to talk to a drug dealer, that's all, but not just any dealer, you dig?"

Darren is totally confused now, and Fletcher's attitude is making him nervous. "Fletch, let me talk to him," I say. Fletcher gives me a whatever look and sits back. "I'm looking for a particular guy, Darren. He may not even be in business now. It's been a long time, but it's somebody who might have been Chet Baker's connection."

Darren glances at Fletcher again and gets another glare that tells him he better tell the truth. He shifts in his chair. "Look, man, I do things for people, you know, just to keep things together. But I don't deal no drugs, really."

"He didn't ask you that," Fletcher says. "But you and I both know you know what's going on in the Quarter."

"Yeah, I hear things," Darren admits. "These are bad dudes, man, bad. You don't want to cross them."

Fletcher looks at me and doesn't even have to say, What did I tell you?

"You won't have to, Darren. We have the name of someone who we think had the same connection. He's called van Gogh."

Darren sits up straighter now. He drops the Shaft persona, as Fletcher calls it. He looks back and forth between us, trying to decide if I'm putting him on. "You serious? Van Gogh? Man, somebody is takin' you down, man." He shakes his head and laughs, but drops it when he sees Fletcher's expression.

"That's the name, Darren, and yes we are very serious."

He pauses, sees Fletcher is waiting for more. "Hey, I could ask around."

"You do that," Fletcher says.

"And then what if he is?"

"Don't worry," Fletcher says. "We'll tell you. You find him, you let us know."

Darren looks at us both, realizes that's it. He's been dismissed. He gets up but doesn't put the glasses back on. "Cool," he says. "I'll be in touch."

After Darren leaves, Fletcher pours us both a brandy. "Man, I must be crazy," he says.

We sit in silence for a few minutes while I think about what I've put into motion, and how slim the chances are that van Gogh is still around or that Darren can find him. "You're kind of hard on Darren, aren't you?"

"Yeah, I guess so. I'd just like to see him doing something else. He's a good kid really."

"Did you know him before or something?"

Fletcher shakes his head. "No, but he's related in a way. Darren is the grandson of a good friend of mine. She knew I was over here and asked me to keep an eye on him when he got it in his head to come to Europe. He had it kind of rough. His daddy left home when Darren was little. His mother died not long after that, and he just got kind of lost."

"He respects you. You know that, don't you? It's easy to see."

"Yeah, I guess. I just haven't done a very good job of looking out for him. Really struck me tonight when he was here. I just don't know what else to do."

"He's going through a phase, maybe. You said he was kind of lost, and with losing both parents, it's understandable."

"Yeah, I guess. I have to do something about him, though." Fletcher stands up and downs his brandy. "Well, that's it for me tonight, man." Before he leaves the room he looks at me again. "You are going to do that gig, aren't you? Whatever happens."

"Oh yeah, Fletch. Don't worry. Whatever happens, I'll be there."

13

I T'S MIDMORNING when Elaine Blakemore calls me. "Evan?
It's Elaine. Are you busy?"

"Hi. No, not really." Fletcher and I spent an hour or so going over some tunes, but my mind wasn't really on the music,
and Fletcher knew it. He gave up and retired to his room to
practice. I can hear the sound of his muffled horn now.

"Good. Sorry you couldn't make dinner with us last night."
The lilt in her voice is only slightly dampened by the phone
line.

"Well, I wouldn't have been very good company."

"Oh? Nothing serious, I hope."

"No, just in one of my minor-key moods."

"Well, let me cheer you up. I looked at the footage Kevin
shot yesterday. Came out very well, the bit with you and
Fletcher playing together. I think we're going to have a good
film here. Fletcher is a fascinating subject."

"That he is."

There's a pause then, as if neither of us knows what to say
next. Finally Elaine takes the reins. "Well, I need to get a lit-

tle background on you, if you wouldn't mind. I was thinking of lunch. If you're busy, we can do it another time, but—"

"No, lunch would be fine," I say. "Sounds like a good idea. Just tell me when and where."

"Great. Let's say one o'clock at the waterfront. There's a place there Kevin told me about. It's called Pier 10, behind Central Station."

"Sounds good. I'll find it. See you at one, then."

"Great. Bye for now."

I hang up the phone and turn around to see Fletcher standing there, an impish grin on his face. I hadn't even heard him come up. "Uh-huh," he says, "uh-huh." He does a little dance all the way to the kitchen, stops, and spins around like Sammy Davis Jr. on a good night.

Pier 10 is just that, and the restaurant is perched right at the end of the pier. Water laps beneath the windows, and I imagine the harbor lights at night would be spectacular. I look around and find Elaine at the far end in a glass-enclosed area, sipping from a goblet of wine and looking out over the water.

"Hi," she says as I reach the table. "Sorry, not quite a deck, but we can walk on the pier after lunch."

"Hi yourself." There's a waiter right behind me as I sit down. I point at Elaine's glass of white wine and say, "The same, please."

Elaine smiles and says, "I told him I was expecting some-one, but I guess he didn't believe me. He's been hovering." She hands me her menu. "I've already decided."

"On what?" I glance at the menu. When I look up at her, she's slightly flushed.

"Oh, I meant lunch."

"I know. So did I."

She looks at me, trying to read my expression, decide how serious I am. "Hmmm, Fletcher told me I should watch it with you. Two minutes, and you're already flirting."

I hold up my hands. "Me? No, just having a little fun." I can't deny Elaine is interesting, attractive, but what she really makes me think about is Natalie and Andie Lawrence.

She laughs then, or it's almost a laugh. The sunlight coming in the windows does nothing to diffuse her clear, rosy complexion. "Well, just in case, I guess I should tell you. I'm kind of engaged."

"Kind of engaged? How does that work?"

"Well, we're pretty committed, David and I. He's a BBC engineer. We just haven't set a date or anything like that, but it's sort of an understood proposition, if you know what I mean."

"I think so." The waiter brings my wine and takes our order. Elaine goes for a Caesar salad. I decide to try the salmon. "So," I say, "you mentioned background."

"Yes, who you played with, little personal history, what brought you to work in Amsterdam, that sort of thing." She starts to take a drink of her wine, then stops and holds up her glass. "To making a good film?"

I touch her glass with mine and nod. "You don't need me for that. You have a very good subject in Fletcher."

"Oh, I know. I met him a couple of times at jazz festivals and once in London, but he always put me off. I was so glad when he finally agreed to do it. And you're a bonus."

I nod. "Well, I don't know about that, but just ten days with Fletcher has been an experience, and this duo thing we're going to do should really be good."

"Yes," Elaine says. "He told me about it. You start this weekend, right?"

"Tomorrow night, as far as I know. We get a kind of trial outing, I take it, and then go from there." I take a drink and look at her. "You coming?"

"Of course. I'm going to see if they'll let me film some, too." She looks out at the harbor. "Fletcher Paige at work with the jazz pianist detective."

I give her a look that wipes the smile off her face.

"Sorry. I was just having some fun too."

The waiter brings our order, and for a few minutes we get lost in eating and making small talk. When we finish, the air is cleared. We push our plates aside and order coffee. "That's all I can manage," Elaine says of her huge salad.

I long for a cigarette but try to resist the impulse, even though smoking is obviously permitted. "So about this background," I say.

Elaine nods and takes out a pen and notebook from her bag. I give her a short thumbnail sketch, including the recording I did before coming to Europe.

"Was that while the . . . serial killer thing was going on?" she wants to know.

"Yes." She waits, but when I don't add any more, she doesn't push it.

"Hard to talk about, huh?"

"I have talked about it, in depth, with an FBI shrink. It's just not something I want to go over again, if you don't mind."

"Not at all," she says. "I understand. So where are you living now? And how long are you staying in Amsterdam?"

Those are both good questions. Where do I live now? I'm staying with Fletcher for the moment, and I guess I'll stay around as long as the gig goes and he'll have me. But what about after that? I haven't even considered future plans.

"I'm crashing with Fletcher for now. Just see how it goes."

"The nomadic life of a jazz musician, huh." She checks over her notes. "What I would like is to have you talk about Fletcher, on camera, maybe how it's different working without a bass and drums."

"That I can do."

"It is different, right?"

"Yes. Like walking a high wire without a net, but Fletcher is a hell of a catcher."

She smiles. "I like that image." She writes it down and puts away her notebook. "How about a stroll on the pier? You can have one of those awful cigarettes in your pocket."

I start to pay, but she puts up her hands. "No, I said my treat. I'll just add it to the budget."

We stroll lazily on the pier. There are more people out now, tourists and probably some locals too, judging by their clothes and absence of cameras, all enjoying the early spring. We stop and sit down on a wooden bench facing the water. Elaine is diplomatic, if nothing else. She doesn't make any disapproving sounds when I light a cigarette.

"I know you don't want to go over old ground, the incident in Los Angeles, but I'm dying to know if you're—looking into, is that the right phrase?—Chet Baker's death."

"Are you now? Fletcher's been talking, huh?"

She smiles. "Well, he did mention something. He seems kind of excited about it."

"Fletcher is too big a fan of mystery novels, I think." I look away for a moment. "It's nothing, really. I was supposed to meet a friend of mine here. He's the one researching Chet Baker, but he's just kind of disappeared."

"And you think something might have happened to him?"

"I've told several people that, including the police."

"The police? So it is serious, then."

"I don't know. It's not like him to just leave like that with no word at all. I think he might have gotten in over his head. He's kind of naive when it comes to the jazz scene."

"Yes, Fletcher told me he met him briefly. Amsterdam is a beautiful city, but it has its dark side like everywhere else. Somebody told me the Zeedijk area used to be called the black hole of the city."

I turn and look at her now. "What do you know about it?"

She shrugs. "Not much. Lot of drug trafficking, users, criminal types, like parts of London, I guess." When I don't say anything, she continues, "Well, it's no secret that Chet Baker was an addict. You think your friend might have gone there, to Zeedijk, hoping to get background material?"

I drop my cigarette on the ground and step on it. "Are you being Elaine Blakemore, filmmaker, or reporter?"

She blushes slightly. "Sorry. Reporter instincts, I guess. I wrote for the *Melody Maker* in London for a while."

"I'm just having fun again. I'm not sure what he was up to. I'd just like to know he's okay and not in trouble." I stand up and look at my watch. "Anyway, he's probably fine and already left town. I worry too much, I guess."

She looks at me closely. "No, I don't think you do."

"Is Inspector Dekker in?" The officer on the desk is the same one as the first day I was here, but I'm not sure he recognizes me.

"A moment, please." He picks up the phone and dials an extension. All I can catch is Dekker's name. He hangs up and says, "Inspector Dekker is coming."

"Thank you."

Dekker comes out and almost sighs when he sees it's me. He has the world-weary look of every big-city cop, and I'm adding to his irritation. "Mr. Horne. I wish I could say I was glad to see you. How can I help you?"

"Sorry, I know you're busy. I just wanted to ask you a couple of questions."

Dekker does sigh now. "Very well, but I don't have much time. Come with me." We go back to his office and sit down. "Now, what is it, please?"

"What can you tell me about the Zeedijk area of the city?"

Dekker leans back in his chair and studies me for a moment, shakes his head. "Most people coming to Holland at this time of year would be more interested in the bulb fields. They are quite spectacular. Tulips of every color as far as the eye can see. But here you are inquiring about a far less attractive area, where drug trafficking took place. Why am I not surprised?"

"Took place? Not anymore?"

Dekker launches into what sounds like a prepared speech for civic leaders. "The entire area has been cleaned up these past few years. Correct me if I'm wrong, but hasn't the same thing happened to Times Square in New York? New developments, restaurants, shops." Dekker pauses, looks at me, and gives up the rhetoric. "Very well, there is still some of that element in Zeedijk, but the restructuring and the new reforms in Amsterdam's drug policy have minimized it. No, Mr. Horne, it is no longer the black hole it was once called."

"And what is this new drug policy?"

Dekker sighs again, digs in his desk, and comes out with a slim blue pamphlet. "It's all in here, Mr. Horne, in English. Not very interesting reading, but full of information."

I take the pamphlet from him. "Thanks," I say.

"Now," Dekker asks, "anything else?"

"Just one thing. Was there any one major drug dealer active in Zeedijk, say ten years ago or so?"

He leans back in his chair and smiles wryly. "Ah, now I see where you are headed. That would be when Mr. Chet Baker died, the famous musician?"

"Yes, although I wasn't thinking just of Chet Baker."

"No? You seem as much interested in him as in your elusive friend. There were many at that time, I believe, some foreign—Cuban, Colombian, African. Very dangerous, very vicious, but most have been put out of business." Dekker reaches across and taps the pamphlet. "I have no specific name, nor can I imagine why you would want to know."

"Just curious. The Zeedijk area was mentioned in those articles in my friend's portfolio."

"Oh course." He stands up, but I get the feeling there's something he's not telling me.

"Has something else happened, Inspector?"

He sits down again and looks at me. "You're so persistent, Mr. Horne." He sees I'm not going anywhere. "Very well. The prostitute, the one who turned in the portfolio, was severely beaten."

"What? Do you know who did it? Can I see her?"

"No, Mr. Horne, you cannot. She's in the hospital recovering, and she is very frightened. She refuses to talk to me about it, other than to say it was the man who left the portfolio in the first place. She doesn't believe we can protect her."

"What's her name?"

"Carmen is her working name. She's from the Caribbean." Dekker leans back and cautions me again. "These people you are stirring up are dangerous, Mr. Horne."

"I know that, and I'm not trying to stir anybody up. I'm just trying to find out what happened to my friend. Whoever stole the portfolio from my room is probably the same one who beat up Carmen."

"I'm well aware of that, and we will take care of it. This is a police matter, so please respect that."

Now it is getting out of hand. This girl Carmen could have been killed. Why? Because she informed the police. There has to be more to it than that, but it's obvious Dekker is not going to let me in on the loop.

"Now, I have many things to do. If you'll excuse me."

"Sure. I'm sorry to bother you again." I start for the door. "Oh, by the way, I'm going to be in Amsterdam a little while longer. I'm starting a new job tomorrow night. It's a place called Baby Grand. Stop by and hear some music. I'll buy you a drink."

"Thank you, but I don't think so."

"Well, if you change your mind." As I go, Dekker gives me a look that says, Don't call me, I'll call you.

Finding a café along Rokin, near the C&A department store, that has outside tables, I sit down with coffee and watch the throng of shoppers, tourists, trolleys, buses, bicycles, and cars that is Amsterdam in midafternoon.

I flip through the pamphlet Dekker gave me. A lot of it is statistics, but there are some nuggets. The coffee bars that sell cannabis, hashish, and marijuana legally are not allowed to sell alcohol, and they have to have special licenses. Despite

Amsterdam's freewheeling reputation, soft and hard drugs are strictly regulated, much like the legal prostitution, but the pamphlet stresses that this does not make Amsterdam a "junkies' heaven," and that, what's more, Amsterdam's approach is more effective than the aggressive War on Drugs strategy applied in other countries. They don't say USA, but they might as well. There are a lot of tables and graphs, information about treatment clinics, methadone centers, and hypodermic exchange programs, highlighting Amsterdam's pragmatic approach to drugs, but there is no mention of Zeedijk anywhere in the pamphlet, so Dekker must be right about the cleanup.

I sit, smoking, drinking coffee, just people-watching, for an hour or so. The pamphlet was interesting but not much help. This is now. I'm more interested in then—the 1980s, when, also according to the pamphlet, Amsterdam was a magnet for foreign drug users, Chet Baker among them.

I'm convinced now it was a dealer, Chet's dealer, that Ace stumbled onto. Knowing Ace, he jumped in with both feet and is finding it difficult to get out once he is in. I know I have to resolve this, and soon, both for Ace's sake and my own. I should know my pattern by now. I get distracted from music, then have to resolve the distraction to get back to music. Same old circle, like the cycle of fifths chord progressions. Time now for the turnaround chords.

I don't really have much faith in Darren turning up anything. Nobody, even Fletcher, seems to know exactly what Darren does. For more definite information, I'll have to call somebody else, and he probably won't be any happier to hear from me than Dekker was.

Detective Engels is at home when I call from the American Express office, but when I ask him about Zeedijk, he sounds like a travel brochure.

"It's Chinatown, Mr. Horne. There is even a Buddhist Temple. Restored buidings, shops, restaurants, and one of two timbered houses left in the city."

"Thanks, Mr. Engels, but I'm more interested in how it was in, let's say, 1988."

"Yes, I thought so. I imagine our Mr. Baker was a frequent visitor then."

"I'm sure. Was there one particular well-known dealer, someone the police were familiar with? Maybe he had a nickname, you know, a special name."

"There were many, and most are gone now, thankfully. I don't recall any name, and they were not all Dutch. Some were Moroccan or from the Caribbean or South America. Why do you ask?"

I pause to think of an appropriate answer. "Oh, someone I just met is doing a documentary film. She heard of it and asked me if I knew. No other reason really."

"I'm sorry I can't be more help."

So am I, I think. Finding Chet's connection, even if he was owed money, is going to be trickier than I thought.

"Go carefully, Mr. Horne. Zeedijk has improved considerably, but there are still places and people just as dangerous as before."

Back at the flat, I find Fletcher and Darren at the computer, arguing about something.

"What's happening?"

Fletcher glances at Darren. "Shaft here thinks he knows about computers. I'm trying to look up something, and he's trying to tell me how to do it."

"Well, I do," Darren says. The jacket and glasses are off now. "Just let me try, okay?"

Fletcher rolls his eyes and stands up. "Okay, but if you fuck up my computer, you're going to pay for it."

"Step aside," Darren says. He sits down and looks at the

screen, then begins typing. "Got to find another search engine for what you want," he says. He types some more, clicks the mouse a few times, and Fletcher and I both watch openmouthed as Darren makes the screen change faster than we can keep up. Finally, he arrives on a jazz site home page. "There," he says, standing up. "You should bookmark places you go back to a lot. It's much easier."

Fletcher stares at the screen for a minute, then at Darren, then at me. "How'd you learn to do that?" he asks Darren.

Darren grins, enjoying the moment. "Just something I picked up," he says.

Fletcher looks at Darren as if he's somebody he doesn't know. He sits down and clicks the menu button.

"What are you looking for, anyway?" I ask.

"I heard Art Farmer was sick," he says. "Just wanted to check to see if there was anything on it."

Fletcher clicks on the news button, and I read over his shoulder. There are some items about upcoming jazz festivals, some new CD releases, and a couple of reviews, but nothing about Art Farmer.

"Whew," Fletcher says. "We're old friends, but I haven't seen him in a while."

"Do me a favor, will you," I say. "Send an e-mail to Margo. Ask her if Ace has been there."

He closes the screen and opens his mail site. Typing slowly with two fingers, he writes a brief message to Margo, then closes down everything and stands up.

"Thanks," I say.

"What are you going to do?"

"Go to San Francisco. I'll try to get a flight out Monday morning."

"Could be tough," Darren says. "Let me try it online, might find something."

"Great, please do."

Darren nods. "No problem. I'll do it at home." He looks at Fletcher. Something passes between them I can't read.

"Come on, Darren," Fletcher says. "I want to talk to you." It's the first time he hasn't called him Shaft.

The Baby Grand is already crowded when we arrive. There's a poster in the front window that reads, "Fletcher Paige & Evan Horne, 8–11." There's some other printing with dates and times and a short paragraph in quotes—some reviewer's words, I imagine.

The restaurant itself is upscale. White tablecloths, silver, glassware, and waiters in white shirts and bow ties. The piano is at one end of the room, and in front, in the curve of the piano, is a stool for Fletcher. No microphones or sound system. This will be acoustic all the way.

I sit down at the piano and run through some chords. The sound is beautiful, and true to his word, the owner has had it tuned. Elaine must have persuaded him to let her film; Kevin is already set up at a front table with his camera and microphone, doing light meter readings with Elaine hovering nearby.

"This is exciting," she says as I come up. "We won't get in your way, I promise."

"I'm sure you won't," I say and let her get back to prepping for the filming. I join Fletcher at the bar, where he's sipping a cognac. He looks thoughtful but not nervous. He's played too many gigs for that. It's something else that's got him quiet, just looking into his glass.

"Hey, man," he says. "Nice setup, huh?"

"Uh-huh. I think we're going to enjoy this. You okay?"

"What? Oh yeah, just thinking." He looks at me. "I haven't told you everything about Darren."

"What do you mean?"

"He's not the grandson of a friend. He's my grandson."

"Whoa. Does he know?" This is starting to make sense now.

"He does now. He pretty much had it figured out." Fletcher sips his drink and stares at himself in the mirror behind the bar.

"That shit he did on the computer today just blew me away. We had a long talk—turns out he works part-time for a computer company here. Can you believe that? Anyway, we talked; I told him the whole story, he liked to broke down and cried. I want to get him off the street, all this Shaft actin' bullshit. Trying to get him to go back home, get established, before he gets in some real trouble." Fletcher shakes his head. "I should have done this a long time ago."

"Maybe he wasn't ready for it then."

"I should have made him ready. This little errand for you is going to be the last of these street deals. Damn, the way he handles himself on the computer, he could really do something."

Eric, the owner, comes over. "So you are both ready?"

"Oh, yeah," Fletcher says. "Let's do it."

We follow him to the piano. I sit down and noodle a bit while Fletcher gets his horn ready and Eric makes an opening announcement. I get a quick smile from Elaine as she bends low behind Kevin.

"So," Eric says to the audience, "Fletcher Paige and Evan Horne."

We'd already decided the opening number would be "It Could Happen to You." There's no count. Fletcher simply glances at me and raises his horn, then we're off on an easy medium tempo, playing counterpoint on the melody. Fletcher takes the first solo, moving through the changes smoothly while I feed him chords and marvel at his tone and ideas. I take two choruses. Fletcher, perched on the stool, listens with his horn across his lap.

On the last eight bars, he stands and waits for the next chorus, then begins playing lines against my own. It quickly becomes a question-and-answer, call-and-response, for two more choruses, then we take it out. The Baby Grand has been initiated.

*   *   *

We're just about to have a post-set drink with the owner when Darren comes in. He nods to Fletcher, even takes off his dark glasses, and beams at Elaine. He catches my eye, comes over, and leans in to speak in my ear.

"Okay," I say. Fletcher watches as Darren goes outside, then turns a questioning face to me.

"Got a little errand to do," I say. Fletcher looks away and sips his drink. Elaine looks at both of us, trying to read things.

"Can I help? You want some company?" she asks.

"No, thanks," I say quickly. "I'll catch up with you guys tomorrow." I turn to Fletcher. "You're going home now, right?" He knows it's not a question and nods.

I head for the door then before anyone can stop me.

14

"Van Gogh?" I find Darren standing in front of the Baby Grand, hands in his pockets, looking at the poster in the window. The traffic has lightened now, and the warm afternoon and evening has become only slightly cooler.

He shrugs as if he doesn't believe it either, but doesn't look at me, just continues to watch cars cruising by. "Old dude, long hair. Draws pictures in charcoal for the tourists. Not very good either, but got that name hung on him." When I just look at Darren and don't say anything, he adds, "Hey, it's Amsterdam. Art and all that shit."

"Okay. And he's a musician too?"

"Yeah, was, a drummer. Guess he used to be okay, but the dope fucked him up too bad. Missed gigs, nodded out. People stopped calling him. Now he just, you know, lives."

Darren sees that I want more. He's uncomfortable about the whole thing, but he's going along with it, mainly, I know, because of Fletcher's insistence. "Look, man, I'm tellin' you what I'm tellin' you. I was told he had the same connection as Chet back then. That and where he lives is all I could get out of him."

"Okay." I didn't really expect Darren to have a direct line to Chet's connection, or to know if he is even still around, so this will have to do for now, and I can't afford not to see where it goes. "You didn't scare him?"

"Nah, man. Just told him somebody, an old friend of Chet's, wanted to talk to him. He wasn't scared of me."

That relieves and surprises me. I don't want van Gogh to go underground. Darren can look intimidating until you get behind those dark glasses. "Okay, show me."

Darren looks pained. "Go with you, you mean?" He glances over his shoulder, as if he's checking to see if someone is watching us. He gives a resigned shrug and sigh. "We need a taxi." He steps off the curb to flag one down and mumbles, "Get this shit over with."

We get in, and he manages some passable Dutch to the driver for directions. "Zeedijk," he says, then a street name I couldn't pronounce if I tried, and a number. The driver frowns and shakes his head but presses the button on the meter.

I look at Darren. "Not a cool place to be goin' after midnight," he says. He slumps in the seat, his gloved hands folded, and stares out the window.

The taxi winds through the narrow streets and over canal bridges till we hit a main boulevard in the direction of Central Station. We make a right in front of the station, then filter down through a maze of streets to a brightly lit underpass north of the station. It comes out along the waterfront, onto a two-lane curved road that meanders for a mile or so, then over another short, narrow bridge with room for only one car at a time. I catch a glimpse of the harbor lights on our left, then we're in a Chinatown section—old buildings, newly restored restaurants, cafés, and shops, wedged between warehouses and drab apartment blocks.

The driver slows the taxi and looks around, trying to read street names. He stops a couple of times, then goes on. After a couple of wrong turns, Darren taps him on the shoulder.

"Here," Darren says, leaning forward to tell the driver to

stop. I pay the fare, and we get out and walk a couple of blocks past rows of apartments and more abandoned warehouses while Darren looks for numbers. The air is chilled from the harbor, and the smell of the sea is strong, fighting for dominance over the odor of Chinese cooking. We walk a little farther, then Darren stops and points. "This one," he says.

Some of the windows are boarded up, some are broken. The front door has duct tape across the glass in diagonal rows where the glass has been cracked. Inside the tiny lobby is a bank of mailboxes, but I wonder how much is delivered here. Most of the name slots are empty; others are scratched out or unreadable. Darren points up the stairs.

The smell makes me not want to breathe. Cigarette butts litter the dimly lit hallways, and fumes from broken wine bottles and crushed beer cans mix with the odor of urine, and some other smell I can't make out at all. We walk up to the third floor and pass doors where muffled sounds from televisions and voices, some even children's, filter through the thin walls.

"Some kind of government housing," Darren says, wrinkling his nose at the stench. "Got projects everywhere."

"You sure this is the place?"

"Yeah. Got the address from another guy. Told him van Gogh owes me money."

"You've never been here?"

"Hell, no," Darren says, like he's annoyed and offended by the question.

He touches my shoulder, and we stop in front of one door and listen for a moment. The brass number 9 is nailed to the door, but the top nail is missing so that the number hangs upside down. I hear a television turned down low and something else—a kind of rhythmic tapping sound. Darren raps on the door with a gloved hand. Inside, the tapping stops. "Yo, van Gogh," he says, glancing down the hallway.

There's nothing but the sound of the TV for a moment, then footsteps, slapping toward the door. "Who is?" the dark, raspy voice says from just behind the door.

"It's Darren, man. Got that guy I told you about. Open up, man. Stinks out here."

The door opens a few inches. Van Gogh's face is deeply lined and gaunt. His long lank hair, shoulder length, flies in all directions off the top of his head. Van Gogh looks at Darren, gives me a quick glance, then breaks into a grim smile. Several teeth are missing, and the remaining ones are yellowish. Cautiously he opens the door wider, sticks his head out to look up and down the hallway, then steps aside to let us in.

He's wearing a tank-top-style undershirt that was probably white once, and faded torn jeans. His feet are in leather sandals with a couple of the straps broken or ready to tear. In his left hand, he holds two scarred drumsticks; in his right, a cigarette, burned down nearly to his fingers. He inspects me as I pass, drags on the cigarette, and exhales a cloud of smoke.

The room, and that's all it is, has a small sink, a countertop, a couple of shelves above it with a few dishes and cups. Lying on the counter next to the sink are a two-burner hot plate, a large jar of instant coffee, an open bag of sugar, and two spoons. I don't see any kind of refrigerator. In one corner is a black iron-framed single bed, a small table, a lamp that barely illuminates the room, and a large white ashtray with the logo of some bar, overflowing with ashes and butts.

Stacked on the floor in a neat pile are several paperback books, the one on top with a garish cover, some kind of horror novel. Propped against the wall is a canvas bag with a couple of framed, smudged charcoal drawings sticking out. A few feet from the side of the bed, a small black-and-white television with a rabbit-ear aerial is tuned low and perched on an old trunk. A movie flickers on the screen. The smell in here is only slightly better than in the hallway.

By the side of the bed is the room's one unusual item, which explains the tapping sound. On a shiny chrome stand, with a circular piece of black rubber at its center, is a drummer's practice pad. Van Gogh sits on the bed, drops the cigarette butt in the ashtray to continue smoldering. In the lamplight, I can see that his left hand is misshapen, the fingers crooked. He places one stick in the crook between his thumb and forefinger of his left hand and curls his fingers around the shaft of the stick.

Without thinking, I flex my own hand. Van Gogh's fingers have been broken at one time and never healed properly, but their movements are long practiced from memory. He cocks his head slightly to the right as I've seen countless drummers do, and continues tapping out rhythms from somewhere in his mind, accenting here and there, but all very quietly, very controlled. The sticks never come off the pad more than a couple of inches. Then, as if remembering some tune he played long ago, he begins to play a medium-tempo ride cymbal beat with his right hand, while accenting with his left.

I glance at Darren. He's taken off the shades, and his eyes flick from me to van Gogh and back again. "You digging this, huh?" he says.

Van Gogh stops the time play then and vamps on a soft press roll. I watch the muscles of his forearms, lined and scarred by a thousand needle marks. He stops the roll then and carefully replaces the sticks on the pad. He looks at me.

"You have one cigarette, please?"

I dig for mine and hand him the pack. He offers me one first, takes one for himself, and lays the pack on the table. He lights us both with a wooden match from a large box next to the ashtray, inhales deeply twice, three times, and exhales clouds of blue smoke. "Ah, menthol," he says. "Very expensive." He picks up the pack and examines it.

"Keep them," I say.

He breaks into another nearly toothless smile and nods. I think of the later pictures of Chet from the portfolio. He and van Gogh could be from the same tribe, some ancient clan for which heroin is the peace pipe. If Chet Baker hadn't been Chet Baker, and he were still alive, would he be in a room like this, playing on an old trumpet?

Darren walks over to the window and struggles for a mo-

ment to get it open and let in some cool air. I sit down on the
bed next to van Gogh.

"You play, huh?"

He shakes his head. "No more, but I remember. I like
this," he says, touching the pad with a finger. "I relax." He
turns his palms up and looks at his forearms. "All the money
is here," he says.

"You played with Chet Baker?"

He nods and closes his eyes, remembering. "Yes, two,
maybe three times. Long time ago. So beautiful, his horn, and
after, together we . . ." He taps his arm again.

"I'm trying to find a man Chet may have owed money to,
his connection—and maybe yours too?"

Van Gogh shakes his head. "No, Chet pays. He has
money." He raises his left hand and tries to close it into a fist
but can only manage halfway.

"A dealer did that?" I say, pointing at his hand.

"Yes, to anyone who no pay. Chet, he pay, he knew." He
pauses, looks at me. "And I no tell."

"What? You didn't tell what?"

Van Gogh just shakes his head, remembering something,
but it's not for me.

"Is that man still in Amsterdam?"

Van Gogh regards me with his version of a perplexed expression. "You want?" he says, looking at my clothes, my face.
"I don't think so."

"No, not drugs. I just want to talk to him. I'm trying to
find my friend."

He glances at Darren, then back to me. "You are not
police?"

"No, no, piano player. I'm . . . I'm just trying to do something for Chet, for a friend." But even as I say the words, I know
I'm here in this junkie crash pad talking to an old drummer as
much for myself as for Ace or Chet Baker. I can't shut it off.

"Ah, piano." He inhales the cigarette deeply again, then
puts it out in a mountain of ash. He picks up the sticks and

begins tapping on the pad, his eyes going to the TV screen. "Listen," he says. "You know this tune?" The tapping begins again, but in a jagged, repeated pattern. He plays it several times. I look at Darren. He checks his watch and rolls his eyes, impatient to go.

Van Gogh moves his head from side to side. His lined face pinches into a deeper frown. He looks up at me, gives me that weird grin. I listen, the rhythm pattern repeating, distinctly. He slows it down for me.

It sounds like, da-da-duh, duh-da-duh-da-di-duh, dada-dadaduh-duh da di.

Then he plays a cymbal pattern with his right hand, accents with his left, and repeats the first pattern again. I sing it in my head, try to put it together; then something clicks—the drummer Roy Haynes doing the same thing. I think it's an old bebop tune, Sonny Rollins.

"Oleo?" I say, making a stab at it. This sends van Gogh into spasms of ecstasy, head back, a low moan coming from somewhere deep inside him, playing hard now, remembering some night on a bandstand somewhere, another time for him. Then silence. He stops, and carefully replaces the sticks on the pad for another time.

I think of something else then and take out the photo I have of Ace.

"Have you ever seen this man?" I ask van Gogh.

He looks at the photo, shakes his head, no, then stands up.

"Come, I show you," he says.

Darren looks at me and shakes his head. "I don't understand this shit at all, man."

Van Gogh ingores Darren. He flicks off the TV and shrugs into an old coat hanging on a hook by the door. Downstairs, back out on the street, it's chilly now. We follow him as he cuts between buildings, down alleyways, until the lights of Central Station are visible.

"We need a taxi?" I call to him. He shakes his head no and keeps walking ahead of us, occasionally looking back over his shoulder to see if we're with him, headed now, I'm sure, for the Old Quarter.

"'Oleo' was the name of that shit he was tapping out?" Darren asks me.

"Yes," I say, keeping van Gogh in sight. He walks ahead of us, sandals slapping on the pavement, head turning side to side, scanning faces, but I don't think he's looking for anyone. He's just looking.

"Damn," Darren says. "How'd you do that?"

"Remind me. I'll show you with Fletcher."

We finally round a corner and stop in front of one of the coffee shops. I know where we are now. Darren and I both look at each other. "Shit, I didn't know," he says.

It's the same one I was in the night I hallucinated. Van Gogh motions that Darren is to stay outside. I start to follow him in, but quickly whisper to Darren first, "Call Fletcher. If he's home, tell him to come over."

"Right," Darren says and reaches for his cell phone.

Van Gogh is waiting just inside the door for me. He motions for me to follow him. We walk toward the back, past tables full of customers sampling, laughing, having a good time, the pungent aroma of several grades of marijuana everywhere. At the far end of the bar, a room juts off in a kind of alcove, two men are seated in a circular booth, as if they've been waiting for me. They both look up at van Gogh.

One of them I recognize immediately. He doesn't have his raincoat or umbrella or satchel, and the glasses are gone, but there's no mistake. This is the same man who gave me directions to the hotel the day I arrived in Amsterdam. He's probably the one who switched my order in this very coffee shop. The other man I take to be the connection. He's late sixties, I would guess, with thick, bushy eyebrows, very dark eyes, and thinning black hair, streaked with gray. Dressed in an expensive suit, he could be a banker. There's a long line, a scar of some kind, down the right side of his face.

Van Gogh shuffles closer, leans in to speak to him quietly.

The man nods and takes out a roll of money, peels off some notes, and hands them to van Gogh without taking his eyes off me. Van Gogh doesn't even look at the money. He just stuffs it in his pocket, turns, and brushes past me. He whispers something to me, but all I catch is "Be careful." Then van Gogh is gone and out the door.

I move closer to the table. "I'm trying to locate my friend, Professor Buffington," I say to the younger man. "That man thought you might know where he is, but since you met me at the train station, you and your partner here probably both do. I've forgotten your name."

The two have a brief exchange, in Spanish I think. The dark man either can't or doesn't want to speak English. He just continues to stare at me.

"Sit down, Mr. Horne," the man from the train station says. "It's de Hass." He has a thin, pinched face and wavy hair and is dressed in more casual but just as expensive clothes. He's much younger than the dark man and from his demeanor, obviously his employee.

He smiles in spite of himself, and his English is excellent, with only a trace of an accent. "You have a good memory. As for your friend, we have no idea where he is at this time. I suspect he has left Amsterdam. We have no further interest in him. Our business is now with you." The dark man looks at him. They have another brief exchange, which I take to be a translation. The dark man nods.

"With me? What did you do, kidnap my friend?"

He gives me an exasperated look. "We persuaded him, Mr. Horne. Kidnapping, as you put it, was not necessary. He came to Amsterdam and attracted a great deal of notice with his questions about Chet Baker—questions that brought up old memories, old debts. Your friend made himself very visible, and eventually, those questions came to our attention. I offered him a chance to talk with Mr. Navarro." He nods toward the older man, who glances over at the mention of his name.

That I was right about everything doesn't make me happy

to be sitting here. "Why? What did his research on Chet Baker's death have to do with you?" I look around the room. There's no sign of Darren or Fletcher, just customers talking, smoking.

De Hass is enjoying himself. "Chet Baker's death was of no concern. Money he owed was. By persuading Professor Buffington to let us assist him with his research, we could protect our interests as well." He looks at Navarro, and his voice inflection makes it obvious he's asking a question. Navarro seems to approve.

"There were rumors, as there are about any celebrity death—rumors about money, long-forgotten bank accounts. People like to expand, add to legends, but there is often truth to these rumors. Chet Baker was a famous musician. His addiction and his carelessness with money were as well known as his music. I think if you were to check with the police, you would find he had a significant record with many police agencies, including Interpol. The needs of his addiction were provided for many times, and because of his celebrity and his earning power, he was sometimes allowed credit. He always paid his debts, eventually, except for that last time."

"And of course, you don't make exceptions." I shift in the booth so I can see the bar.

"No. I would never have allowed credit to begin with, even for Chet Baker. It's not good business. Mr. Navarro did on occasion. Perhaps he had a misguided soft spot for Chet Baker." His smile is chilling, menacing.

That would be a first. A drug dealer with a soft spot. "And this time you're talking about, it was just before he died?"

"Yes, so Mr. Navarro blames himself partly for the loss."

"Chet Baker's death?"

"His death?" De Hass laughs and shakes his head. "We're talking about money, nothing more. I know you talked to the police. Chet Baker needed no help from anyone. He avoided Mr. Navarro, perhaps unintentionally, one too many times. But no, Mr. Navarro had nothing to do with his death. Chet Baker was already dead, evidently by his own hand. Mr. Navarro was looking for him, but he was too late."

And van Gogh never told. Now I know what he meant. *I no tell*, van Gogh had said. Maybe he had warned Chet, helped him hide from Navarro, and maybe for his trouble, his hand was crushed. But I also know he brought me here not to find Ace but to deliver me to these two, out of fear and need—a few guilders, another fix. Never trust a junkie.

"How much did he owe?"

"Let's just say it was a significant amount, enough that it was worth exhausting your friend's leads, to clear the books, so to speak." He pauses and looks around at Navarro, who says nothing but shifts in his seat and waves his hand in an impatient gesture. The younger man nods and turns back to me.

"Now we come to you, Mr. Horne. Mr. Navarro doesn't want to bother, but I think there is money and that you can find it. For obvious reasons, I cannot make inquiries of bank records." He pauses for a moment, then continues. "So, unless you wish to make good on that debt yourself, or know of some other way it can be paid, we are going to insist that you make those inquiries for us." He glances up then, over my shoulder. I turn and see Fletcher and Darren slide onto a couple of stools at the bar.

"What do you mean, you insist? You forced my friend to—"

He puts his hand up. "Forced? No, Mr. Horne. Your friend cooperated willingly. You perhaps don't know him as well as you think. He told me from the beginning that you had agreed to help him with his research, and there you were, right on schedule. As a musician it was obvious that you would have more success than he would have, so we simply speeded things along."

"He told you that?"

He nods, but even before he does, I know he's telling the truth. Now it all suddenly starts to make sense—Ace's disappearance, the missing portfolio, his avoiding me, the impersonator at the archives. This was the man Helen thought was

Ace. Ace and I were the puppets, and de Hass pulled the strings. Only, I had been the main puppet.

"You thought there was some money, that my friend knew something about it?"

"His words were, I believe, 'If it's there, Evan Horne will find it.' We had no other interest in Chet Baker or you or your friend." He seems amused by the notion. "I don't even like his music. He was simply someone who owed a debt, an old one but a debt nevertheless. Your friend was sure this money existed somewhere and that you would find it."

I listen to this man, talking dispassionately about Chet's death, his addiction, how his needs were provided for, how he didn't even like his music, and feel anger boiling up inside me. If it suited them, they would coldly order someone beaten or killed without a second thought for not paying. I want to dive across the table and smash his face, and Navarro's. No, they didn't lure Chet Baker into a life of drugs—he'd done that himself—but they could be talking about anyone. That voice in my head is screaming, This is Chet Baker we're talking about, you idiot, one of the great trumpet players of jazz! Futile thoughts, I know, but I can't get them out of my mind, and Chet has no one to speak for him.

"There is no money, at least none that I know anything about. You also know Chet Baker spent his money freely, and a lot of it went to your ugly boss."

He studies me, his jaw muscles tightening, and for a moment I think I've gone too far. "I won't translate that remark, Mr. Horne. As for the money, we are not convinced it doesn't exist, and Mr. Navarro wants to close the books on Chet Baker."

"Suppose I go to the police. Tell them you forced my friend to cooperate with you, that you—"

"You are not listening, Mr. Horne. Tell them what? That your friend, in his eagerness to get a scoop—isn't that what you call it?—for his book, miscalculated? Anyway, your friend is no longer here to corroborate any such story you might tell the police, and I doubt that he will be back in Amsterdam any-time soon."

That is no doubt also true. Ace was probably "persuaded" that leaving Amsterdam was a good idea. He is probably on a plane to California or already there. I sit back and digest all this, my mind turning over de Hass's words. I have an even better reason to find Ace now than when I thought he had disappeared and was in trouble—and I know where he is.

The man takes my silence for agreement. "Yes, I think you realize the truth, Mr. Horne." He speaks to Navarro briefly, then turns back to me. "We must go. I'll expect to hear from you regarding the money."

"And if you don't?"

He carefully reaches into an inside pocket for his glasses, puts them on, then leans forward, folding his hands in front of him on the table. "I'm not one to make idle threats, Mr. Horne. The man who brought you here . . . it's not only because he draws pictures for tourists that he's called van Gogh." He pauses, continues to stare at me, until he sees that I know what he means. "You have until Monday to make the money available to me or convince me that there is none. Otherwise . . ." His voice trails off. He holds up his hands and gives me another cold smile. My imagination can do the rest.

The two of them slide out of the booth and stand up. They straighten their clothes, but before they go, the man leans over and taps his fingers on the table. "According to some of the articles in your friend's portfolio, Chet Baker made a great deal of money the last two years before he died. He owed Mr. Navarro $23,000. That's the amount we expect. No more, no less."

He turns then, and the two men simply walk out, right past Fletcher and Darren, without so much as a backward glance.

They watch them go, then come over and join me in the booth. "Well?" Fletcher says. "What did you find out?"

"More than I wanted."

I tell Fletch and Darren what de Hass wants, what he's told me. They listen quietly. Fletcher shakes his head; Darren's features harden into defiance.

"They're bluffing," he says.

"Darren, shut up," Fletcher says.

Darren leans back and shakes his head. "Well, they are. What are they going to do?"

Fletcher and I both stare at Darren. I find myself clenching my right hand, thinking about a rubber ball I once used as therapy.

"What?" Darren says.

Fletcher puts his head back, closes his eyes, and sighs. "Did they threaten you? Say anything you could go to the police with?"

"No, not in so many words." But the threat was there nonetheless. I have no doubt Navarro would have had Chet killed if he felt like it, and I'd seen for myself what he'd done to van Gogh for not cooperating—even if I hadn't seen under his long hair except in my mind now.

I could run, get out of Amsterdam—and then what? Leave Fletcher to deal with de Hass? Stay, and look over my shoulder until one night in some dark street they catch up with me?

I get up slowly, suddenly very tired and washed out, as the impact of what I've been told slowly seeps into my mind. I can't decide yet what bothers me more—the threats, the demands, or that Ace sold me out.

We walk to Fletcher's car and say good-bye to Darren there. He's relaxed now, back to his old cocky self, and doesn't really understand what's just gone down.

"Thanks for calling Fletch and being here, Darren," I say.

"Nothin', man. We could have handled those dudes," he says. "That old guy wouldn't give nobody no trouble."

"There was nothing to handle, Darren," I say.

Fletcher glares at him. "Darren, shut the fuck up and get out of here. We gotta think."

Darren takes several steps backward, his hands over his

head like Fletcher has a gun pointed at. "Okay, man, that's cool, that's cool. No problem. I'll be in touch."

Fletcher watches him go and shakes his head. "I got to do something about him, get him out of here and back to the States."

"He came through, Fletch."

On the drive home, I don't have much to say. I try to wrap my mind around what Ace has done, searching for some valid, reasonable explanation, but there is none. Fear? Had they actually done something to Ace? The threat of violence would have been enough for Ace. I think back to London, turning Ace down flat. If I'd agreed to help, we might still have run up against Navarro. Maybe, but it could have been avoided. I would have handled things differently. But now there's no turning back.

Fletcher lets me alone till we're almost home. "You could just leave, you know. Get on the next plane out of here."

"Yeah, I could, but then what? They might come after you. And what about the gig?"

Fletcher stops for a red light and turns to look at me. "The gig? I know Dexter Gordon said playing bebop was a life-or-death thing, but he didn't mean something like this." He drives on. "Maybe Darren is right. Maybe they are bluffing."

Who could I call and ask to wire me $23,000? I don't want to pay them twenty-three cents. Then I flash on something else—bank inquiries. "I could call their bluff."

"Huh?" Fletcher turns into a parking lot near the waterfront and turns off the engine. "Man, we got to talk about this shit." We get out of the car and walk to the edge of the pier. We both light cigarettes and watch two cargo ships docked and a crew of longshoremen busy unloading with cranes and dollies. The work lights cast long shadows over the dock.

What had de Hass said? *For obvious reasons, I can't make inquiries about bank records.* "You have any banker friends here?"

Fletcher looks at me and squints. "I got a couple of accounts, I have some money wired back to a bank in the States occasionally. Why?"

"Anybody at the bank owe you a favor, or would do you one?"

Fletcher considers. "Maybe, long as it wasn't illegal. One guy is a big fan, kind of took a liking to me. Why?"

"It's not exactly illegal, just sort of stretching things." I lay it out for Fletcher then, improvising as I go, thoughts, possibilities, choices coming fast, flooding my mind. "What do you think?"

Fletcher takes it all in and grins. "Hell, it just might work. They might buy it. I'll call him in the morning."

"If it does, then I have to make a quick trip back to the States."

"Well, make it fast. The man told me tonight, we got a weekend off, then we're good for three months at the Baby Grand if we want it." Fletcher turns and grins at me and holds out his palm. I slap it.

Three months. Not many jazz gigs like that. "I'll be ready," I say.

Fletcher's smile fades then. "Hey, man, I'm sorry about your friend."

"You know?"

"I guessed, from what you told me about him."

"It's just something I have to do, Fletch, but I'll be back."

Fletcher grins again. "Hey, I'm not worried. You ain't going to pass up a chance to play again with Fletcher Paige."

"No, I'm not."

We get back in the car and continue home. Fletcher turns into the parking place by the canal, but neither of us makes any move to get out of the car. We watch a small boat, its running lights reflected in the canal, move by slowly under the bridge.

It's a long time before he says anything. "You know how Chet died too, don't you?"

"Yes, I think I do."

Wednesday, May 10, 1988, Rotterdam

The Alfa Romeo, lost again. Wandering around in the night, his teeth hurting, his heart hurting, thinking maybe it's time to go home for a while, to Oklahoma, see his family, his friends. Diane is gone too. At the police station again, he calls his agent.

"Stay there, Chet," he says. "I'll have someone pick you up. I have a place for you to stay until the concert Friday."

"Okay," Chet says. He hangs up and waits outside, pacing, feeling the itch, thinking he'd like to play. When the car comes, the agent's friend introduces himself, asks Chet what he wants to do.

"I need something," Chet says.

"I will try," the man says. They go to the house. There's another man there Chet thinks he knows. They talk, but Chet is restless, craving, waiting for some word, but none comes. Chet wants to play, so they all go down to the Dizzy Jazz Café and go inside. Nobody notices as he walks in, his horn under his arm.

Bad Circuits is playing, a kind of fusion group, but the pianist is good, Chet decides after listening for a few minutes. Chet floats to the bandstand like an apparition, unaware of how bad he looks. He suddenly appears next to the pianist but doesn't register the surprise on the young musician's face as he recognizes Chet. "Do you mind?" Chet asks.

The pianist says, "No, please." He glances at the bassist and drummer, who have also become aware of Chet's quiet presence.

They play two tunes. On the second, "Green Dolphin Street," the pianist is nervous—this is Chet Baker—but devotes himself to comping for Chet. It doesn't help—Chet has no strength. The notes he tries for elude him, and he plays so quietly, the drummer strains to hear. The saxophonist is unimpressed. It just isn't happening. He takes the horn from his lips, smiles his thanks to the pianist, and disappears as quickly as he came, shaking his head, stuffing the horn back in its bag. He knows the tune so well, but tonight it's like a stranger.

"I'll see you back at the house," he tells his two companions. They know it's useless to try to talk him out of it. Outside again, he stands quietly, unsure of what to do next. He wanders some more, then finds himself in a coffeehouse, thinking he must get back to Amsterdam, score, get straight, get ready for the concert with—did the agent say Archie Shepp?

Thursday, May 12, 1988, Amsterdam

It's late afternoon when he gets off the train and makes his way through Central Station. He'd slept through most of the day in Rotterdam, but he can't make it anymore. Tonight with Archie Shepp—but he has to find a connection first, then a hotel. He heads for Zeedijk, makes a buy, then hears that someone is looking for him, someone he should avoid unless he has money. He can't remember who it is. All he cares about now is to get to a hotel and fix.

He tries the usual haunts, but it's busy everywhere—some holiday, he's told—and all the hotels are full. Finally, near Central Station, traffic whizzing by, trams bearing down on him, he tries the Prins Hendrik. Yes, there is a room available, on the second floor.

He checks in, fixes; finally there is relief on this very warm evening, the mix of cocaine and heroin taking away the awful craving. He makes some calls and leaves for the Old Quarter, wanders around the Dam Square, feeling the warmth of the drugs as the sun sets on Amsterdam.

Back in the room, he smokes, dials numbers, turns on the television, and watches darkness settle over the city. He plays a little, gets the window open after a struggle and sits on the ledge, watching below, leans out to glimpse the canal, smiling and waving at a young girl on a bicycle, but she doesn't wave back, doesn't see him. Seeing the girl makes him think about Diane, all the hurt he's feeling, wondering how much longer he can play with the dentures.

He should call the promoter, let them know where he is. There's the concert with Archie Shepp. They'll be waiting, but it's slipped his mind, and there's time. There's always time, but it's so dark now, way after midnight.

He's lost all track of time, and now it's Friday the thirteenth. He hears nothing, but then he's leaning more, starting to nod off. It isn't supposed to be like this.

Did he hear something behind him, feel something pushing him, a voice, or was it all in his mind?

Then, suddenly, it makes no difference. He's flying, the cobblestone alleyway rushing up to meet him.

15

'M UP early, way too early for Fletcher. I slip out the door and just walk until I find a café, sit down outside with a large mug of coffee, and think about going to San Francisco. I could write Ace a letter, tell him that I know everything, end it like that, save myself money and the trouble of a trip, but I know I won't. This is something I have to do in person. I want to see his face, hear what he says when I confront him.

I sit there for nearly an hour, going over conversations in my mind, trying to rationalize, make excuses, come up with some acceptable explanation, but none of them work. There is only one way to do this, one way to close it down for me, answer all the questions I have, including the big one. I have to hear Ace Buffington say why. I pay my check and head for the Old Quarter. There are other things to do first.

I don't expect to find Inspector Dekker at the police station on Saturday, so I'm surprised to catch him coming out of the station in casual civilian clothes as I round the corner. He's carrying some file folders under his arm and seems in a hurry, like a man on a mission.

I call to him from across the street. "Inspector Dekker."

He wheels around, and his face drops as he sees it's me. "Ah, my favorite visitor to Amsterdam. Please tell me this meeting is an accident."

"Well, not quite," I say. "If I hadn't caught you, I would have tried to find you at home. Let me buy you breakfast. It's important. Please."

Dekker sighs, sees there is no escape. "When is it not with you, Mr. Horne? Very well, but I've promised my wife a day in the country, so I haven't much time."

"Great, thanks." I point to a nearby café. "How about there?"

"Fine," Dekker says, and walks along with me.

We order coffee and breakfast. While we're waiting, I give Dekker a short, heavily edited version of my meeting with van Gogh and the two drug dealers and what I've found out. I leave out de Hass's demand and threat if I don't come through.

Dekker is incredulous. "But how?" he says. He leans back in his chair and studies me. "No, never mind. I don't want to know."

"Let's just say I made some contacts. The older man's name is Navarro. He didn't actually talk to me, but his partner did. His name is de Hass."

"Navarro . . . Navarro." Dekker stares out the window, trying to dredge up the name. "Yes, I know the name, but he's been inactive for a long time. We have a file on him. De Hass I certainly know. He stays in the background for the most part. He is right, however. It's impossible to make any charges against him, since your friend has left Amsterdam."

"I know. I'm not concerned with that now. What I want is to confirm that my friend has really left Amsterdam. I'd feel better if I knew for sure."

The waiter brings our order, and Dekker dives into toast and eggs. "I see," he says. "Let me guess. You want me to make an official inquiry with the airlines to confirm that your friend was on a flight to America."

I smile at Dekker. "You've a very good detective. I'd appreciate it. They wouldn't tell me. Otherwise I wouldn't bother you."

Dekker just mumbles and wolfs down the toast and eggs. He puts his plate aside and studies me as if I'm an abstract painting he's trying to decipher.

"Mr. Horne, you are truly quite amazing."

"No, not really. Just persistent and sometimes lucky."

"I won't argue with that," Dekker says. "I think you missed your calling. Very well. Anything else?"

"Well, actually, yes. I'm sure de Hass is responsible for the prostitute's beating."

"Yes?" Dekker says, his interest intent now.

"How is she?"

"Her friends tell me she will be fine. She's going home tomorrow."

"Good. I'm not the only one who'll be relieved to hear that. I'm meeting with de Hass again." Dekker starts to protest, but I push on. "In broad daylight, in a very public place. If you were to be there as well, it might discourage him, perhaps make him a little more wary, bring him out of the background." It would also make me a lot more comfortable to have Dekker along. I can't risk telling him everything—he'd stop me in a second—but this he might go for.

"And what is this public place?"

"A bank."

"A bank," Dekker says. "I'm sure there is more to it than you're telling me, but . . ." He shakes his head for a moment, thinking. "I must be out of my mind," he says. "When?"

"Monday morning, if it all works out. I'll call you."

Dekker nods and pushes his plate aside.

"There's one other thing."

"I'm not sure I want to hear it," Dekker says. "I'm an old man, Mr. Horne. My heart."

"Oh, this is easy. I'd like to have the portfolio. I want to return it to my friend in person."

Dekker frowns. "You're going to see him? I can understand your feelings, but what will it accomplish? I know you have strong suspicions, but are you sure that—"

"Yes, there's no mistake. It may not accomplish anything, but it's something I have to do."

Dekker's expression changes then. "I'm truly sorry, Mr. Horne. As I told you the first time we met, friends sometimes do strange things."

"Yes, I guess you were right." I look away and wonder why it had to be Ace.

He wipes his mouth with a napkin. "Well, I must go," Dekker says. "What was the name of that place where you are performing?"

"The Baby Grand."

"Yes. I have the portfolio at home. Suppose I bring it to you this evening. Frankly, I'll be glad to see the back of it."

"Thank you, Inspector. I appreciate it. Then I'll be out of your hair for good."

"No," Dekker says. "That will only be when you leave Amsterdam."

Fletcher is just signing off on his computer when I get back to the flat. "I sent an e-mail to Margo," he says. "If she's around, she should answer soon. I'll keep checking." He picks up his horn and snaps it on the chain around his neck. "I want to try a couple of tunes if you've got time."

"Sure."

"I want to do 'Lament.' You know it?"

Perfect for Fletch, I think. Beautiful tune by J. J. Johnson. "Yes, I think so."

"Well, let's go find out." We go into the living room, and I sit down at the piano, remembering the changes, playing through them quickly. Fletcher starts on the pickup melody notes, but before I can play the first chord, there's a knock on the door.

"Damn," he says, and goes to answer it.

I hear Darren's voice, and Fletcher's, but more friendly than I've ever heard him with the young black man. "Hey, man, come on in."

They come back to the living room, joking around like old buddies. Darren nods at me and hands me a slip of paper with flight information. "Best I could do, man, on such short notice."

I look at it. Amsterdam to San Francisco. Much less than I expected to pay, and sooner than I thought possible. Monday afternoon.

"Hey, thanks, Darren. This is great."

"Nothin', man. Now you do me a favor."

"Sure. What?"

He glances at Fletch. "Show me how you knew what that song was—'Oleo,' you said it was—by just listening to van Gogh tap it out on that drum pad thing he was beating on."

Fletcher looks at me. "What the hell is he talking about?"

I laugh. "The old drummer I told you about. He was tapping out rhythms, seeing if I knew what tune he was thinking of. Darren wants to know the secret."

"Ah," Fletcher says. He puts the horn in his mouth and blows the first eight bars of "Oleo" while I tap out the rhythm with my hands on top of the piano. It's a very jagged, syncopated line that lends itself to catching the tune from just the rhythm, a jam session tune that most musicians know. Darren watches and listens to Fletch's horn and my tapping, but still looks puzzled.

"You got that from just the rhythm?"

"Well, it was a lucky guess."

"Oh, no," Fletcher says to Darren. "This cat has some ears."

"Dig it," Darren says. He looks at Fletcher more seriously now. "Look here, okay if I listen to you rehearse?"

"Well, sure," Fletcher says, a bit surprised. "I thought you liked that hip-hop rap shit." He looks at me and raises his eyebrows. Might be hope for this boy yet, his expression says.

We go over two other ballads besides "Lament," and one jump tune I don't know, something Fletcher says he played with Basie called "Moten Swing." I'd heard it, but never played it.

"Just lay waaay back," Fletcher says. "Basie style, smack on the beat, almost behind, like you're Benny Moten, just sauntering down Vine Street in Kansas City."

I follow his lead but find it's difficult. I play on the top of the beat, edgy, so it takes some adjusting. It almost feels like we're dragging the tempo.

"There," Fletcher says, "now you got it," as we go through it for the third time. He laughs then. "We had a sub trombone player for a week once, cat from Maynard Ferguson's band. Now, you know how frantic Maynard plays. This cat was already to letter C before we got out of the first eight bars. We had to cool him out."

I laugh and think every time Fletcher tells a story like that, I'm reminded of who I'm playing with and how lucky I am to be with him. It's like joining the Giants as a rookie and looking to your left and seeing Willie Mays giving you the thumbs-up sign.

Darren applauds our efforts and stands up to go. "I'll be by tonight," he says.

"All right," says Fletcher. "I'll be looking for you."

When he goes, Fletcher says, "You know, he's a good kid."

We get some lunch then, and after we clean up the dishes, Fletcher checks his e-mail.

"Here we go," he says. "Margo must be up late." I read over his shoulder.

Hi Darlin,

I got a couple of nights at a pizza joint, and yes there's some professor called me, trying to get me to sit down and talk about Chet. I put him off but guess I will talk to him. Seems like a nice guy. You know him? Hope your gig is going well and glad to hear you found a piano player you like. You are soooo picky.

Bye Sugar.

"Well, there's your answer," Fletcher says. "Ace has landed." He closes the screen and shuts down the computer. "Yeah, there's my answer."

I spent Sunday going over the bank scheme with Fletcher— bouncing ideas off him, trying to anticipate the unexpected— until we were both mentally exhausted. By the time Fletcher called the banker friend, I was having second thoughts and doubts about the whole thing. What if de Hass didn't show up? What if he saw through the entire scheme or wasn't satisfied I'd made enough of an effort? It could all blow up in my face.

I listened to Fletcher turn on the charm while I paced around the living room, wanting it all to be over. Finally, when I couldn't stand the suspense any longer, I went for a walk. When I came back, I could tell from Fletcher's tired smile he'd pulled it off, but he looked totally wrung out. I heaved a great sigh of relief and listened to Fletcher recount his conversation. The banker friend had been reluctant at first, but in the end, he caved in under Fletcher's persuasiveness, the promise of some rare records, and unlimited guest privileges for the length of our stay at the Baby Grand.

"This shit's gonna cost me," Fletcher said, "but Hoke Moseley would be proud." He got up then and headed for his room. "Even if they do find Glenn Miller, don't call me."

As soon as his door shut, I punched the air and said, "Yes!" I made a quick trip to the coffee shop to leave word for de Hass with the bartender. I described him, but I really didn't have to—the bartender knew who I was talking about.

"Just tell him Evan Horne said Credit Banc of Netherlands at ten tomorrow morning."

He had just nodded and wiped down the bar like he didn't want to know any more.

I called Dekker, left him the same message, grabbed some dinner, came back to the flat, and fell into bed, hoping my mind would turn off till morning.

But now, as I walk into the bank, the reality of the situation hits me, and all my doubts return. There's no sign of Inspector Dekker yet, but the bank is already humming. People are in line for the teller windows, filling out forms; voices and footsteps echo on the marble floors up to high ceilings; and sunlight streams through the plate-glass windows of the old building.

When I ask for Mr. van Lier, I'm directed to a desk off to the side in a kind of bullpen area reserved for bank officers. Van Lier joins me and sits down. He has wavy gray hair and tortoiseshell glasses and is dressed in a three-piece suit, with a pocket watch on a chain, which he checks several times. He couldn't look more respectable or official.

"Mr. Horne?"

"Evan, yes. Fletcher Paige said everything is in order."

Van Lier looks around a bit nervously. "Yes, it's very irregular, but I believe you will find this satisfactory." He opens his desk drawer and hands me two sheets of paper. I look at them and see dates, amounts, some embossed bank stamps, and the magic name. Everything else is in Dutch, and it looks official as hell.

"All you have to do is just confirm what I say," I tell van Lier. "I really appreciate this."

"Is he coming soon?"

"Yes, any minute."

Van Lier swallows and checks his watch again. He probably hasn't had one of Amsterdam's major drug dealers at his desk—at least, not that he knows. "Would you like some coffee?"

"Yes, please."

He gets up and goes to the back just as the doors swing open. De Hass strides in, dressed in a suit and tie, looking like any prosperous merchant, and Dekker is right behind him. They both spot me and come over, glancing at each other when they realize they're headed for the same desk. They sit down on either side of me in front of van Lier's desk.

"I don't like to be summoned," de Hass says to me, leaning closer. "Who is this?" He glances at Dekker, who looks back, but there's no recognition in either of their faces.

"I'll introduce you in a minute. How else was I supposed to contact you?"

Before he can answer, van Lier comes back, carrying two coffees. When he sees my companions, he almost drops them.

"Here you are," he says, setting them on the desk. He pulls up his chair, and I lean forward slightly. Time to go to work.

"Mr. van Lier, this is Mr. . . . I'm sorry, I've forgotten your name," I say for Dekker's benefit.

De Hass glares for a moment but recovers quickly. "De Hass. Edward de Hass."

"Yes, that's it. And this," I say, gesturing to my right, "is Inspector Dekker of the Amsterdam Police."

It's almost worth all the trouble just to see the expression on de Hass's face. He shifts in his chair and suddenly becomes fascinated with the floor. Dekker nods at van Lier and stares at de Hass while I press on.

"I've explained to Mr. van Lier that I'm acting on behalf of the Baker family, and that we simply want to confirm that the account in question has been inactive for several years, and that any claim on that account, by any creditor, would have to be examined. I've cooperated fully with the police, since the account holder was not Dutch, and they have been very helpful in tracking down information."

"Yes," de Hass says. "My company is appreciative of that." He smiles at van Lier, one businessman to another, but avoids looking at Dekker.

"Certainly," van Lier says. He produces the two sheets and

hands them to de Hass. "It's a very old account, so I've taken the liberty of checking our records and made a printout of the last transactions."

De Hass takes the sheets. He reaches inside his coat for his glasses and examines the documents van Lier has created out of thin air. He's close enough for me to see the papers. Van Lier has made it look good; Chesney Henry Baker's name appears at the top, then a series of numbers, the account identification. The second sheet is a notice of some kind. De Hass examines and reads through each very carefully.

"I'm sorry, I don't read Dutch. What does it say?" I ask de Hass.

He glances up at me. "The account has been closed due to inactivity. The balance was used for bank charges."

"Yes, that's correct," van Lier says. "As you can see, it's been more than ten years."

De Hass looks up. "And there are no other accounts?"

"No," van Lier says. "I did a complete search of our records." He steals a glance at me for approval of his improvising.

"I see," de Hass says. "This is very disappointing."

I hold up my hands and smile. "Sorry."

"May I keep these, for our company records?" de Hass says.

"Of course," van Lier says. "Those are copies."

"Well, thank you." De Hass stands up and shakes hands with van Lier, ignoring me and Dekker. He says something to van Lier in Dutch. The banker answers and smiles.

We get up, and I walk de Hass to the door, leaving Dekker and van Lier to compare notes. "Well, I found it, but that's all there is."

"Yes, very disappointing. Some advice to you, Mr. Horne."

"Yes?"

"Stick to music. It's much safer."

I put my hand on his arm. "Now here's some advice for you. You bother me or anyone I know, and Inspector Dekker over there will be on you so fast you won't know what hit you."

I hold de Hass's gaze for a moment. "And that will be much safer for you."

He doesn't say anything, just stares back at me, then glances over his shoulder at Dekker and van Lier, who are still talking. He pushes the large glass door open then and walks out, clutching the papers.

I turn back toward van Lier's desk. He's still standing, watching. I walk over but don't sit down. "What did he say to you—in Dutch, I mean?"

Van Lier smiles. "He said he doesn't like dealing with Americans."

Out of the corner of my eye, I catch de Hass. He's stopped in front of the large window by van Lier's desk, looking in at us.

"Don't look now, but we're being watched. Keep smiling and shake my hand," I say. When I look again, de Hass is gone. "You did fine. Fletcher and I both thank you."

"Yes, I did, didn't I," van Lier says. "It was rather exciting."

"You don't know how exciting. Thank you again."

Dekker follows me to the door. "Mr. Horne, I . . . I . . ." He can't finish the sentence. He turns and walks out, and I breathe a huge sigh of relief.

I'd packed the night before, so I'd planned to just come back, get my bag, and get a taxi to the airport. I hear Fletcher's horn, but the minute I open the door, he comes flying out.

"Well? How did it go?"

"Like clockwork. I don't think we have to worry about de Hass."

Fletcher holds out his palm for me to slap, then does his little dance. "Well, come on. I have to take you to the airport," he says.

"Oh, you don't have to do that. I can take a taxi."

"No big thing, man. I'll take you. I want to hear all the details."

We share a cup of coffee, then Fletcher goes off to get dressed. There's some minor tension in the air. I know Fletcher hates to see me go and is afraid I might not come back.

I put my hand on his shoulder. "Fletch, don't worry. I always make the gig."

He smiles. "Okay. Give me ten minutes," he says.

"Sure, we got time."

I get the rest of my things together—one small carry-on bag and Ace's portfolio. I pause at the piano, hope I'm going to see this old upright again soon, and play the first eight bars of "Oleo."

"You ready?" Fletcher says.

It's nearly an hour's ride to Schipol Airport. I give Fletch a complete rundown of the bank scene and have him laughing most of the way. When we pull in to departures, he stops the car. "I'm not going in," Fletcher says. I get my bag out of the back, and he comes around.

He holds out his hand. "Get this over with quick, and let me know when you've got a return flight. I'll pick you up."

"Thanks, Fletch. See you in a few days."

"I hope so," he says. "We've got some music to play."

I watch him drive off, then go inside to check in. Darren has gotten me a window seat, and I plan to kill time by sleeping as much as possible on the long flight—over ten hours, and that puts me into San Francisco in midafternoon.

I spend the flight enduring two movies, three meals, and two snacks but no cigarette. Instead, I get up periodically and walk the aisles. I drink coffee, pick at the meals, try to read, but keep seeing the same words over and over. I even skim through the articles in the portfolio again, thinking that this is what started it all.

When the films run, I get some headphones but doze through most of them, not even sure what I'm watching. Finally I give up altogether and fall asleep the rest of the way until I hear the pilot tell us we're on the final approach to San Francisco. It seems to take forever to clear customs and passport control, but eventually I'm standing outside, breathing in San Francisco's cool spring air and having my first cigarette in thirteen hours. Maybe I could quit.

Shaking off the jet lag, I go back into the terminal and call Coop from a pay phone. "Hey, Coop, you just lounging around eating doughnuts?"

"Evan? Hey, where are you?"

"San Francisco. Got a little business up here, then I'm heading back to Amsterdam." I fill him in on Fletcher, the upcoming gig, and my beef with Ace. "He sold me out, Coop."

"Are you sure? Doesn't sound like Ace."

"Oh, I'm sure. Just have to tie up some loose ends and let him know where we stand."

There's some silence on both ends as we think about it. I take a deep breath then.

"Coop, you have a number for Andie?"

He laughs. "I knew you were going to call one of them. Just didn't know which one. My money was on Natalie. Frankly, I'm surprised."

"Yeah, well, so am I."

"Hang on a minute." While he's away, I tell myself this may be a dumb thing to do, but that's never stopped me before, and it's something else I have to do. When Coop comes back, he says, "Okay. Got a pager number, that's all."

Yes, I think, maybe she'll be too busy to answer. But I write it down in my book. "Thanks, Coop. On the way back maybe I'll stop through L.A."

"I doubt it. Hey, don't be too hard on Ace."

"Bye, Coop."

I hang up the phone and walk outside for another cigarette, watching cars and buses pulling up, dropping off, picking up, people waiting impatiently for rides, remembering when Andie and I arrived here, what now seems like ages ago. The FBI car and agents waiting for us, Andie driving us into San Francisco, the Travelodge, the unlocked door.

Then I go back in and dial Andie's pager, punch in the

numbers of the pay phone, and wait. I decide to give it fifteen minutes, but it takes only five for the phone to ring. I let it go. Two, three rings, then pick it up.

"Lawrence." Strong, businesslike voice, probably annoyed at interrupting whatever she's doing, wondering what somebody wants on a Monday afternoon.

"I thought all you agents were special?"

"Oh, my God—Evan?"

"Yes, how are you?"

"Where are you?"

"SFO. Just flew in from Amsterdam. I've got some business here, and—"

"Are you free? Can I see you? Oh, my God."

"Well, sure, I guess that's why I'm calling."

"I live fairly close to the airport. I'll pick you up. What airline?"

I tell her, and she says she can be there in thirty minutes. "Evan, I'm so glad you called. I'll be there as fast as I can."

"So am I," I say, but she's already gone.

While I'm waiting for Andie, I arrange for a rental car, to be picked up tomorrow morning. I take a map they give me and go outside, find a seat on one of the concrete benches, and study my route to Margo Highland's home in Monte Rio, north of San Francisco. Maybe a two-hour drive, it looks like. I just hope Ace is not gone already.

In a little less than thirty minutes, Andie's car skids to a stop. She jumps out, waves off one of the security guards, and ignores the "This is a loading zone only" announcement over the PA system.

"I can't believe it," she says, running over as I stand up. She gives me a big hug, and we both look at each other. She's in jeans, sweatshirt, and tennis shoes. Her hair is a bit longer than I remember, and she looks great. "Come on, let's get out of here." She takes hold of my arm and walks me to her car. I throw my bag in the back as the parking security guy comes over to lecture Andie for leaving her car unattended. She digs in her purse and flashes him her FBI badge. "Back off."

He stops in his tracks, glances at me, and puts his hands up. "Hey, no problem," he says, and backs up several steps.

Andie looks at me and smiles. "Hey, it comes in handy sometimes."

We get in the car, and Andie roars off.

On the drive from the airport, Andie keeps stealing glances at me, making small talk but avoiding any serious questions, as if she isn't sure where to begin. I don't either, and for a minute, I wonder if this isn't a mistake. We try to overcome the awkwardness, but it's going to take a while. I briefly go over the past few months and try to get her talking.

"So how long have you been in San Francisco?"

"Since right after L.A.," Andie says. "I wanted a transfer and to get away from profiling for a while after . . . So this came up, and I jumped at it."

"What are you doing now?"

"Bank robbery detail."

At a stoplight, her elbow on the door, she rests her head on her hand and looks at me. "So how are you, really?"

"I'm okay. I talked to a shrink in New York, one of your people. She was good, talked me through a lot of things."

Andie is nodding, still looking at me, when the light changes. The car behind us honks. She glares into the rearview mirror and stomps the accelerator.

"Andie, I haven't called or talked to Natalie since I left."

I watch her face relax. "I didn't want to ask," she says. "I was afraid to."

"I know."

She makes a sharp right up a steep incline, pulls into the driveway of a small apartment complex, and parks. "Are you hungry?"

"As long as it's not on an airline tray. What I really want is a hot shower."

"Okay. I'll run out and get a few things and throw something together here. You can shower and take a nap."

"I'm not going to argue with that."

We go inside, and she shows me around. I recognize some of the things from her L.A. apartment—the books, prints, and the ever-present laptop on her desk. "Not much of an improvement, huh?" she says.

"I imagine you don't spend much time here anyway."

"More than you think. Well, towels are in the bathroom, then take your pick, bed or couch. I'll be back soon. Make yourself at home."

The minute she's out the door, I strip off my clothes and stand under the hot water for ten minutes, feeling it wash the jet lag away, marveling at the varieties of shampoo Andie has. I get into some jeans and a T-shirt and stretch out on the couch. I don't hear her come back, nor any of the noises she's making in the kitchen, until I open my eyes. She comes over and sits on the arm of the couch, watching TV with the sound down.

I watch her for a few minutes, glad now that I called. "Hey, how long have I been out?"

She turns and smiles. "About an hour. Feel better?"

"Yeah, I think so." I swing my legs off the couch and sit up, trying to get reoriented. "Now I'm hungry."

She stands up and goes to the kitchen. "About five minutes," she says.

I go in the bathroom, run cold water on my face, and start to feel human again. Andie is setting the table when I come out. "How about a beer?"

"Sure." I watch her bustle around the kitchen and bring the food to the table.

"Nothing special," she says. "Just some pasta and a salad."

"Sounds good." I sit down and take a long pull on the beer. Andie joins me, and we clink bottles.

"I can't believe you're sitting here," she says.

"Neither can I. My mind is still in Amsterdam."

"So are you going to tell me what this is all about?" She fixes me a healthy plate of pasta and points to a couple of bottles of salad dressing. She eats and listens; I eat and talk, telling her about Ace, the gig, and Chet Baker.

She dabs at her lips with a napkin and shakes her head. "You and dead jazz musicians. Just can't resist, huh?"

"I'm beginning to wonder. I would never have gotten into this if it weren't for Ace disappearing."

"It's going to be hard. You're old friends."

"Yes, I know."

"So, how long are you staying?" Her eyes meet mine.

"Long enough to have things out with Ace. I've got a job to go back to in Amsterdam. Then I don't know."

She doesn't comment on that, just nods and asks if I want coffee.

"Sure, and someplace to smoke."

"Right out there, although I'm tempted to let you smoke anywhere you want."

I go out on the small patio. There's a table and chairs. She brings coffee out, and we sit down.

She shifts in her chair, stands up, walks to the railing, then turns around. "I can't stand this, Evan. I want to tell you so much. If I had known where you were, I would have called, even come over there if I thought we had half a chance. I grilled Cooper, but he either didn't know or wouldn't say."

"Well, don't be too hard on him. He gave me your number."

"Yes," she says. "And you did call me." The same look is there that I remember the day we sat in a car staking out Gillian's brother, the day we talked about timing.

"It's much better now," I say.

"What?"

"The timing."

"Is it? God, I want to believe that."

"Just let it happen, Andie. Just let it happen."

Later, I look over at Andie asleep, her hair tousled on the pillow. I get up, slip on my jeans, and go out on the patio to smoke. I hear the door slide open behind me and Andie's voice.

"This isn't where you slip away, is it, leave me a note or something?"

I turn and look at her and smile. She has her robe wrapped around her. "No, wasn't planning on it."

"No regrets?"

"None."

She shivers and pulls the robe tighter. "God, you smokers will endure anything. Hurry up and finish."

"What's the rush?"

"We need to work on that timing some more."

16

ANDIE WON'T hear of me renting a car. "Take mine," she says. "I've got some time off coming and I don't need it. And besides," she says, "this way I'll get to see you again for sure."

I don't protest too much, probably for the same reason. I cancel the rental car and promise to call Andie. By late afternoon, I'm ready to go. Andie stands in the driveway waving as I pull away.

From her place, I get back on 280, heading for the city, and remember how to exit on Nineteenth Avenue, then follow the signs for the Golden Gate Bridge. I've missed most of the rush-hour traffic, but the jet lag is getting to me as I cross the bridge and continue north on 101. I see the first sign for Santa Rosa. Nearly fifty miles, and according to the map on the seat beside me, a few miles beyond that to the River Road exit.

I punch up the radio and get a San Francisco talk show for a while—anything to make the miles go faster. Then, closer to Santa Rosa, something called KJAZ, but it's all smooth—Kenny G and clones. I turn the radio off and think about what

I'm going to say to Ace. As Andie said, we've been friends a long time. How do you confront a friend when you know he's lied but want to believe him?

For one brief moment, I almost hope he's already gone, but even if he were, I know my next trip would be to Las Vegas. This can only be done in person. Plus, I want to talk to Margo as well and close the book on Chet Baker, at least for me. Something else I have to do.

There's some slowing in Santa Rosa, but finally I break free of the jam, take the River Road exit, and head west for Guerneville and the Russian River resorts. The road winds through open country, vineyards, farms, redwood groves, and past the Korbel winery as I get closer to the Russian River. The sun in my eyes fades quickly, and finally the lights of Guerneville come into view. Monte Rio is four miles farther.

I crawl through Guerneville in the slow traffic. Everything seems to be on three blocks. When I stop at a crosswalk, I look to my right, and my eye catches a "LIVE JAZZ" sign in the window of a pizza place called Main Street Station. Through the glass I can see musicians on a small stage and a singer in front of them. I think I recognize her.

I circle the block, find a parking place, and walk back. There's only a few people inside. I don't recognize any of the musicians. I go in and stand by the door, listening for a minute. Margo Highland, backed by bass, drums, and guitar, is finding her way through "Body and Soul." Fletcher was right. She does sound like a little girl who once saw something or experienced something she shouldn't have, and she does it all without a microphone. I notice then there's no bass amp, and the guitarist is playing a classical instrument. They take their acoustic music seriously at Main Street Station.

Margo finishes to light applause. The tall, white-haired drummer stands up and says, "Margo Highland, a beautiful girl for many years. She'll be back again, so I hope you stay around." He sits back down, and the trio launches into "The Peacocks." I watch Margo walk to the back and take a seat at the bar.

I follow and sit down next to her. She turns and gives me a friendly smile. I remember the pictures at her place in Amsterdam. It's easy to see she was once a model and quite beautiful. It's still there. "Margo?"

"Yes, do I know you?" Her voice is light and there's a slight accent or drawl. She leans away slightly and looks at me.

"No, but Fletcher Paige in Amsterdam told me to look you up." Her smile gets bigger.

"No way. You know Fletcher?" She stares at me for a moment. "Oh, my God, you're Evan."

"Yes, and I've been sleeping in your bed. Can I buy you a drink?"

"Well, sure. Glass of red," she says to the bartender when he comes over. "Hell, I haven't had anyone as young as you in my bed in a long time, even if I wasn't there." She laughs. "Hey, don't mind me, I'm just a crazy old Texas gal."

"I'll have a draft beer." I turn to Margo. "I'm looking for a friend of mine." As soon as the words are out of my mouth, I realize that may not be for long. "Fletch asked you about him in the e-mail. I guess he's already been here and talked with you, about Chet."

Her smile fades, and she looks around at the band. "He's a friend of yours, you say?"

"Yes, I've been trying to track him down. Is he still here?"

We both turn at a loud crash of cymbals. The drummer stands up and addresses the audience again. "Steve Weber on bass, Randy Vincent on guitar, and yours truly, Benny Barth. I hope we've enjoyed playing for you as much as you've enjoyed listening to us." Nobody really gets it, but he continues. "We're going to recharge our batteries and come back for another set."

"Benny is insane," Margo says, laughing. Then she turns back to me. "Been here? Your friend has been driving me insane, asking me about Chet. He didn't mention you much, though. Hell, I might have talked to him more then."

"No, I'm not surprised," I say.

"You want me to call him?" Margo says "I've got his number. I know he'd want to come down. He's just up in Monte
Rio."

"No, I want to surprise him," I say quickly. I don't know if
Margo really buys it, but she gives me directions to Ace's hotel.

"Just turn left by the movie theater, over the bridge, and
left again at the first street. It's about halfway down on the
river side."

"Thanks," I say, and start to go. "Hey, you sing good."

Margo smiles and nods. "Thank you, that's sweet. Come
back and sit in. That old piano has a few tunes left in it."

"Thanks, I just might do that."

I pass the Northwood golf course and start looking for the
bridge turnoff. The road winds along the river for another
mile or so; then I see the lights of Monte Rio. There's not
much to it—a nursery, a hardware store, an old church, and a
convenience store that used to sell gas. The pumps are still
there but obviously inoperative.

At the stop sign, I see the movie theater on my left. It's an
old Quonset hut of corrugated metal with a mural painted on
the side. I cross over 116 and turn left over the bridge, crossing
the Russian River for the third time. After the bridge, I make
another left and find the hotel at the bottom of a slight grade,
redwoods towering around it. I park opposite the hotel, turn off
the engine, sit quietly for a moment, and light a cigarette.

Now that I'm here, my anger at Ace rekindled, I also dread
this meeting. In the back of my mind is the faint hope that he'll
have some logical explanation, something I can rationalize and
forgive. But I know in reality that's not going to happen. Ace
lied, sent me chasing around Amsterdam, and delivered me to
a drug dealer to get himself out of trouble. Survivor instincts?
Fear? Yes, but it could have all been avoided.

I finish my cigarette, get out of the car, and walk across
the street. It's dark now, and the redwoods loom high, black

silhouettes in the star-filled night sky, the almost full moon peeking through. There's nobody at the front desk, but there is a small sign next to a bell: Ring for Service. I do and hear footsteps almost immediately.

"Yes, can I help you?" The clerk is late twenties, short hair, and an earring in his left ear. "I'm afraid we're full up."

"Oh, no, I don't want a room. Friend of mine is here, I think. Just want to surprise him. Charles Buffington."

He opens a small ledger and runs his finger down a list. "Yes, he's in number five." He points to the river side. "Just out that door and along the walkway."

"Thanks, I'll find it."

The walkway connects the two buildings and takes me along the side of the inn. I can see the lights of the bridge I just crossed up ahead. I don't have to go much farther. Outside what must be number five, I see Ace, his back to me, sitting in a deck chair, his feet propped up on the railing. He doesn't hear me or is lost in thought. When I get a little closer, I stop, look at him for a moment, then toss the portfolio. It lands with a loud smack on the wooden deck right behind his chair.

Ace jumps up as if he's been jerked by a wire.

"Hello, Ace."

He falls back in the chair, grabs the arms, then struggles to his feet again. "Evan? How did . . . what are you doing here?" He doesn't even look like the Ace I've known for years. There's an outside light, and in the shadows that play across his face, I see panic, shock, even fear.

"Surprised you, huh? I guess you thought I was still in Amsterdam. Too bad we never connected, but then you left kind of suddenly, didn't you?"

"Evan, I didn't know you'd come here, I . . . I don't know what to say. How did you know I was here?"

"Margo Highland told me. I just saw her."

He looks around, as if he's searching for an escape route, but then he shrugs, pulls up another chair. There's resigna-

tion in his movements now. "The people in these two rooms
are out, so we might as well stay out here." I ignore the chair
and lean against the rail. "Evan, I know it must seem—" He
leans forward, runs his hands over his face, and risks a glance
at me. "God, where do I start? If you're here, you know—"

"Know what, Ace?"

"Evan, I know you're probably angry. Things just . . . got
out of hand. I don't even know how, really."

"No kidding. They just happened, huh? Got out of
control?"

He looks at me again. His face is awash with guilt and
embarrassment. "You're not going to make this easy, are you?"

"Any reason why I should?" I try to restrain the impulse to
grab Ace and throw him over the rail into the Russian River.
Instead I light a cigarette and glare as darkness settles over
the river. "You really had me going, Ace. I got involved with
the police and ran all over Amsterdam looking for you. Man,
don't you get it? I thought you were missing, really in trouble.
Do you understand that?"

"Yes, yes, I do," Ace says. "And I was in trouble." His
voice is quiet, but it sounds loud in the stillness of the river
and the redwoods. A beautiful setting wasted on this ugly
confrontation.

"I want to know why, Ace."

"First, you have to know how disappointed I was when
you turned me down in London."

"I had good reason. You know that."

"I know, I know. But when I got to Amsterdam, I ran into
problems almost immediately. I didn't have any contact for
musicians. I had this portfolio full of notes and ideas but no
way to follow through on them. I got lucky in getting the
room Baker stayed in, I visited the Jazz Archives, saw that
film. Then . . ." His voice trails off.

"Yeah? Then what?"

"I don't know, I still thought, hoped, there was a chance
you might change your mind, become intrigued yourself." I

look away, at the river, see cars crossing the bridge, and realize I'm looking for a canal. "I didn't know you'd be staying at
the same hotel. When you did, I knew you'd at least see the
plaque, maybe even stay in that room yourself."

"That was sheer accident. The promoter booked me
there. I didn't connect it as your hotel until I got there. When
they told me you'd checked out and didn't leave any word,
yes, I was intrigued and puzzled. I looked in the room, found
your portfolio—but you were counting on that, weren't you?"

Ace shrugs. He pushes back in the chair, scraping it on
the deck, trying to put more distance between us. "A joke that
got out of hand. If you didn't find it, well, I was just going to
go back and get it."

"But I did find it, and you knew I'd think it even more
strange that you'd left it. You knew I wouldn't think it was an
accident."

"Yes, it kind of backfired, the whole thing. I decided to
play it out, leave that note at the archives, see if you followed
up, and of course you did."

I lean in closer, see his eyes darting everywhere. "You used
me, Ace, to do your research for you by making me think
something had happened to you. You knew I'd go looking for
you, and to do that I'd have to retrace your steps. Looking for
Chet Baker to find you."

"No, it wasn't like that. I checked back with the archives—that girl, Helen, she told me you'd picked up the
note. After that de Hass went in my place. I know I should
have just stopped it right then, but I didn't know how I could
just show up at your room and say, Hi, wasn't that a funny
one? I tried to get in your room while the maid was cleaning,
but she caught me, wouldn't let me look around. I'd already
copied all the articles and notes, so I wasn't worried about
this." He picks up the portfolio. "After I saw the film, I decided to just follow the chronology of Chet's last days. You
know, go to Rotterdam, those other clubs, try to account for
the missing time." He pauses and shakes his head. "I guess I

talked too much, asked too many questions, and that's when I met the guy de Hass. After that, well, he ran everything. Checked me into that other hotel and—"

I snatch the portfolio out of his hands. "In the meantime, I reported you missing to the police and got into trouble with them for withholding the information that I had the portfolio, at least for a while." I throw it down on the deck again. The sound is like a shot, and Ace jumps. "I called UNLV, your house. I even had Danny Cooper checking on you."

"I know, I know, it just . . . escalated until I couldn't stop it. I thought I had an in to talk with Chet's dealer, something I could use for the book, and then—"

"Before that, Ace, you could have stopped it anytime you wanted. All you had to do was show up and tell me you were not missing. Jesus, what else did you think I'd do?" I walk away a few steps, then turn around. "The police found your jacket, the portfolio. I was expecting them to find your body next." I drop my cigarette on the deck and step on it.

Ace shakes his head. "I know, that was the stupid part. You know, I've never smoked pot in my life, and here was a chance to really satisfy my curiosity. God, it hit me hard. I got out of there, left the jacket in the booth, I guess. I had no idea anybody would turn it in. I didn't even remember leaving it there."

"No, Ace, that wasn't the stupid part. Letting me think you were missing was the stupid part."

He takes another deep breath. "You think I don't know that? I don't have any logical explanation that would make you understand or satisfy you. All the advance research I did, and I still didn't have anything good enough to interest a book editor. I needed more. I didn't want to go home empty-handed." He looks up at me. "I'm sorry, Evan, I'm really sorry."

I don't say anything for a moment. I just stare at him. I want to forgive, say everything is okay, but I can't. "I'm sure you are, Ace, but that's not good enough."

"I know it's not, but it's like when you haven't called

someone for a long time. The more time passes, the more embarrassed you are to call, and it just goes on. Then de Hass and that other guy were pushing, threatening me." He looks up at me, his eyes pleading. "I was scared, Evan. I didn't know what they were going to do."

"They wouldn't have known about me unless you told them." My voice is louder now, echoing in the quiet of the river. "Where did you get the idea there was money, anyway?"

He shrugs again. "I don't know. There were rumors that Chet had opened bank accounts and forgotten about them."

"You told de Hass that?"

"Yes, what else was I going to do? I was scared, I just wanted to get out of there then. Can you understand that?"

"Yes. Thanks to you, I met Navarro and de Hass. Those aren't people to play around with. So what did you think was going to happen to me once you'd given me up?"

"I don't know. I didn't think, I guess."

"No, you didn't. The moron who stole the portfolio back from my room stopped on the way to visit one of the prostitutes. He left it there, and she turned it in to the police. When he want back for it, he beat her up."

A kind of moan comes out of Ace. "Oh, God," he says, wringing his hands, shaking his head. He gets up, walks to the railing, and leans over. For a minute I think he's going to be sick. "I didn't know, Evan, I really didn't. Is she all right?"

"She got it pretty bad, Ace," I said quietly.

His face is full of anguish now; the words spill out faster and faster. "I didn't know what to do. By then the police were involved, and I got nowhere on my own. De Hass forced me to keep track of you until he was finally convinced I didn't know anything about money. They let me go then, thank God. I didn't know, well, I should have known, I guess, you'd track them down. I admit it, Evan, I was damn scared. Coming here was a last resort. I was going to talk to Margo, piece things together, and hope I could get enough to satisfy the publisher."

"Goddammit, what were you going to tell me? Jesus, I can't

believe you're still thinking about a publisher." I walk away for a minute, clenching and unclenching my fists. When I turn back, Ace is still standing there, staring out at the river.

Then we hear footsteps coming along the walkway. It's the desk clerk. "Everything all right here?" he asks. I know what he sees. Me standing in front of Ace, tensed. Ace cowering against the railing.

"Yeah, we're fine," I say, to the clerk. "Don't worry about it."

He's not sure, but he retreats back to the office. I lower my voice and move closer to Ace till I can almost hear his breathing. "Margo doesn't know that much, Ace. Nobody does."

He looks up at me. "But you do."

"You really want to know?"

"I'm ashamed to say it, but yes, I do."

"Chet Baker just fell out of that window. No, he was pushed. No, I'm just kidding. He was depressed and killed himself. Don't you get it, Ace? Nobody knows. That cop in the film was right. The only person who knows what happened is Chet Baker, and he's dead."

Ace watches me for a moment. "But you know, don't you?" His eyes are bright now, like a cat's in the darkness that envelops the river.

"No, Ace, I don't."

"But you must. You talked with musicians, friends, you went to Rotterdam."

"Yes, I did. I did everything I would have done if I'd agreed to help you and more. I also looked for you. But I didn't come here to tell you that. I came hoping you'd say something to make me believe you didn't betray our friendship, but you haven't, Ace."

He puts his hands up, then holds them together. "Evan, is there any way—"

I put up my hand to stop him. I take a deep breath and look away. It's like kicking a puppy. I have what I came for, but there's no satisfaction, just hollowness. "I don't know, Ace. It's going to take a long time." I walk over to the railing. "I told you in London I didn't want anything to do with your book, and I'm telling you again now. I don't want my name mentioned in any way. I want to be clear about that." Ace nods silently, keeps his head down. "But you were right about one thing. I did get intrigued. Not to help you with any book, but to satisfy my own curiosity. You knew that and used it, Ace. That's what I can't forgive."

He doesn't look at me now, but sits, shoulders hunched, head down. Suddenly, I've had enough. I just want to get away. "I hope it was worth it, Ace. I really do."

He sits down again, and his voice is quiet now. "You're not so different from me," he says.

"What?"

"You want to know just as badly as I do. It's not about a book for you, but you're just as obsessed." He looks up at me then. I feel myself tense again. It's all I can do not to slap him across the face. I see him steel himself and I know I have to get out of here.

"Maybe you're right, Ace. Maybe I am. But there's one difference between you and me. I wouldn't want to know at your expense. You talk to Margo if you want, but I don't think she's going to be much help."

His head drops again. He doesn't even look up when I turn around and walk away. I glance back once. He's still slumped in the chair, staring out at the river.

I sit in the car for a few minutes, thinking about what Ace said. Maybe he was right. Maybe we are no different. If Ace was wrong, then I would simply drive back to San Francisco, but I know even as the thought crosses my mind that I'm not going to do that, leave this unfinished. I can't still this feeling until I know. I looked for Ace, and now I'm looking for Chet Baker, the answer to one last little nagging question. The money.

Fletcher's guess was a good one, and when I'd checked the list of donors who contributed to the plaque and sculpture, I was sure of it. Helen at the archives said the biggest amount came from an anonymous source, someone who adamantly stipulated that as a condition of their contribution. I know who it is now, but I want to hear it directly from the source too.

I drive back to Main Street Station just as things are breaking up. Margo Highland, a stack of music under her arm, is just getting to her car when I pull up.

"Margo, wait a minute."

She turns toward me. "Oh, hi. Did you find your friend?"

"Yes, I did."

She laughs. "I bet he was surprised."

"Margo, I need to talk to you about Chet."

Her face darkens for a moment. She shifts the music from one arm to another, and I see her car keys in her hand. "Chet?"

"Yes, it won't take long, but I need to talk."

Her head drops for a moment, then she looks up at me. "You know, don't you?"

"Yes, I think I do."

She sighs as if a weight has been lifted off her shoulders. "All right, I guess it's time I told somebody. We'll go to my place. It's not far—you can follow me."

We drive back the way I've just come, through Monte Rio and over the bridge again, but this time we go to the right, past a small market and opposite the Pink Elephant bar. There's a group outside that looks like they've moved straight from Haight-Ashbury to Monte Rio, several men and a couple of women standing outside the bar, talking, smoking, joking loudly with each other while loud music streams out onto the street.

At the corner, Margo slows. I follow her as she turns right and goes down a mile or so, then takes a turn off and down another smaller road to her house, nestled in the trees with other similar dwellings. Three or four cats stir on the porch, and inside we're greeted by a small white dog and two more cats. "Hello, darlin'," she says, leaning down to pet the dog.

The living room is carpeted in a dark burgundy color, and

there are heavy drapes to match. Dark wood paneling covers the walls, and the room is crowded with heavy furniture, not unlike her place in Amsterdam. She drops her things on a chair. "Make yourself at home. I'm going to make some tea. Would you like some, or a drink?"

"A drink sounds good."

"I've got some brandy, I think."

"That would be fine."

She goes off to the kitchen, and I look around the room. There's a fireplace on one wall, and on the mantel is a duplicate of the photo I'd seen in Amsterdam—Margo and Chet, sitting on a wall, probably taken right here in her backyard. She sees me looking at it when she comes back with my drink. "I can't believe that was taken almost twenty years ago," she says. She holds it up and looks at it with a sad smile, then returns it to the mantel.

"I saw it in Amsterdam," I say. "By the way, thanks again for your hospitality."

She smiles. "Oh, that was nothing. You did me a favor keeping Fletcher company. How is that old rascal?"

"He's fine, playing better than ever. We're going to do a duo gig when I get back."

"All right," she says. "You must be damn good. Fletcher is particular about piano players."

"Well, I've learned a lot from him already." There's a whistle from the kitchen.

"Oh, there's my tea. I'll be right back."

I look around some more. There's an old upright piano. I touch the keys and wonder if Chet ever played it. There's a stereo system, soft comfortable chairs, and a large sofa. I look through the CDs. On the top of the stack is one in a plain white cover with Chet's name in marker pen.

"He did that right here," Margo says from behind me. "I had a little studio in the basement then. God, what a night that was." She hands me the brandy, and I sit down on the sofa. She sits opposite me and absently strokes her dog.

"It had been raining for three days, Monte Rio was flooding, and there were a few inches of water in the studio. It's a wonder we didn't all get electrocuted. Chet could hardly stand up, but God, did he play beautifully, as always." She picks up the CD and looks at it. "I had a few copies made from the master tape. I probably should do something with it, but . . . You want to hear a little of it?"

"Yes, please." I sip the brandy and watch her at the stereo.

"Just don't pay any attention to the singer." She laughs.

The recording quality is not that good, but Chet's horn oozes feeling on "My Foolish Heart." He plays the melody line so mournfully, hearing it makes me think he believed it was the last time he would play it. Then, backing Margo, her voice younger and fuller than I'd heard at the club, he sways behind her, gently easing, nudging her through the tune. "The second track is "The Thrill Is Gone," and just as haunting.

I watch Margo listen, remembering that rainy night in Monte Rio. Her eyes well up, and she tries to cover it by patting her dog.

"He stayed right in that room," she says, pointing to a door in one corner. "He spent a lot of time up here. We had a gig at a place—it's not there anymore, just some little dive—nobody would have believed Chet Baker was playing there. But when the word got out, a lot of people came around. It was just insane. You should talk to the piano player too. Terry Henry. He was good friends with Chet."

"Did he know about the sculpture?"

"You know, I'm not sure," she says, continuing her confession, not even trying to hide anything now. She blinks her eyes, trying to clear away the tears. "Your friend told me you were something of a detective. I guess he was right. I promised I'd talk with him tomorrow. You think I should?"

"That's up to you, Margo. He's trying to write a book about Chet."

She has a faraway look in her eyes. "Nobody will be able to do that, not the real Chet, because nobody really knew him."

"But you did."

"Yes, I knew him, but . . . what he was really like I mean. Nobody will capture that."

"What about the sculpture, Margo, the money?"

She leans back in the chair and closes her eyes. "Chet got paid in cash whenever he could. Everybody knew that, but I kept telling him it was dangerous, given the people he ran with when he was trying to score. Drug dealers are drug dealers. Gawd, don't forget he nearly got killed right here in San Francisco. That was insane. Anyway, I finally got him to let me hold his money when he went to cop. He took enough to pay for whatever he needed. You know, he did get off for a while. He was in a methadone program." She shrugs. "But, when he went back to Europe, well . . ." Her voice trails off, as if she's thinking about what might have been.

"Then of course, he'd get high, disappear for days at a time sometimes, get another gig, get paid more, and the whole cycle would start again." She shakes her head. "Well, I didn't want to hold all that money, so I opened an account for him in both our names. I could hardly get him to fill out the signature card. He didn't even like to sign recording contracts."

I nod, remembering the record producer saying the same thing in the film.

"Well, it just kept mounting up, with interest, and I did some investing. He was feeling so bad after that gig in Rotterdam, that woman leaving him—"

"What woman?"

"They'd been together before, when Chet was here. He wrote her a letter before he left for Europe that last time. He never mailed it, though, and I found it. He just left it there on the desk."

She gets up and goes out of the room, returning in a minute with a sheet of paper. "Here," she says.

I skim through it, reading Chet's careful script, but several phrases jump out at me like they've been highlighted.

I wanted more than anything to make you Mrs. Chet Baker, and I know in the long run you would break my heart. . . . You can take me to the gates of heaven one day and toss me in a bottomless pit of agony the next moment. . . . I know now it could never be so I'm going back to Europe to settle there. I will never come back to this country . . . am in withdrawal and my body is writhing in pain. . . . No one will ever care for you as I have. . . . I'll just have to keep telling myself that I'm Chet Baker and that I am important to many people throughout the world. . . .

I hand the letter back to Margo. "He had it bad for her," I say. "Did you know this woman?"

Margo nods and sets the letter aside. "I met her once, and I couldn't really see it, but who knows why anyone falls in love?"

"Well, they did get back together. He talks about her in a film I saw."

"Yeah, but she broke it off again just before he died. Oh, I'd love to see that film," Margo says.

"It's at the Jazz Archives in Amsterdam. Ask for a woman there named Helen when you go back."

"I will, I will."

"So, you were saying about the money?"

"I decided it was time to let him have it, maybe use it to go home, see his family. He needed that, to get away from Europe for a while. I knew he was coming back to Amsterdam, but before I could . . ." Her voice trails off, and her eyes well up again. "I know a dealer was probably looking for him to get his money."

"How much was there?"

She looks at me, back from her musings. "You won't believe it, but it was over $87,000. Hell, I couldn't believe it. After he died, I closed the account, paid for the sculpture, and I've been trying to decide ever since what to do with the money." She shakes her head. "I should have sent it to his family, but everybody came out of the woodwork after he died, making claims, filing suits. I didn't want to see it go to lawyers, so I just kept putting it off."

She seems lost for a moment, as if she doesn't hear me.

"What do you think, Margo? Did he jump? I know he wasn't pushed."

"Are you sure of that?"

"Yes. There was a dealer looking for him, Margo, but he didn't find him." I tell her about van Gogh. "He must have seen Chet sometime that night, knew where he was, but he didn't tell anyone."

Margo sighs and smiles slightly. "Well, bless his heart."

"He's in bad shape now. Maybe some of the money could go to him, help get him straight."

Margo doesn't answer for a long moment. She's perfectly still, then she raises her eyes to me and lets me see pain, longing, sadness, and finally relief, all in one brief gaze. "I hope to God he just fell and didn't know anything."

It's so quiet I can hear the wind rustling through the trees outside. I reach across and touch her arm. "I think you're right, Margo. I don't think he knew anything."

She lays her hand lightly on mine for a moment. "Thank you," she says.

She gets up and puts the CD on again. She kneels in front of the speakers, her hands clasped together, and listens with her eyes closed. I listen too, as Chet Baker's horn fills the room with melancholy, reaching down inside both of us somewhere, touching us without even knowing he does it. I watch Margo for a moment, feeling now like an intruder. I quietly let myself out and close the door behind me, the painful strains of "My Foolish Heart" still ringing in my head.

I don't think she cares or even knows when I leave.

Coda

Y OU MIND if I sit in?" I turn and find Johnny Griffin leaning over at my shoulder, his tenor saxophone in his hand. Fletcher hasn't even seen him. We're between tunes, and Fletch is talking to somebody at a front table.

"Hey," I say and almost fall off the piano bench. "Well, yeah, sure." The Little Giant, as he's called, straightens up then and grins Fletcher's way. Fletcher sees everybody looking behind him. He turns toward us, sees Griff, and throws up his hands.

"Oh, man," Fletcher says and runs over. I watch the two of them embrace and laugh. They're cut from the same cloth, and all eyes are on these two now as they have their public reunion. Fletcher finally looks at me. "Man, can you believe this?" His face must hurt from grinning. "Damn, let's play something."

There's a quick discussion of tunes and keys until they eventually decide on a fast blues. Fletch snaps his fingers for the tempo. "About here?" Griff nods, and we're off. They're like a pair of racehorses out the gate, heading for someplace I've never been. Neck and neck through the line twice, then Fletch nods and steps away. Griff smokes a half dozen choruses and I just hang in, listening, slotting the chords. On his last one, Griff points his horn at Fletch, who's been standing there listening to Griff's blistering lines, nodding, grinning. He gives him a look, like, Oh yeah, well listen to this. Fletch steps up and answers back with six of his own. It's a tie. Fletcher Paige and Johnny Griffin. Griff comes back, and they trade choruses, then four measures each, then two, holding the audience spellbound, until finally Griff waves his hand at Fletch in mock surrender. Then they both turn and point at me.

I manage a half dozen of my own, and when I look up to signal I'm done, they're both snapping their fingers. "What'd I tell you?" I hear Fletcher say. "Go on," Griff says, and that's all I need. I look up at them at the end of my last chorus to let them know I'm done, and they come back, chasing each other for a couple more, and finally take it home. The audience hardly matters. Fletcher steps aside then and holds out his hand: "Ladies and gentlemen, Mr. Johnny Griffin," but it isn't really necessary. Everybody knows. They're all on their feet now, clapping and yelling.

Damn, Fletcher Paige and Johnny Griffin.

We break then, and while Fletch and Griff catch up at the bar, I go outside and take in the Amsterdam night air.

This is our third weekend, and everything has gone to plan. The crowds have been good; the owner loves us and is already talking about an extension. My playing is probably the best it's ever been, thanks to Fletch. It's like working with a great actor, being pushed and prodded beyond your normal limits, and my hand has responded well.

But some things have changed since I came back, and some people are gone. Darren, for one. "We had a long talk," Fletch told me. "He's gone back to the States, to get in a computer degree program. Finally made him see he's wasting his time here and it was time to go back. Forget all that Shaft shit."

"And I'm sure it helped that you encouraged him," I said.

"Well, maybe. I hope so. I owe him."

I talked to Margo Highland a couple of times. She decided to set up a Chet Baker fund for aspiring young musicians with some of the money, and promised to return to Amsterdam soon to get things rolling. Navarro and de Hass are nothing but bad memories now, and Inspector Dekker has assured me they are both being investigated. De Hass will have slipped up somewhere, but that's for Dekker to worry about. That I am leaving to the police.

I tried finding Van Gogh again, but nobody knew where he was, only that he'd left Amsterdam.

Now, as I turn to go back inside, I see Fletch and Griff coming out, shaking hands, saying good-byes.

"Nice to meet you," Griffin says. "And play with you." He winks at Fletch. "Is he paying you right?"

"Oh, yeah," I say. "Pleasure is all mine, Griff." It's all I can do to not call him Mr. Griffin.

"Well, you take care, Fletch." He turns, and we watch him walk toward the taxi stand.

"Damn," Fletcher says. "That was good. Come on, let's walk a bit. We got time."

We walk down to the canal and cross the bridge. The lights from tour boats glitter and shine on the water, and we can hear voices carrying across the water.

"I had an e-mail from Margo today," Fletch says.

"Yeah? Is she coming back?"

"Uh-huh, sometime next month, if she gets all her shit together."

"Guess I'll have to find a place of my own."

"No hurry," Fletch says. He looks at me. "You going to stay, then?"

"For a while. I haven't thought about it much—I'm just enjoying the moment."

"Yes," Fletcher says, "so am I. What about your FBI girl-friend?"

"She might come over, at least for a visit." I shrug. "She has a career too."

Fletch smiles. "Uh-huh, and I think I see San Francisco in your future."

Fletcher could be right.

Once I'd had it out with Ace and talked to Margo, I drove back through the wine country, and somewhere in the back of my mind, I could see myself living there. So did Andie.

I'd boarded the return flight to Amsterdam with an advance copy of my CD, courtesy of Paul Westbrook, some promises from Margo Highland, and the scent of Andie's perfume. We'd spent another night and day together, and although neither of us knew exactly where it was going, we'd made a good start. The timing was certainly getting better.

"You have to see Natalie, at least talk to her," Andie said before I left. "I want to know, I want you to know, then we'll go from there."

She'd dropped me at the street check-in. "I can't go in there. Let's just say good-bye here."

"Okay." There'd been the usual crush of cars around us, unloading bags, vying for a space at the curb. When she looked at me, I saw her eyes well up. "Hey, c'mon now. We'll be fine."

She pulled a tissue out of her handbag and wiped her eyes. "Damn, an emotional FBI agent." She managed a smile then. "You know how much I'd like to get on this flight too, don't you?"

"Yes, but this time it's different."

"Yes, it is, isn't it?"

I pulled her close and kissed her. She leaned her head against the seat for a moment. "God, you are a champion kisser. Now get out of here before I make you miss your plane."

It wasn't the same as with Natalie—maybe nothing ever would be—but it was good, and sometimes that can be enough.

"Who knows? I don't like to predict anything anymore." I look at my watch. "Hey, Mr. Paige, let's play."

Driving back from the Baby Grand, relaxed, feeling that good tired feeling that comes over me after a satisfying night of playing, we pass the Prins Hendrik Hotel. I tell Fletcher to pull over. "Just for a minute," I say.

"Damn," Fletcher says, "haven't you had enough of that place?"

I get out of the car. "Just want another look."

I walk over to the hotel. There aren't many people out now, but just behind the hotel, I know the Old Quarter is bustling with activity. I look at the plaque again. The hotel and streetlights make the inscription just readable.

It should be in Yale, Oklahoma, I think—Chet's hometown—or maybe someplace in California, where he spent so much time. But where? The Haig, where he began with Gerry Mulligan, is gone, and so is the Lighthouse, Shelly's Manne Hole, like Birdland and the Five Spot in New York, or the Blackhawk and the Jazz Workshop in San Francisco. All gone. Like so many musicians before him, and so many after, Chet Baker came here to play his music where it's appreciated best, so maybe a foreign country is appropriate.

The words on the plaque stay with me as I walk back to Fletcher's car. *He will live on in his music for anyone willing to listen and feel.*

We like our heroes to die young dramatically, or if they live, confess and show remorse. Chet Baker did neither.

Well, Chet, a lot of people are still listening, still feeling.

I get in the car and catch Fletcher's look. "You okay?" he asks.

"Yeah, I'm fine now."

Fletcher says, "Cool." He puts the car in gear, pulls away, and starts humming a tune that's vaguely familiar.

"What's that?"

"'The Peacocks.' Stan Getz and Jimmy Rowles's record. Young tenor player, old pianist. We got just the opposite going. You know that tune?"

"Not yet, but I can learn."

"Yeah, man," Fletcher says. "You learn fast."

Chet Baker Selected Discography

*The Best of the Gerry Mulligan Quartet with
  Chet Baker.* Pacific Jazz, 1991.
Quartet: Russ Freeman and Chet Baker.
  Pacific Jazz, 1956.
Chet Baker: The Pacific Jazz Years. Pacific Jazz, 1994.
Chet Baker in New York. Riverside, 1958.
In a Soulful Mood. Music Club. 1997.
My Favorite Songs: The Last Great Concert.
  Enja, 1988.